TWO PRINCES

The Biker and The Billionaire

(Sons of Sanctuary MC, Book 1)

Victoria Danann

Published by 7th House Publishing
dba Imprint of Andromeda LLC
U.S. Copyright Office Copyholder
Print Edition

Read more about this author and upcoming works at
VictoriaDanann.com

INCLUDES BONUS PREQUEL:
Be sure to read
A Season in Gemini, Introduction to the SSMC
first.

Victoria Danann

SUBSCRIBE TO MY MAIL LIST

Website

victoriadanann.com

Black Swan Fan Page

facebook.com/vdanann

Facebook Author Page

facebook.com/authorvictoriadanann

Twitter

twitter.com/vdanann

Pinterest

pinterest.com/vdanann

AUTHOR FAN GROUP

facebook.com/groups/772083312865721/777140922359960

New York Times and USA Today Bestselling Romance Author

2013 and 2014 Winner BEST PARANORMAL ROMANCE SERIES – *Knights of Black Swan*

Thank you to my BETA READERS

Anne Rindfliesch

Becky Burciaga

Christine Olesinski

Dee Bowerman

Debera Smith

Diane Matlack

Ellen Sandburg

Fawn Phillips

Joy Whiteside

Lisa High

Nelta B Mathias

Pam James

Rebecca Stigers

Robyn Byrd

Tifinie Henry

Yolanda Tull

Yvette Grimes

Melvena Asa

***Intro** to the Sons of Sanctuary MC*

Garland St. Germaine had way too much fun celebrating graduation from Dartmouth with her sorority sisters. They had, apparently, managed to singlehandedly revive Dartmouth's reputation as the rowdy Ivy League institution. As a result, Garland's father had given her a choice of accompanying him on a three month business trip to Austin, Texas or finding a substitute for the lavish lifestyle her allowance provided. After several tantrums unworthy of a college graduate, she left Park Avenue wearing sunglasses and a huff, and got on the company plane bound for the Yellow Rose Country Club and Resort. She was sure there had to be more to life than an adult version of being grounded.

Brant Fornight had made up his mind that he wasn't interested in the life his dad's motorcycle club could offer him. He wasn't overly interested in money, especially not if it came with the risk of a prison sentence. He thought of himself as a simple guy even though he often pondered some of the great philosophical questions while he worked as a mechanic. He liked working with mechanical things and hadn't needed a formal education to do that. The Sons of Sanctuary had topped off the natural born talent by mentoring and letting him work on their vehicles.

After high school, he drifted from one Austin repair shop to the next, accidentally improving his resume with each move that earned a better title and more money. When he was twenty-four, he took a job as Head Mechanic at the Yellow Rose Country Club and Resort. It never occurred to him to wonder if there was more to life.

CHAPTER 1

DAVID ST. GERMAINE had sent a van and two guys to move Garland out of her primo room at the sorority house. He was extremely proud of the fact that she'd been voted Panhellenic Rep by her sorority sisters. He'd told her that it was a more impressive accomplishment than any other office because she was the embodied statement that her sorority wanted to make about their chapter at joint Greeks meetings. Garland liked having her father's approval when getting it didn't interfere with what she was going to do regardless.

Every day for the ten days between finals and graduation she'd packed a few things in preparation for the final move-out. She was torn between having loved university life and wanting to get on to whatever came next, even though she wasn't clear about what that was. Certainly she'd never planned to use her B.A. in Classical Studies to gain actual employment. She could read and write Greek and Latin, sketch an Ionic column, explain Socratic Method, and accurately recount the biography of even the most obscure demigod.

A quarter million dollars of education and related

expenses later, that degree and a few dollars would buy a Starbucks. But livelihood wasn't a concern. She was the only child of a rich widower who rarely denied her anything.

She showed the movers to her room and pointed out what should go. After one last look, she plugged her phone into the console of her wine-colored Maserati, selected the music playlist she'd entitled ROAD TRIP, and pointed the car south toward New York thinking that traffic wouldn't be bad on a Sunday. At least not *as* bad as usual. She could probably do the trip in four and a half hours with one potty stop enroute. After four years, she knew where to stop for a decent restroom.

THE NEW YORK TIMES still printed society pages on Sundays, only the new current title was "About Town". It included celebrity sightings along with traditional news about Social Registry members. Charity galas and Arts League balls were always popular. The concession to modernity was that in recent years there had been sensationalism-creep. The news had begun to treat society's best more like celebrities, in the sense that scandals were printed right alongside who was seen with whom at balls, galas, museum exhibit previews, and art show openings. It had become a gossip column thinly disguised as the time-honored tradition of setting aside valuable print space for flattering the moneyed elite.

GARLAND PULLED UP in front of her building, grabbed the

rolling suitcase with essential stuff, smiled at Max, the doorman, and gave him the car keys so that he could have the car parked in a two thousand dollars per month garage nearby. She might not use the car again for weeks, or even months, but it was nice to know she could.

She took a deep breath and called out to anyone who might be in the penthouse.

"I'm home!"

Since it was Sunday that would probably be either her father or no one.

She walked the length of the kitchen and beyond to a small, but elegant and sunny breakfast room that overlooked Central Park and was rarely seen by anyone other than Garland, her father, and the staff.

"I say, 'I'm home!'", she repeated as she flopped into a chair opposite where her dad was having coffee and reading the paper.

David St. Germaine looked over the top of the Wall Street Journal. "So I see."

"Wow. Welcome home."

He slid a section of the Sunday Times toward where she sat across the glass top table. "I second the 'wow'."

Before looking down at whatever he wanted her to see, she could tell that he was the farthest thing from happy. When she'd seen him two days before at graduation, he'd been delighted, either with her or his date for the day. There was no point in remembering her name. Her father rarely saw women more than once.

On the cusp of fifty, he was still handsome, with a

little silver above his ears and a tan that never faded completely because he kept a boat at the Yacht Club and made a point of sailing, when weather and business permitted. He'd been referred to as 'eligible bachelor' more than once, but Garland doubted the veracity of that claim. Since her mother's death, he hadn't given anyone reason to think he was 'eligible'.

She looked at the paper. The front and center color image was of none other than herself wearing a short sparkly dress that had ridden *far* too high as she fell backwards, spilling a colorful beverage as she went sprawling into the laps of laughing friends.

The headline read, "Germane Enterprises Princess Out on the Town. Daddy's little girl lets her hair down and her skirt up."

As she stared at the page, her father said, "Nice dress," in a tone dripping with sarcasm.

Without looking up, she said quietly, "We were just having some fun, celebrating graduation."

"How many times have I told you that what you do reflects on me? And, by extension, on Germane Enterprises?"

She raised her eyes to meet his glare. "Thousands."

"That's right! Thousands. You would think a girl capable of graduating Dartmouth summa cum laude would get it after mere dozens of times."

"Everybody else…"

"You're not everybody else though. Are you?"

She lowered her eyes. "No."

"With great privilege comes great responsibility."

She bit back a comment that tried to take possession of her mouth. Something about using condoms and clubbing with a designated driver. But she decided that sort of retort would make her sound weak and juvenile. So she said nothing. After a few seconds of staring, he continued.

"Christ, Garland. You and your miscreant friends got thrown out of some cheap dive? That's pretty hard to do. Places like that host Ladies' Nights to attract young women to come in." He let out a frustrated breath. "What are your plans?"

"My plans?"

"Yes, Garland. As in, what do you plan to do when you wake up tomorrow?"

"I just finished school. I was thinking I'd take a couple of weeks. Maybe do some shopping and get together with friends before…"

"Before what?"

Truthfully, she hadn't gotten to that. Her vision began and ended with lunching and shopping. "I haven't worked that out yet."

"Good. Then you won't be inconvenienced to have to cancel anything."

"What do you …?"

"I've made plans for you. I'll be spending most of the summer at the property we're expanding in Texas. You're coming with me."

"To Texas!?!" She looked as horrified as if she'd just

been told she'd be summering inside a tank on a war torn border somewhere between the remnants of Arabia and the remnants of Persia.

He went on as calmly as if she hadn't spoken. "This…" He glanced down at the tattling paper. "…is an indication that you're not ready to make your own choices. So I'll make them for you. Austin this summer then Wharton School this fall. Thank goodness your GPA is high enough. I'll have to call in some favors *and* donate a fortune, probably, but you *will* get in."

"To Business School? I don't want to study business. I can't think of anything less fun. And Philadelphia? Really?"

She saw the traces of a smirk appear around his mouth. "This has nothing to do with fun, Garland. It's about being a productive member of this family and, by extension, a productive member of society. When you have an MBA from Wharton, you'll be ready to step into a position with Germane Enterprises and do something worthwhile with your life."

Her eyes flashed. "You can't make those decisions for me. I'm not a little girl."

His face softened slightly, but was no less serious "No. You're not. And you're welcome to show me your independence by walking out that door with your clothes and the college degree you just earned. You can start at home plate, like I did. Instead of on third base. Like you did."

The range of limited options flew across her vision

like a rapid-sequence music video. And she didn't like anything she saw.

She wanted to be the girl who took that option. She wanted to stand up and say, "Okay. I'm out." But she didn't think she was cut out for pioneering a whole new way of life.

"I guess you win then. I'm not prepared to be homeless."

"It's not a matter of me '*winning*'. It's about what's best for you." He snapped the paper and went back to reading. "We're leaving in two days. You can shop and play with your friends until then." He lowered the paper again long enough to say, "Do you think you can manage to stay out of the news for that long?"

Since the question was rhetorical and there was nothing else to say, she rose and left the room. It was the adult version of being grounded.

Garland didn't hate her father. She believed he loved her in his own distant, detached, heavy-handed way. She'd also spent enough time in the homes of friends to know that warmth and affection had been missing in their household since her mother died.

Visiting with friends was a great vicarious pleasure for her. She loved observing the dynamics of families where love was shared openly and without agenda. She wanted that for herself someday.

CHAPTER 2

BRANT FORNIGHT WAS a third generation Austin native and everything about the town suited him just fine. He wasn't one of those people who lived in the mountains, but dreamed of a house on the beach. Or vice versa.

Dry air, hills, and live oak was good enough for him.

He'd made up his mind that he wasn't interested in the life the club could offer him. Since he'd grown up in and around his dad's motorcycle club, he was able to make a truly *informed* choice.

Brant didn't have the kind of angry fire in the belly that motivates a man to choose that path. He wasn't overly interested in money, especially not if it came with the risk of prison. And he hadn't experienced the sort of injustice that had caused the original seven members, all Vietnam vets, to band together with a third finger prominently raised at particular aspects of society.

Brant thought of himself as a simple sort of guy even though he was an avid reader of classics and secretly pondered some of the great philosophical brain-scramblers while he worked as a mechanic. He'd been born with the talent for it, loved taking things apart and putting them back together in better condition than before. The Sons of Sanctuary had nurtured that gift by mentoring and letting him tinker with their vehicles.

After high school, he'd drifted from one Austin repair shop to another, accidentally improving his resume with each move to a larger shop, new title and more money. When he was twenty-five, he took a job as Head Mechanic at the Yellow Rose Resort. It required a double skill set: mechanic *and* manager of fuckwads who needed a babysitter more than a supervisor. Even though he was younger than almost all the guys who reported to him, he handled it. One way or another.

He smiled about that. It was exactly the sort of thing his old man liked to say. *Get it done. One way or another.*

It never occurred to Brant to wonder if there was more to life, and maybe he never would have, if Garland St. Germaine hadn't gotten lost while exploring the resort grounds. Occupied by her own dark thoughts, not looking at much but the pavement in front of her, she'd wandered far afield of the guest paths. When she looked up, she was in front of the huge vehicle maintenance facility known as "the shed". She didn't know how she got there and had no idea how to find her way back.

Since she'd been in Austin for a week, she'd acquired a golden tan that would be the envy of any lotion ad. Her ash blonde hair had also lightened several shades and taken on some dramatic, but still natural, highlights. Wearing a tank top, knee length shorts, she flip flopped through one of the open bays and came face to face with

Brant Fornight.

He was wearing jeans and a black tee with the Yellow Rose logo and text that simply read CREW.

He looked her over too quickly to be accused of leering at a guest. And everything about her screamed guest, from the small diamond studs in her ears, to the designer sunglasses, to the skin that had that look of perfect nutrition and expensive lotion.

"What can I do for you, darlin'?"

The endearment was politically incorrect according to the new standards, but if she complained, he could always say it was just part of the local charm.

Looking at the twin fires in Brant's striking black eyes, she temporarily forgot what she needed. It was hard to tell whether the amusement on his handsome face was a permanent expression or if he was having fun at her expense.

She cleared her throat. "I was having a look at the, uh, property and I guess I got turned around."

"Yeah." He gave her a slow smile that had all her lady parts perking up and standing at attention. "We don't get many people who start out lookin' for the pool and wind up here," he drawled, while wiping his hands on a rag.

She scowled. "I wasn't looking for the pool. I was just..."

"Havin' a look at the property." He smiled. He pointed to a black and green vehicle that also bore the Yellow Rose logo. "Hop in this golf cart and I'll drive you back."

"I don't want to put you out."

He laughed out loud and shook his head. “This is the best thing that’s happened to me this year. Come on. I’ll go fast enough to get the breeze goin’ and cool you off.”

She had gone past attractive glow to full on sweat. As if on cue, she was reminded of that when she felt a trickle of perspiration run between her breasts. His promise to ‘cool her off’ caused a blush for, what she was sure was the first time in her life.

“Well, it is hot out here,” she said, looking around as if someone might argue. Or intervene.

He looked over at the temperature gauge. “Only ninety-six in the shade. ’Course that’s the way they report temps. In the shade. But…”, he looked down at her feet, “…it’s really about one fifteen where you’re standin’. On that asphalt. In the sun.”

Following his eyes down to the tarmac beneath her feet, she realized that she did actually feel as if she was slow cooking.

“Thank you. I appreciate it.”

His grin was heart-stopping. He turned his back long enough to open a refrigerator, withdrew a bottle of water, and set it in the cart’s drink holder when he got behind the wheel. After Garland seated herself on the passenger side of the cart, he handed her the ice cold bottle of water. “All part of the service, ma’am.”

“Thank you.” She accepted gratefully. But as badly as she wanted to drink, she wanted to feel the cold bottle against her skin even more. She held it to her chest, closed her eyes and moaned. “You’re an angel in disguise."

When she opened her eyes and saw the change in his expression, she realized that calling attention to her breasts may not have been the smartest move.

Brant tore his gaze from the water bottle. It may have elicited a moan that would haunt his fantasies forever, but even he knew that ogling guests was crossing a line. He wasn't sure whether he should be glad that he'd given her a cold compress, or curse himself for it, but the view above her neck was just as interesting. She'd removed her sunglasses and stuck them on top of her head, which left him exactly sixteen inches away from amber-colored irises that were stunning, and so unusual with her blonde locks that she looked almost exotic. At the moment they were also questioning why he wasn't starting the engine.

He pushed the ignition button and they lurched forward. When they started down the hill, the cart picked up speed. The air movement did cool the feeling of scorching skin. She took a big swig of cold water and laughed. "You're right. This feels good. You could sell rides to the overheated."

He smiled, steering and stealing glances at the unlikely passenger and the strange, but welcomed turn his morning had taken.

"So where to?"

"You know where the hotel is?" He raised one eyebrow. "Well." She laughed. "Of course you do."

They coasted down a hill then laughed when the cart struggled to climb up the next. On reaching the top, the hotel came into view, sitting on a ridge as if presiding over the Yellow Rose's five championship golf courses.

She pointed to the right of the eighteen-story hotel. "We're in one of those villas next to the hotel."

He whistled long and low. "So I'm guessing you're not using a stay-two-nights-get-the-third-free coupon."

She laughed because she had no other response, not knowing if there was such a thing or if he'd just made that up. "Oh, you know. My father is here overseeing some business development. Told me to either come for the summer or look for a box under a bridge."

When Brant looked over, he seemed to be studying her. He suspected that she was early twenties. So what she said about being there with her father didn't really make sense. "You in a box under a bridge. Can't see that."

"Hmmm. Well, it could happen. You remember the story about that ex movie star who was living in the bushes in Central Park?"

"No. I guess I missed that."

"You must not watch 'Entertainment Tonight'."

He chuckled. "Guilty. Or not guilty. Take your pick."

She indulged in a leisurely look at his tan profile. He had lashes so long and thick that she would think they were fake on a woman. But she thought that, if she was reading signals right, there was nothing fake about Brant Fornight. He had an open, easy-going manner that put her at ease. Running her eyes over the dark hair that threatened to reach the ribbed neck of his tee, and following the line of his straight nose and strong jaw, she decided he could be vying for the title of the best-looking man she'd ever seen.

"What's your name?"

"Brant Fornight. What's yours?"

"Garland St. Germaine."

His eyes slid sideways. "Pretty name. And unusual. I don't think I've ever run into a Garland before."

"It was my grandmother's maiden name. The one good thing about it is that it doesn't lend itself to cute nicknames." She chuckled. "The closest anybody ever came to making one stick was this guy at school who used to call me Garfield."

Brant puzzled at his reaction to that. His gut had tightened. Apparently he didn't like getting an image of another guy calling this girl anything. Once he realized that he would probably never see the beautiful girl with the terrible sense of direction again, he slowed the cart down as much as possible without raising suspicion.

When they reached the walk to the door of her villa, she turned toward him. Her hesitation made him wonder if she was just as reluctant to end the unlikely encounter.

Her smile was warm, but he couldn't tell if it was a friendly smile or an 'I'm interested' smile. "Well. I guess this is me."

"I guess so."

"Thank you for the ride, Brant."

"It was my pleasure, Garland. Whenever you get lost anywhere around vehicle maintenance, this chariot will be at your disposal."

She grinned. “Flowery words for a vehicle maintenancer.”

“Maybe I’m not one-dimensional.”

She stared as if she was trying to read his mind. “Maybe you’re not.”

She got out and walked to the door knowing that he was watching her rear end under the pretense of seeing her safely home. She swiped the card key and opened the door then turned to smile and wave. In return she was rewarded with a macho chin jerk that made her smile even bigger.

CHAPTER 3

BRANT SET THE torque wrench down, wiped his hands, grabbed his keys and pulled the bay door down. Like always, he waited until everyone else was gone so he could lock up. As he started his car, he turned his attention to what he might do with a Wednesday night. He could throw together some Hamburger Helper and watch the tube. He could grab a shower and stop by the Hawg Stop for a burger and a beer. Or two. Depending on who was there.

He was seven minutes from home, still running through options with no stand-out choice, when he saw a BMW pulled off the roadside with the driver side door open. Being a car guy, he noticed the car, but it would be pretty hard to ignore the shapely derriere that was bending over the seat.

As he slowed, he was thinking that a damsel in distress with a killer ass could be just the thing he needed to get Garland St. Germaine out of his head. As he pulled close to the Beemer's bumper, the owner of the heart-shaped butt stood up and looked to see who was there.

"God's balls," he muttered to himself. How was he

supposed to forget about Garland St. Germaine when she made a habit of turning up unexpectedly, wearing the juiciest look of vulnerability?

She looked a touch wary about the car that had stopped, until he opened the door and set one booted foot on the gravel. When she recognized him, her face broke out in a smile that put sunshine to shame. And his heart squeezed in his chest like it was caught in a vise grip.

"Brant Fornight! Just when you need a mechanic..."

He couldn't help but return the smile, flattered that she'd cared to remember his name. "Trouble?"

"No. It's Garland. Garland St. Germaine."

He chuckled and shook his head. "So you say. But I'm thinkin' I got it right." Her grin revealed teeth so perfectly white and straight they could easily be featured in a toothpaste ad. "Man. You have beautiful teeth. I'm guessin' you don't chew."

He intended it as a joke, but she looked confused. "Chew? Doesn't everybody?"

He laughed. "Let's see what's goin' on here."

"I couldn't figure out how to open the hood. Not that I'd know what to do after that."

"Why'd you pull over?"

"The gearshift popped out of Drive and wouldn't go back in." She paused, seeing the look on his face. "That expression is telling me that this is not good."

"No. It's not." Looking through the open car door he spotted a mobile phone. "You tried callin' somebody?"

"Yeah. No luck."

"Figured. It's hard to get service through this stretch. Is this a rental?"

She looked down at the car. "No. It's a loaner for while I'm here. Some business associate of my father's."

"Hmmm," he said, like it was the most natural thing in the world to know people who loan practically new BMW sedans to the grown children of business associates. "Well, get your stuff and come on. I'll get a tow truck to take it to a shop that specializes in Germans. They know me and won't try to rip off your dad's friend."

"You're going to give me a ride?"

"I'm not leavin' you out here to walk."

"That's nice of you, Brant."

As she smiled, he was thinking that maybe, if she knew what all he'd like to do to her, she wouldn't think he was so 'nice'.

When she pulled her purse out of the car, he said, "Were you running away?" Those little lines formed between her brows. He pointed at the bag. "That's gotta be the biggest purse I ever saw."

"It's Sequoia Paris," she said defensively.

He chuckled, but said, "Okay," in a maddeningly placating way.

When she settled into his car, he realized that he liked the way she looked in the passenger seat way more than he should.

When she closed her door she realized that, in a vehicle without open-air sides, he was a really big guy who took up a lot of space and made proximity feel very, very close.

"What kind of car is this?"

"It's a 1968 Camaro. Original everything."

"I like the color. What do you call it? Slate?"

"No. I call it gunmetal gray."

She nodded and threw his placating reaction back at him. "Okay."

When he started the engine, Garland felt the vibration rumble through her body like a purr. Not a kitten's purr. More like a panther that had flopped down next to her and proceeded to rub his big head into her lap like she was catnip.

"Wow."

"Exactly." He turned to grin at her and watched her throat as she swallowed. He hoped she wasn't afraid, but truthfully he could just eat her up. As he pulled back onto the road he said, "So where were you goin'?"

"Oh. This woman at the pool told me I'd be missing out if I didn't go to the Bee Caves Shaman while I was here and get a tarot reading."

He laughed out loud. "New Age Hoodoo?"

She cut her eyes his direction and smiled slightly. "Maybe."

"You still want to go?"

Garland's big eyes widened. "You mean drop me off there?"

He glanced away from the road long enough to appreciate her surprised look. "Well, no. I'll wait for you and take you back to the Yellow Rose."

"You'd do that?"

"Conditionally."

She narrowed her eyes. "What conditions?"

His lips twitched at the corners. "I have two. The second one is that I need to be fed first. It's been a long time since lunch."

"You're going to make me ask you about the first, aren't you?"

"No ma'am. I've had the pleasure of workin' a full day without benefit of air-conditioning. I need to stop by my place and grab a quick shower." He could feel her tense up without even turning his head to look, so he cautioned himself to soft pedal. With a slow smile he said, "I'm not a serial killer, Garland."

"That's what all the serial killers say, Brant. And death may not be the thing I'm most worried about."

He slanted his eyes toward her while still wearing a smile. "You can wait in the car. Won't take long. I promise." She relaxed visibly. "Then I'll take you out for the best Mexican food in the Great State of Texas."

"Really?"

"No shit. And it's just five minutes from the Shaman."

"Oh. So you know where to find New Age Hoodoo?"

"All the locals know about Foss Carley. Comes from a family of famous musicians. Well, at least they're famous in Texas."

"Is Foss a guy?"

"Yeah. Went to high school with him."

"Really? Was he super spiritual back then?"

Brant almost guffawed. "Hardly."

Brant's house was on a bluff overlooking Bee Caves Road, ideally located halfway in between two ice houses frequented by the Sons of Sanctuary. That would be fifteen minutes to the Hawg Stop at Bee Cave and fifteen minutes to the Watering Hole at Dripping Springs. A nice easy ride either way, especially at sunset, when the warm air would rush around a biker like a ravishing lover. It was also just three miles from work at the Yellow Rose.

At the top of the hill, Brant turned onto a gravel and caliche drive. The house was small, but made entirely of local white river rock. It looked substantial enough to withstand a siege.

"The three little pigs might as well not bother," Garland said.

Brant looked at her like she'd lost her mind. "What?"

"You know the story. Right?"

"I do know the story, but since I live here, you must think I'm the wolf who ate the pigs and claimed their house." She laughed. "You sure you want to wait out here? It's cool inside. I'm just gonna make a call about your car and shower quick."

She hesitated, the wariness returning. But after another look in his eyes, she decided to go with her instincts. "Okay." She opened the car door and got out before she could change her mind.

He entered first. "Well. Be it ever so humble… Come on in and cool off."

When she stepped in, the cool air enveloped her in blessed relief.

There were ample windows, but it was dark inside.

"Do you always keep the shutters closed?"

"Just during the eight months when I'm trying to keep the cool air in and the hot air out."

"Oh."

Brant stood watching for her reaction to his casita. It was simple, but it was paid for and it had a coveted eastern view over the tops of trees that was valuable beyond price.

Garland took it all in. The house had two rooms, a large combined living with kitchen at the end away from the front door and, what Garland supposed was, a bed and bath down a short hallway.

The interior was a version of rustic chic. It had the requisite bachelor leather furniture, but the floors were distressed wide plank hardwood. His housekeeping was neater than she would have guessed. No clutter to speak of. No dishes in the sink. But the thing that made the biggest impression by far was the giant black shiny motorcycle sitting in the middle of the living room.

She pointed to it. "Is this an expressive art piece or does it have a practical application?"

He chuckled. "I guess both. I do ride it if that was the subtext of that question." The look she gave him caused him to say, "What?"

She shook her head. "Nothing. Sometimes you just surprise me when you use words like 'subtext'."

He stiffened. "Because you expect me to have a vocabulary of one hundred words or less."

"No. I…"

"Forget it. I'll make the call and be out in five minutes."

She listened to Brant tell his acquaintance where to find the car and where to drop it off. Then he made a second call to the guy who specialized in "Germans".

He didn't look back at her before making his way down the hallway. He hadn't exactly stormed off, but he'd left little doubt she'd bruised his ego.

In his absence, there wasn't much to do but look around. She walked around the bike and the sofa to get to the far wall where she'd spied the second most interesting thing in Brant's house. Two well-stocked bookcases.

She expected to see titles about carburetors and lug nuts. Maybe sex how-to's. She wasn't prepared to find Heidegger, Kant, Nietzsche, Kierkegaard, and Jean-Paul Sartre to name a few. He seemed to have a complete collection of the works of famous philosophers with some epic literature and even a few plays. The man was delightfully enigmatic.

She was so intent on reading titles that she didn't hear him come into the room.

"You ready?"

His voice startled her, but not noticeably. She hoped. "Sure." She waved her hand toward the books. "You've got eclectic taste."

His smile was guarded and didn't completely reach his eyes. "I know how to read, Garland." Standing there with his hair wet, he looked fresh in clean jeans and a tee that couldn't disguise the rugged outline of the physique underneath.

She canted her head to the side. "I didn't mean to hurt your feelings, Brant."

He gaped at her. "Hurt my... You didn't hurt anything. Look, maybe..."

She knew that she needed to do some damage control if she wanted to have dinner with the sexiest man who'd ever crossed her path. So she cut him off before he could finish that sentence.

"I'm looking forward to the best Mexican food in Texas. And I'm holding you to the claim. How far is it?"

Brant looked like he was thrown off his game for a minute. "Uh... it's only five minutes away. Just down the hill and to the right."

She gave him her most dazzling smile. "Good. I'm starved."

It only took Brant a second to decide whether he wanted to be indignant or happy.

"After you." He motioned to the door and that time the smile did reach his eyes.

"OH MY GOD," she gushed. "What do you call this again?"

He chuckled. "Chimichanga."

She'd eaten an entire basket of chips and salsa before

the real food ever arrived. And downed a large frozen Margarita. When Brant had learned that she'd never had Mexican food before, he'd ordered two different combination plates so that she could try some of everything. And *everything* got rave reviews.

"This place is a *find*," she said with her mouth still full.

"Well, Chuy's is not exactly a secret around here. Lots of people have already found it."

"Smart, smart people," she said seriously as she took a bite of a chile con queso stuffed hatch pepper. "Oh my God. This is the best thing yet."

He laughed. "You've said that about everything you've tasted."

"Here!" She held the rest of the pepper out to him. He obediently opened his mouth and let her feed him from her hand. He chewed with amusement, enjoying witnessing her rapture. "Well?!" He shrugged. "Oh come on. You know this is the *best* food anybody ever ate."

"Glad you approve."

"I'm having another Margarita."

He made a face. "How can you stand it? Tequila tastes like shit."

"There's something wrong with you, Brant. It's the best thing ever."

"That's what you said about the flauta." He laughed at her. "You're gonna have to make a choice. The Shaman closes at nine. So it's either the Margarita or tea leaves and shit."

She pouted. “I want both.”

He laughed. “I know you do. You strike me as the kind of girl who likes it her way. You want it all.”

“Well. Who doesn’t? So how about you? What do you want?”

“I haven’t given much thought to it.” She started laughing. “What’s so funny?”

“You read Kant and Heidegger, but you’ve never thought about what you want? You’re an unusual guy, Brant.”

“Unusual peculiar? Unusual creepy? Or unusual extraordinary?”

As Garland watched the playful expressions flit over his handsome face, her grin resolved into a smile. “Extraordinary. Definitely.”

For the second time in a couple of hours, he felt the squeeze in his chest. He wondered if Garland St. Germaine was merciful with the hearts she took captive.

“What are you thinking?” she asked.

“That I’ll bet you’ve left a trail of broken hearts.”

“Brant Fornight. You’re flirting with me.”

“Does it show?”

“Not enough,” she replied.

He laughed, a deep throaty rumbly laugh that reminded her of the Camaro’s purr.

“Next time I see you, let’s go for a ride on my bike.”

Her expression went instantly serious. “I can’t.”

“Why?”

“I promised my father I would never get on one.”

"Why?"

"Too dangerous."

He squinted, mulling that over. "How old are you?"

"Twenty-two."

He gave a little nod and looked at his beer. "Garland, everything in life that's fun or worth doing comes with risk."

"That's not Margarita talk. Too deep." She looked over the railing, where they sat outside at a patio table. "I'll think about it."

"Whatever you decide. The choice should be yours. You're grown up. Right?"

"Sometimes it's not as simple as that."

"Sure it is." He grinned.

She giggled as if to prove, on cue, that she wasn't grown up at all.

GARLAND CHOSE A second frozen Margarita over a visit with High School Foss.

They laughed and talked about how different their lives were, but the more they talked the more they found that, improbable as it seemed, they agreed on important things.

One of the things they had in common was an attraction to each other that pulled like a magnastar.

At ten o'clock, Chuy's shut down. One of the bus boys motioned to the patio gate.

"They're kicking us out," she reported to Brant.

"Looks like," he replied.

WHEN BRANT PULLED up in front of Garland's summer residence, he handed her a note with information on where the BMW had been towed for repair and said, "I guess it would be presumptuous to ask if you want to see me again?"

At that, she surprised the hell out of him by leaning across the console and giving him what might as well have been his first kiss. She ran her fingers through his hair and gave a soft little moan of approval. He didn't know if that moan meant that she liked the kiss, or his hair, or him, but he hoped it was all three.

When she pulled back and smiled, he tried not to look as breathless and discombobulated as a thirteen-year-old.

"I could manage to be free Saturday. How about you?" He nodded and tried to pull her back for another kiss, but she laughed and opened the passenger door. "Save it up for me. What time?"

He tried to get his brain to work through a fog of lust and enchantment. "Uh, twelve. Wear jeans and a long-sleeved shirt over a bathing suit."

"Jeans and a long-sleeved shirt? In this heat?"

"Trust me."

"Hmmm." She didn't look too sure about that. "Okay. I'll meet you at your house."

"Can you find it?" He narrowed his eyes. "You ashamed to be seen with me?"

"No!" She shook her head vigorously, which turned out to be a bad thing after two potent Margaritas. "My dad likes to decide who I spend time with and our ideas about that rarely intersect."

"Okay." He pulled the piece of paper back from her hand, opened the glove box to retrieve a ballpoint pen, and wrote his address on the back. "Here's the address. And here's my phone if you get lost."

"I'm not a complete ditz. I can read a map. I think." She giggled. "Just kidding. Saturday noon."

When Brant drove away, it struck him that he'd just had the best date of his life. The fact that it took place fully clothed with no more contact than a goodnight kiss made him laugh out loud. It didn't seem like those two things, best date and fully clothed, should exist in the same sentence.

He had to admit. She was something special. Really special.

He didn't care for the idea of sneaking around, but if he had to steal the princess from the monster who tried to keep her locked in a tower, he wouldn't be above it.

CHAPTER 4

AT A QUARTER past twelve, Brant restlessly paced in his living room listening for the crunch of gravel under tires. Maybe she couldn't find it. Maybe the old man had caught her trying to sneak away to live her own life. Maybe she'd changed her mind. Maybe she got a better offer. Those and a dozen other possibilities went through his mind.

He was just about ready to open a bottle of Jack when he heard the telltale crunch of gravel. He froze, wanting to run for the window, but having too much manly pride to do it.

Garland had only knocked once when the door flew open. She found herself locked in a kiss with strong arms holding her tight against an incredibly hard body. When he pulled back, he smiled like the cat who thought he stole a saucer of milk.

When he let her go, Garland laughed a little breathlessly. "So you're glad to see me."

"I could play hard to get and say no, but I'm not good at subterfuge."

"Me either. But I don't want you to think I'm easy."

"Why not?"

She giggled. "Because."

"Is that an answer?"

"What's the plan?" she asked, smoothly changing the subject.

"Step back and I'll show you."

He started rolling the motorcycle out the door, into the sunshine reflecting off the white stones.

"Wait a minute," she protested. "I didn't say I agreed to get on that thing."

"You didn't. But you dressed for it. You look beautiful, by the way. The braid is perfect for what we're doing."

"And what is that?"

"Don't want to be surprised?"

She thought about it for a minute and decided that spontaneity could be a sweet change. "Okay. Surprise me."

After showing her where to put her feet and giving her instructions about hanging on, leaning when he leaned, etc., he started the engine. Garland didn't know whether to be more excited about the sound or the lovely vibration traveling through the seat and making contact with her most intimate places.

Brant took her hands and wrapped her arms around his middle.

"You smell heavenly," she yelled, to be heard over the engine noise. "What is that I'm smelling?"

"Just plain old Old Spice."

"I'm investing in that company on Monday. Where

do you get it?"

He chuckled, charmed that she liked the way he smelled and charmed that she was open enough to say so. "Any five and dime. Hold on tight," he said over his shoulder. "And don't let go."

She nodded, but looked anxious. He hoped that would fix itself in a few minutes. When he started away slowly, her arms tightened around his ribs so that he could barely breathe.

By the time they were down the hill and on a stretch of flat road, she was beginning to get the feel of riding. She shifted her weight as he did, so that they were perfectly in sync. When her death hold gave way a little, Brant grinned.

He turned east on 2244 so that he could catch Barton Springs Road all the way to South Congress. He thought he'd show her his town the way it was meant to be seen. When he turned north on Congress, the view of the Capitol across the Colorado River was magnificent. When they stopped at the intersection of 6th Street, he pointed to the right.

"What?" she asked.

"Best music in the world. I'll bring you down here one night."

Garland looked where he pointed, but it wasn't the idea of music that caught her attention. It was his proclamation that he was planning a third date. Or at least a second *planned* date.

When Congress dead-ended at the Capitol grounds,

Brant took a leisurely turn around the circle, then headed away from downtown toward a spot where the Colorado River widened at Bee Creek. Pulling onto a grassy embankment underneath a two-hundred-year-old oak tree, he smiled because, just as he'd hoped, no one else was there.

He turned the Harley off and soaked up the quiet.

"This is pretty," she said.

He looked around and imagined seeing it through her eyes. "Yeah. You gonna get off?"

"Oh. Okay. Sure."

It was a little awkward, but she managed to get both feet on the ground without falling on her ass. Barely.

"Good job, Grace."

"Come on. It's my first time. Let's see you do it." He swung off the bike in a fluid motion like he'd done it a thousand times before, and she supposed he had. The performance was topped off with a look of male satisfaction. "Oh. Easy to be smug when we're in your element."

He laughed. "Let's go swimming." Garland turned around and looked at the still blue water like she'd forgotten the instructions to wear a swim suit. "You did bring somethin' to wear."

She turned to Brant with a look of confusion. Right up until her face broke into a huge grin. "Gotcha," she said as she pulled her long-sleeve knit top over her head. Her jeans were stripped away leaving flawless, delectable skin and curves that had been hiding underneath the clothes protecting her from sunburn and, heaven forbid, road rash.

She ran toward the water taunting him. “You’re in *my* element now, Buster.”

The sight of a bikini-clad Garland had left him dumbstruck. The best reply he could think of was, “Buster?”

He managed to get his own clothes off and jumped in with an impressive cannonball. He swam in her direction, but when he got there, she was out of reach. Again and again, he tried to catch her but she was always just out of reach and laughing.

“Fucking hell. Are you a mermaid?”

“Sort of. Swim team.”

“Yeah? Well, it shows. Guess I’m at your mercy.”

“Ooh. I like that!”

“Well, I’m just going to stay right here while you decide what to do with me.”

It didn’t take Garland long to decide that she wanted to wrap her legs around his waist and tease him with a slick wet body and a kiss that made the one in the car seem like a dry peck. It was long and hot with tongues tangling and heartrates racing. But when he tried to reach under her bikini bottom, she pushed off him with a mighty backward lunge and swam away.

Brant decided to swim under the shade of one of the trees where the water was cooler and think about his next fix-up project, a 1963 GTO he had parked at the Club. He hoped that would get his erection under control before he had to get out of the water.

When he thought he was presentable, he turned toward her and raised his voice. "We better get out before the sun turns us lobster red."

"You're the only one in danger. I've been lying out by the pool every day."

"Suit yourself."

He pulled two beach towels out of one saddlebag, laid them down on the ground and sat down to watch the show. When Garland decided to get out of the water and join him, he was glad to be exactly where he was. If he'd ever seen anything in his life more appealing, he couldn't think what it might have been. He was glad that he'd put on sunglasses so she couldn't tell just how much of an effect she was having on him.

She smiled all the way from the water to the towel, like she knew exactly how much she was being appreciated.

"That was fun," she said as she sat down on the towel next to Brant. "The water, the sightseeing, *and* the motorcycle."

He slanted a smile her way. "So you admit it."

"I do," she said, mimicking his smile. "I also like holding on." She reached over and lightly stroked one of the ridges in his abdomen to make the point that she was referring to his midsection.

His mouth twitched. "Better stop that. You're makin' me horny as a fourteen-year-old."

She giggled. "Okay. What's next?"

"What do you want to do?"

Garland's eyes darted from Brant's eyes to his mouth while she considered the question. "Let's go get some of those things from Chuy's and go back to, um, your place."

Brant swallowed down the flash of a dozen images that came to mind, not wanting to look too eager. It was one thing to joke about being teen prick horny. It was something else to act it out.

"Some of those *things*?"

"Yes."

"Okay," he said slowly then started naming things he'd seen her eat. "Would that be enchiladas? Chalupas? Chimichangas? Flautas?"

She shook her head after each suggestion. "No. You know the ones."

"Describe them."

"They had kind of a crispy envelope with yummy meat stuffing and lettuce and tomatoes and..."

"Tacos?"

"That's it!"

He laughed. "Okay. But I warn you. If you eat tacos every day, you may not always look like..."

"Like what?"

"You know."

"Tell me. Look like what?"

"You already know you're beautiful, Garland. You don't need me to say it."

"I *do* need you to say it."

Seeing that she was perfectly serious, he took off his

sunglasses. "You're one of a kind, Garland. Beyond compare."

"Wow," she said. "I was hoping for something like, 'Yeah. You're cute enough'."

He smiled. "Over the top?"

"Not if you mean it."

"I mean it."

In that sudden way that he was beginning to learn was uniquely Garland, she rolled on top of him without warning and began planting kisses all over his face, neck, forehead, and chin. He grabbed her under the arms and pulled her up his body until she was positioned in just the right spot for… that was when two pickup trucks full of teenagers pulled in whistling and hooting. And interrupting.

She rolled off Brant and walked toward the bike to get her clothes. When he joined her, she said, "My suit is still wet, but it will probably just help me keep cool."

Brant smiled. "Your braid has survived a bike ride and a dip in the river."

"I flew my hairdresser in this morning on the company plane." She looked so perfectly serious, Brant started to doubt that she was joking.

"You didn't really."

She looked at him with a perfectly straight face, until it was a suddenly-Garland moment. With a big grin, she said, "Of course not, silly. Every girl knows how to braid hair."

He just shook his head while he pulled his shirt on

and tied a bandanna around his head to keep his hair from whipping in front of his face. He straddled the bike first and held out a hand to help Garland on.

"Tacos won't be good if we try to take them out. We'll stop off long enough for tacos and that frozen shit you like. I could use a cold one myself."

"Hurry. I'm hungry. And thirsty." She was absently tracing each ridge of his abs one by one while talking about hunger and thirst.

"Oh. So now you want to go *fast* on the motorcycle." He laughed.

"Things change. You make me feel safe." Brant knew that was just banter, but it did funny things to his stomach anyway. He liked the sound of making Garland St. Germaine feel safe. "And rebellious."

"Fast and *rebellious* it is. But you've got to stop that if you want to live to eat another taco."

"Stop what?"

"You know what."

She buried her face and her laughter between his shoulder blades, but stopped exploring. "Okay, boss. Touchy, but no feely."

He looked over his shoulder and dropped his voice. "That's not a permanent rule. It's a just-for-riding rule. When we get back to my place, feely will be welcomed."

She rewarded him with a throaty bawdy, unladylike laugh that made him wish he could push a button and hear it again.

GARLAND COULDN'T DECIDE what kind of tacos to get, so Brant finally ordered a la carte for her. One crispy chicken. One soft with chicken fajita meat. One crispy beef picadillo. One soft beef al carbon. One crispy fish. One crispy black bean. And one crazy thing with shrimp. He figured she could try each one, choose the ones she wanted and he'd eat the rest.

By the time the tacos arrived, she'd gone through a battery of personal questions, some of which he didn't even have an answer for.

"What's your favorite color?"

"Don't know, Garland. What's yours?"

"Red. I think your favorite color is brown."

"Why would you think that?"

"Because everything in your house is brown, your hair is brown, your eyes are brown, and most of Austin is brown."

He chuckled. "Well it is at this time of year. But you're wrong, my favorite color isn't brown."

"Well?"

"Well what?"

She threw a tostada chip at him. "What is it?"

He pinned her gaze. "It's whatever you call that." He pointed at her eyes.

She stopped eating, which, Brant thought, was a minor miracle, given the way she ate tacos like she'd just discovered food. "My eyes?"

He nodded. She blushed, and knowing that she was blushing made her blush all the more. Girls jaded by fine hotels, restaurants, and world travel don't blush. Unless they're discombobulated by sexy handsome bikers who come from another world.

Brant chuckled, liking the way the blush looked on her. In fact, he liked just about everything about the girl who sat across the table. He liked the way she hummed when she gobbled tacos to indicate how much she was enjoying them. He liked the way her eyes lit up when she noticed he was watching. He liked her laugh, her silly questions, and the way she seemed oblivious to all the male attention she garnered. She acted like the two of them were the only two people in the world. And he liked that. A lot.

"This is my favorite." She held up a fish taco.

"I'm really glad you feel that way because I don't like to waste food and, as far as I'm concerned, fish tacos are cat food."

She laughed. "Lucky cats. What's your middle name?"

"Stonewall."

"Stonewall?!"

"Yes. My grandfather was a big fan of Stonewall Jackson. It was kind of an offering to keep the peace when I wasn't named after him."

"That bad, huh?"

"Horace."

"Ouch. Here's a toast to your parents for having the good sense to name you Brant instead of Horace. Although… Horace would lend itself to an unusual nickname for a boy."

"Funny."

"Where did Brant come from?"

"Was Mom's idea. I've been told it's Old Norse. Means sword of fire or somethin' like that."

"I knew it!"

"You knew what?"

"You're a Viking!"

He laughed. "Garland, I'm not a Viking."

"You are! I can totally see you in a helmet with horns, riding on your bike."

"Really?"

"Yes!"

"Hate to rain on that parade, but Vikings didn't actually have horned helmets."

"Don't tell me that. I don't want to hear that."

"So what's your middle name?"

"I don't have one."

"Yes. You do."

She shook her head vigorously.

"Okay." He shrugged. "We'll revisit that at another time, when we're not in a public place."

She laughed. "What does my middle name have to do with being in a public place?"

"Well," he said slowly, opening his hands in explanation, "if we weren't in a public place, I could hold you down until I'd located your most ticklish spot, then torture you until you gave up the information."

"You're a dangerous man. With or without a sword."

"If the horns fit..."

"What's your favorite movie?"

"Enough about colors and movies and middle names and imaginary childhood friends. Tell me something real about your life."

The quickness with which she stopped chewing, went still, and lost all sign of happiness was disturbing. She stared at him like that was the last thing in the world she wanted to talk about.

"That bad, huh?" He mimicked her question from earlier.

She looked at the half taco she held in midair, set it down on the platter in front of her, then said, "It's not fun." She looked up. "I mean, sometimes it is. College was great. I was a long way from New York. I had friends who came from a lot of different backgrounds."

"Mostly privileged?"

She smiled. "Yeah. Mostly privileged." She looked down at the tacos in front of her, but didn't pick one up. "Then I graduated."

She sat back with a sigh and Brant was sorry he'd brought it up, but thought that once you're already cold and wet and in the water, you might as well get the swim you came for.

"What happened then?"

She pressed her lips together in a half smile. "My friends and I had fun celebrating graduation. So much fun that it made the Sunday New York Times and embarrassed my dad."

Brant was trying to put himself in her shoes and process how a night out could end up being a newspaper item, much less how it could ruin somebody's life, as it seemed to have done with Garland.

"What happened?"

"I was told that I'd be accompanying my dad to Austin for the summer. His company is investing in renovating the Yellow Rose and developing this whole area for touristy draw." Brant nodded for her to continue. "He also called in favors to get me a last minute spot in the Wharton School of Business MBA program. For September. First, I've never been interested in business, but he says it's time for me to start getting serious about citizenry or something like that. Second, I don't know anybody in Philadelphia. That's where the Wharton School is."

"So you didn't want to come here and you don't want to go there."

She smiled. "I didn't want to come here, but that was before I found out about Viking mechanics who ride big rumbly bikes." He acknowledged the compliment with a small smile and a nod. "And, yes, I don't want to go to Philadelphia or study business. But he gave me a choice. It's that or a box under a bridge."

"Garland, you have a degree from a fancy pants college. And even if you didn't," he waved at the world around them, "lots of people get by with a hell of a lot less and they don't end up in boxes under bridges."

"I know. But I'm not them. I'm, like, handicapped."

Brant looked confused. "Handicapped. What are you

talking about?"

"I never expected to have to work. At least not like the people you're talking about."

"You mean not like being a mechanic or," his eyes darted around, "being manager of a place like this."

Her voice was quiet. "Yeah. Like that."

She looked away for a minute, like she didn't want to face him. Brant didn't like that any more than he liked the idea of her old man being an asshole to his own daughter, treating her like she was chattel because she partied out a milestone.

"Your tacos are not goin' to be fit to eat if you keep ignorin' them." Her eyes drifted back to the plate in front of her. "Go on. Try the al carbon. It's one of my favorites even if it doesn't qualify as real Texmex. Not that fish tacos do either."

A little of the light came back into her eyes as she reached for the one he pointed to. "Enough about my sob story. Tell me something real about *your* life."

Brant's gaze drifted over to the rock face cliff on the other side of the road. "I went to high school about fifteen minutes from here."

She seemed delighted by that tidbit and started a rapid fire series of questions without giving him a chance to answer. "You did? Did you ride a big bad motorcycle to school? Did all the girls want to get in your pants? Did you play football? I'll bet you did. How big was your school?"

When she paused for a breath and looked at him expectantly, his lips spread into a slow smile. “One at a time. Pick the one that’s most important to you first.”

“Okay. Did all the girls get in your pants?” Her face was alight with mischief.

“Of course not. Only the knockouts.”

She laughed. “Did you ride a motorcycle to school?”

“Not usually, but I had a hot car that turned heads.” She shook her head. “What? You think I’m makin’ that up?”

“No. I think it wasn’t the car that was turning heads.” She was watching for his reaction, so there was no missing the little flush that pinked his skin. She almost choked on a taco. “You’re blushing!”

“I’m not blushing.”

“You are!”

Brant saw the people at the next table turn to look. He leaned toward Garland and lowered his voice. “Maybe I have a little sunburn from the river, but I’m not blushing. Men like me don’t blush. You might as well call me a pussy.”

Garland sat back. As her face froze into a serious expression, she looked more intense. She stared into his eyes for ten full seconds before calmly saying, “Pussy.”

“You did not just say that.”

“I did. Want to hear it again?” She giggled. He stood up, threw cash on the table, grabbed her by her arm and started pulling her off the patio and onto the parking lot. She couldn’t stop laughing. “Sticks and stones. Sticks and stones.”

"Sticks and stones, my ass."

"Where are we going?"

"Someplace where I can smack you on your beautifully formed behind if you call me a pussy again. Christ, Garland. I would hospitalize you for that if you were a man."

He got on his bike, but before she climbed on, she said, "It's just a word, Brant."

"Words can be weapons, Garland. All women know that."

Minutes later they pulled up to Brant's front door. He didn't bother to roll the bike in. He pulled Garland inside and slammed the door with his foot.

Towering over her, he said, "Want to say it again?"

Her gaze drifted from the challenge in his eyes down to his mouth and lingered there. "Maybe. Kiss me first."

She didn't have to ask twice.

He nudged her against the wall behind her until she could feel every inch of his body pressing into hers. When she gasped at the contact, Brant's mouth smashed against her parted lips. He growled deep in his throat. Garland had never before kissed a guy capable of making a sound like that. She was sure of it. It was an expression of earthy masculine supremacy that made a direct connection with the nerve endings in her core.

When her tongue battled his, Brant was so delighted with the blatant push back that he had to suppress a chuckle. He didn't want her to misunderstand and think he was laughing at her. He wasn't. He was simply euphoric that he'd found a woman with enough fire to call him a pussy then try to take control of sex. Girls like that didn't cross his path every day. He knew, in fact, that such a thing could easily happen only once in a lifetime.

Bending at the knees, he grasped the backs of her thighs and lifted her so that she could wrap her legs around his waist. When he started walking them toward his bedroom, she tightened her grip and nipped his earlobe.

"Christ, woman."

Brant was glad he'd gone to the trouble of changing sheets and making his bed. Just in case. He hadn't known for sure that the day would bring them to that moment, but he knew he wanted to make a good impression. A girl like Garland shouldn't lie down on dirty sheets and he knew he'd feel the same way if she didn't come from money.

When he set her down on her feet, she pulled away and looked around. The bedroom was on the back of the house with a view toward Austin. A gorgeous view.

"Wow. This is…" She didn't finish. Brant was behind her pulling her damp tee over her head and kissing her neck. When she was left in a damp bikini top, she almost immediately started shivering. "Ahhh! It's cold in here. Either take me back outside or get me out of these wet clothes."

"Hmmm. I pick B."

"Good choice."

They hurried out of wet clothes as fast as they could

and scrambled to get under the covers of his bed, each playfully trying to shove the other out of the way. They burrowed under his sheets and black satin comforter, covered in goosebumps, and unable to stop laughing. The cold had pulled Garland's nipples into hard beads just begging to be touched. And laved.

Within minutes the body heat had them both pushing at the covers instead of clinging to them. When Garland felt the substantial evidence of Brant's arousal, she reached between them to take him in hand and stroke.

"Good God, man. This thing is scary big." He laughed into her neck. "Don't you dare leave marks on me."

Brant hesitated. He was fast coming to the conclusion that he wanted to keep this girl. Marks that branded her as his would be a nice bonus.

He pulled away and looked at her. "Leave all the marks you want. I'll wear 'em proudly."

The look on her face told him he was going to destroy the mood, but he knew a couple of ways to get back on track. He'd joked about high school girls getting in his pants, but the truth was that he'd never had any trouble in that department. Women liked him. Maybe it was his looks. Maybe it was an attitude. He'd never cared one way or the other, but he found himself wondering if it would be possible to get Garland St. Germaine interested in a permanent kind of way.

THEY SPENT THE rest of the afternoon in bed. Exploring.

Experimenting.

"You hungry?" Brant asked. They were lying on their sides facing each other.

"I'm in an orgasmic stupor. Couldn't begin to tell you if I'm hungry or not."

He chuckled. "It's dark out."

She sat up and looked out the window a few feet from the foot of the bed. Some of the lights of Austin twinkled back at her. "Wow, Brant. This is gorgeous."

He ran the back of his hand down the curve of her side. "Not nearly as gorgeous as this."

"It's too late to sweet talk me. You already got what you wanted."

"How do you know what I want?"

"Hold on." She held her hand to her forehead. "My ESP tells me you want food."

"You wore the tacos right off me."

"How romantic." She laughed. "So. Are you cooking or offering something out of a box?"

He cocked his head at her. "Don't know yet. Do *you* know how to cook?"

She threw herself backward on the bed laughing. "Don't be ridiculous. Of course I don't know how to cook."

"It's not ridiculous. It's a basic survival skill, Garland. A way to keep from ending up in a box under a bridge."

She stopped laughing. "You may be right. It's just not a skill I've needed to survive before now." She leaned up on an elbow. "So you know how to cook?"

He grinned. "Well, I'm not a gourmet. The only French thing I can cook is French *fries*. But I can throw some stuff in a skillet and have it come out edible."

"Good enough for me. You got some dry clothes I can put on?"

He gave her a pair of cotton boxers and a Harley tee shirt. Both swallowed her, but he found a safety pin to help hold the boxers in place. Half an hour later they sat down to a Hamburger Helper pasta mix with a few green peppers and carrots thrown in.

"This looks like a mess, but it's yummy."

"Yeah?" His eyes twinkled at the compliment. "Well, it's not special or anything."

"It is special." She smiled. "It's my birthday dinner."

His jaw went slack. "This is your birthday?"

"Yep. I'm a Gemini baby. Sign of the twins."

"Why didn't you say somethin' earlier? I would have planned… I don't know. Somethin' else."

"Why? This was the best birthday ever. I did things I've never done before. I rode on a motorcycle. And not just any motorcycle, a big bad black work of art." He grinned. "I swam in something that's not a pool or an ocean. I got river mud between my toes. Okay. That part was kind of, ew, but it was still a new experience."

He laughed at the way she scrunched up her nose.

"That's all good, babe, but what about cake? And a wish candle? More important, why didn't your dad have a plan?"

She shrugged and looked away for a second. "He forgets more often than not. Since my mom died, and since I didn't have birthdays during the school year, there was nobody around to make a big deal out of it. So, you know, it's not a big deal." She paused. "Plus…" She made circles in the air with a finger pointed at Brant. "I got beefcake." She wiggled her eyebrows.

Ignoring her attempt at humor, he said, "It *is* a big deal." After a few seconds he got up and started looking through drawers and cabinets. He found a candle in a holder fashioned from recycled iron, and a lighter. He pulled a piece of paper out of a little spiral notebook, scribbled something quickly, and folded it up.

Moving her plate aside, he set the candle in front of her and said, "I don't have a good singin' voice, but happy birthday. Make a wish for what you want more than anything."

Her eyes searched his for a few moments until they grew bright with unshed tears. When her eyelids closed slowly, it forced a single tear down her cheek. She opened her eyes, blew out the candle, and then swiped at the stray tear, trying to make light of the incident and cover with quiet self-deprecating laughter.

"Hey," he said. She felt the timbre of that one word, as he pulled her to her feet and wrapped his arms around her. He reveled in the feel of her relaxed warmth and braless body. "Your wish makes you sad?"

"No. Well, yes. It's just… you know I can't tell or it won't come true." She dropped her head back so she could look up into his face. "When's your birthday?"

"October. The first."

"Fall. My favorite time of year. At least it is in New

England. There's always this one day when you get up and look outside and, somehow, the shadows look different and you go, 'It's here!'."

Brant ran his thumb over her cheek. "You a poet, Garland?"

She smiled. "We're all poets in our own way."

"Maybe."

He handed her the piece of folded paper.

"What's this?" She looked as excited as if it was a diamond necklace.

She quickly unfolded the paper and read…

Happy Birthday, Beautiful. This coupon is good for one night on the town. On me. - B.F.

She gave him a sweet kiss that went on forever. "Thank you. And I have it in writing that you're taking me out again."

"Every chance I get."

She placed a kiss on his bare chest as she slid both hands into the rear pockets of his jeans and gave a suggestive little squeeze.

"You comin' on to me?" He looked down through hooded eyes, but she didn't miss the twitch of the corners of his mouth.

"What makes you think that?" she said as one of her hands casually drifted around to the copper buttons on the front of his jeans.

CHAPTER 5

THE DAYS OF summer went by faster than Garland would have imagined possible. When she'd gotten on the plane for Texas, eleven weeks had seemed like an eternity, but after Brant entered the picture, she found herself wishing it was eleven years. Or eleven decades.

Whenever an errant thought like that surfaced, she shoved it down hard and focused on something else. Anything else.

When her father wanted to give small dinner parties at the villa to entertain business contacts, he had Garland stand in for a wife with menu planning, table arranging, and, of course, charm. Occasionally he also "asked" her to join golf outings. She suspected that he liked to show off the fact that she was a damn decent golfer. She liked golf and wouldn't have minded so much if it wasn't for the fact that temps were hitting triple digits every day.

As Brant told her, people who weren't born and bred to heat had a hard time acclimating.

She spent every available minute she could with Brant, which meant anytime he was off work and her father hadn't put in a demand for her time and talents.

Brant spent his days looking forward to seeing Garland at night. He was teaching her how to cook simple stuff, which was more fun than he would have thought. From his point of view, Garland made things fun just by being present.

She never spent the night, but the time they had together was good. Whenever Brant thought about the probability that the end of summer meant the end of Garland, he had difficulty breathing.

One night in late July he made good on his birthday promise of a night out. There was a particular band that he wanted to share with his girl.

She arrived in a red sundress pretty enough to wear to a cocktail party. She parked next to the Camaro and noticed that it was shined to sparkling perfection.

Brant saw her from the window and walked out to greet her wearing his sexy smile, a black AC/DC tee shirt he'd gotten at a concert in San Antonio the year before, and black jeans. Garland thought he looked perfectly scrumptious, and would have been okay with skipping birthday night.

"You look gorgeous."

"That's my line," he said as he drew her into his arms.

"You'll be sorry if you kiss me. This dress-matching lipstick will give you a permanent case of punch mouth."

"Hard choice. The lady or punch mouth." She smirked. "I'm thinking you wearin' that could be a spankable offense."

"Not unless you want that to be the last time you

touch me."

"Uh oh. Hit a nerve. Let's get back to kiss talk."

"Tell you what. Give me drinks and feed me. I won't reapply, which means that after dinner I'm all yours."

"Likin' the sound of that better."

"So where are we going?"

"Your coach awaits." He gestured toward the Camaro.

"I'm thanking the birthday gods that you don't expect me to ride the hog in this dress."

"No, baby. The only hog I expect you to ride in that dress…" She stopped him in mid-sentence by slapping at his stomach. "Ow."

She laughed. "Do not pretend that hurt, Mr. Steel Body."

"Garland, you say the damndest things."

He shut the door after she'd tucked her skirt in.

"So where did you say we're going?"

As he pulled out he glanced back and forth between the road ahead and his beautiful passenger.

"There's a historic hotel downtown, The Driskill. It's got a grill and it's only a couple of blocks from the best live music in the world."

"Nice. So what makes it the best music in the world?"

"This is where the innovators come to be heard before they either make it or get broken to bits by suit-wearing accountants who don't know the first or last thing about music."

BRANT SPENT A big part of dinner entertaining Garland with tales of colorful events that happened in the hotel.

She laughed. “Do you believe this stuff?”

He smiled. “Just because it’s folklore doesn’t mean it’s not true.”

She sat back. “Whew. I’m stuffed.”

“Too bad.”

“What do you mean, too bad?”

“You’re about to find out.”

Right on cue, the waiter set a plate in front of her with the biggest piece of fudge cake she’d ever seen. In the middle was one red candle, which he lit, saying, “We hope you enjoy your birthday, Ms. St. Germaine. It’s been a privilege to have you as our guest for your special occasion.”

“Thank you,” she told him, cutting her eyes to Brant.

“Happy birthday, baby. You don’t have to make another wish if you don’t want to, but if you have one that makes you happy when you think about it…”

She blew out the candle without taking her eyes away from Brant and gifted him with her most radiant smile, the one that made his heart swell so big it felt like it would break his ribs.

Brant took her hand as they left the restaurant, making their way across the lobby to the door that led out to the street. Garland’s eyes were sparkling with that special light he treasured, when Brant heard someone behind them call her name. She froze, stopped walking, and her grip bit down on his hand like a vice.

A middle-aged man was coming straight for them with a scowl on his face. Brant put it together in a heartbeat. It was the dick who confused fatherhood with slaveholding.

David St. Germaine stopped in front of the two of them and gave Brant a once-over that couldn't possibly have conveyed more contempt.

"So this is what you've been doing with your spare time?"

"Dad. This is Brant Fornight. Brant, this is my father, David St. Germaine."

Normally Brant would have extended his hand, but decided to make an exception.

Since he was three inches shorter than Brant, St. Germaine tilted his head in a practiced way that gave the illusion he was looking down anyway. "You're out with my daughter. What? On a date? And what do you do, may I ask?"

"Well," Brant drawled, "I like watching "The Price is Right" and going for long moonlight skis on the lake."

Garland's father gave him a look dripping with disdain.

"You're being rude, Dad."

"I don't need etiquette lessons from you, Garland. Go home. I'll talk to you later." He walked away, leaving the impression that there was no question his command would be obeyed. They'd been dismissed.

"Garland?"

She glanced at Brant. "Well, there went a perfectly

lovely evening. I'm so sorry it was spoiled."

"It's not spoiled unless we allow it. Let's go do what we came to do and forget him."

Garland hesitated. She looked more than doubtful. She looked worried. "Okay. You're right. He's not ruining my birthday."

"That's right."

"At least not until later," she murmured.

"Baby. You afraid of him? Does he hit you?"

She shook her head. "God no. If he did then maybe I'd have the courage to… Never mind. Let's go find some music suitable for slow dancing."

"We can try, but that's asking a lot for 6th Street on a Saturday night."

GARLAND DID HER best to appear like she was enjoying a lighthearted night out. She didn't want Brant to be disappointed, but she never stopped thinking about the run-in. It was around midnight when they pulled into Brant's drive.

When the car stopped, neither one moved to get out.

"Comin' in?" he asked, but had a sinking feeling that he already knew the answer.

She turned toward him. "Not tonight. There's going to be an argument when I get home and I want to get it over with." She paused. "I'm so sorry about the way he acted."

"Don't apologize. You're not responsible for the fact that your old man is an asshole. You've got my number.

Call me if you need me."

"I will."

When she reached for the door handle, he put his hand on her arm. "Will I see you tomorrow?"

"Of course. Tomorrow's Sunday. We always spend Sundays together." The words caught in her throat when she realized that over half their Sundays together were gone, and the rest were going to be threatened since her father knew about Brant.

He pulled her in for a quick kiss. "Countin' on it."

GARLAND'S FATHER WAS sitting in the living room with an ankle resting on one knee and a highball glass resting on the other.

Waiting. For her.

She decided that the best course of action was to take the offensive.

"You were rude to my friend tonight, demonstrating exceptionally bad manners. What you do reflects on me, you know." She loved having the opportunity to turn those phrases around on him.

Unbothered by her feeble attempt at independence, he smirked. "I brought you down here to keep you out of trouble this summer and you decide to use the time to go slumming?"

"Do you even hear yourself when you talk?"

"I do. That's why I'll remember telling you that you will not be seeing that garbage again."

David St. Germaine rose and was almost out of the

room when he heard her say, “Yes. I will.

“You said I had to come here for the summer. Nothing was *ever* said about choosing my friends or specifying how I’d spend my time. I’m an adult. It’s time to let me make a few decisions for myself and, if I make wrong ones sometimes, it doesn’t make me bad. Just human.”

“You don’t have the luxury of being ‘human’.”

“Do you think Mom fought to stay alive? Or do you think it just got too hard to not be human?”

His face was devoid of all emotion, his eyes hard and cold. He left the room without another word. As far as he was concerned, he’d made his desires clear and that was all that needed to be said.

BY NOON THE next day Brant was getting worried that she wasn’t coming. When he heard engine noise outside, he closed his eyes with relief and felt his shoulders relax. He wasn’t happy to see how tired she looked when he opened the door.

“Sorry I’m late.”

“You look like shit.”

That got a little smile. “Thanks a lot. You look incredible. Like always.” She stepped into his waiting arms and let him rock her back and forth on her feet. “Hey. I finally got my slow dance. You’re pretty good at this.”

“Want to tell me about it?”

“Sure. He said I’m not to see you again. I said that wasn’t part of the deal.”

“That’s it.”

"You don't really want a reenactment."

"I want whatever will make you feel better."

"*You* make me feel better." The words were out of her mouth before she thought about the ramifications. That was not the kind of thing you said to a casual summer fling.

Brant knew it, too, and he didn't want to leave her alone in her confession. "I feel the same way, baby. When you didn't come this morning.... Well, you're here. That's what counts."

He kissed the top of her head. "What do you want to do today?"

"Just stay here exactly like this."

"Okay. If you get tired or hungry or thirsty, let me know."

"Well, now that you mention it, I could use a slow hot screw and a fast frozen Margarita."

"It just so happens I know where to get both those things."

They started their Sunday with unhurried, thorough lovemaking. Brant insisted she keep eye contact with him. The combination of that and his excruciatingly slow thrusts made emotion bubble to the surface. It broke free in the form of big hot tears. He rocked her through sobs, murmuring sweet nothings about how he was right there with her, how everything would be alright.

"Brant, I..."

"What, baby?" When he could see she wasn't going to finish the sentence, he said, "There's nothin' you can't tell me."

She nodded, but didn't say more.

MID-MORNING ON MONDAY the shop phone rang and somebody yelled that it was for Brant.

"Mr. Fornight, you're needed at H.R."

"Right now?" He looked over at the electric maintenance vehicle he was working on.

"Yes. Mr. Fornight."

Brant wiped his hands and hopped in one of the golf carts. When he walked into the air-conditioned offices, the receptionist pointed him to the right.

"In there."

Brant didn't remember ever seeing the guy who sat down across the desk.

"Please, sit down." He gestured for Brant to sit across from him.

"Getting right to the point. I'm afraid we have a breach of policy to bring to your attention. We *strongly* discourage fraternizing with guests, Mr. Fornight."

He gaped. "Fraternizing with guests?"

"It has come to my attention that you're seeing one of our guests socially." He stopped to wrinkle his brow as if he was remembering what face to make when. "So I'll be honest. You've done good work for The Yellow Rose and we don't want to let you go, but we will have to insist that you curtail any plans to see our guests on your off time."

Brant gave the guy a hard look. "Look," he pointedly looked at the nameplate on the desk, since no introductions had been made, "*Doug*. What I do on my off time is *my* business. What guests of The Yellow Rose do on their time is *their* business."

Doug pursed his lips. "It would be a mistake to take that stance. We won't have any choice but to dismiss you."

Brant clenched his teeth. "Do your worst."

"You sure about that, son? Jobs like yours don't grow on trees."

"Anything else?"

Doug shook his head like he was a principal who was disappointed in a student demonstrating bad behavior. "Two weeks' severance. One month insurance. You can opt in for COBRA if you want, but you have to let us know now."

Brant got to his feet. "Yes to the money. Yes to the insurance *and* COBRA. I'd like to say no to the screw over, but looks like it's too late for that." He let the door slam against the wall on his way out.

It wasn't that Brant cared about that job in particular. It wasn't particularly better or worse than any other shop. It was the principle of St. Germaine using his influence to try to manipulate Garland that made Brant see red. When St. Germaine hadn't been able to bend her to his will directly, he'd tried to use the indirect approach.

At least Brant knew what he was dealing with. Garland's father was a slick, well-dressed thug.

"Hey, Boss. What's up?" Apparently Ricardo could see that Brant didn't look happy.

"I've been canned, man. Made a VIP mad."

"No. Really?"

"Yep. Gettin' my stuff and I'm outta here." Brant paused and looked at Ricardo. "If you want my job, you should hightail it up to H.R. and apply."

"Doesn't seem right."

"Hey. Somebody's gonna get it. Might as well be you. I'm done with The Yellow Rose in this lifetime." Brant threw him the key. "Treat everybody fair."

An hour later Brant was sitting on his sofa staring straight ahead and pulling on a cold beer when the phone rang.

He answered. "Talk."

"Sounds like you're in a bad mood?"

"Aw, baby. Didn't think it was you. I figured you'd think I was at work."

"I did. There were leftover sandwiches from this golf thing I went to this morning so I brought them to you for lunch. One of the guys told me you were fired, like under his breath."

"That's the long and short of it."

"I'm so sorry this happened."

"No need to apologize, babe. We both know you didn't do it. And we both know who did."

There was a slight pause. "You don't think my father…"

"They gave me a choice. Stop 'fraternizing with guests' and keep my job. Or not."

"Oh no. He wouldn't."

"Oh yeah. He did."

"You chose seeing me for another month over keeping your job?"

He sighed into the phone, not really understanding that she didn't take that choice for granted. "Of course."

After a lengthy silence, she asked, "What are you going to do?"

"Actually, I was just sittin' here thinkin' about that. When I see you I'll tell you all about it."

"Come get me."

"Come get you? Yeah. I guess we're done sneakin' around."

"He can't put me in a cage, but he did take the wheels away."

Brant clenched his fist thinking about St. Germaine and his overbearing tactics. "Look for me in twenty minutes. Bike wear."

Garland was watching for Brant from the front window of the villa. When the Camaro came to a stop, she was already out the door and running toward the car. She jumped in and threw herself into a kiss he'd never forget.

"What was that about?"

"You chose me."

Brant's eyes half closed when he raised his chin. "Yeah. I did." Pulling away, he headed out of the resort via the immaculately groomed, tree-lined boulevard. "You already had lunch?"

"No. I was planning on having sandwiches with you. At the shed."

"Well, where are they?"

"I left them for the others."

He smiled. "I'll bet they're even more in lust with you than before."

"Pffffft. Doubt it."

"So you could eat?"

She grinned. "Have I ever said no?"

"We still talkin' food?"

She played at smacking his bicep. "Are you saying I'm slutty? Right now I say no to everyone, but you."

"As it should be."

"Do you?"

Brant glanced at his passenger and saw that she was serious. "Garland, I haven't even thought about being with anybody else since the day you turned up lost and hitched a ride in a cart. Jesus Christ. Don't you know that?"

She smiled with bright satisfaction and nodded slightly. "I wanted to hear you say it."

"So what do you want?"

"What do you mean?"

"For lunch. Remember?"

"Do not speak to me as if I have dementia. I'm a Dartmouth graduate."

"So you are. Do they teach question evasion at Dartmouth?"

"Something hot. Spicy hot."

He smiled. "I know just the place."

He pulled into a roadside dump with a tin roof and a

sign hand painted in irregular letters, Ragin Cajun.

The place was open air with a stained concrete floor. Big ceiling fans turned lazy revolutions, fast enough to move the air around, but not fast enough to blow napkins off laps. The table tops were made of something that looked like gray plastic linoleum.

"You sure it's safe to eat here?" She looked ready to run.

Brant laughed and leaned down to whisper in her ear. "Pussy."

"Don't start with the name calling because you know it will not end well for you."

"Feisty." He smiled and guided her to a table in the back.

"Must be seat yourself."

"Yeah." He nodded toward the chair in front of her. "So sit those very fine hindquarters down in that chair there and grab a menu."

Garland gave her order to a waiter with red sauce on his apron and a missing front tooth. She asked for the tamest thing she could find on the menu. Grilled chicken. Boiled potatoes. Corn on the cob.

"I thought you wanted spicy."

She looked around at the lunch clientele. "This place is plenty spicy. So you were going to tell me what you're thinking you'll do next."

He grabbed a hot hush puppy out of the basket that had just been set on their table. "You know that GTO I told you about? My next hobby car?" She nodded. "Well I got to thinkin' about how much money I make whenever I restore a classic car and sell it. Then I was thinkin' that if I took all the hours I spend workin' at a shop and spent that time on the business of makin' hobby cars for rich guys, I'd make more money than I have been." He took a swig of beer. "And I'd be my own man."

"That's a phenomenal idea. Phenomenal and entrepreneurial."

"I can use the shop at the club, which means I won't have any overhead."

"The club?"

"I never told you about the club?" He looked down at the hush puppies. "Huh. Well, I know I told you my family lives close by."

"You did tell me that, yes."

"So." He cleared his throat. "Here's the thing. My dad is really involved in a motorcycle club. In fact, he's the president."

Her eyes widened. "You mean like Hell's Angels. He's in charge of a gang?"

"It's not a gang. It's a club. And no. It's not like Hell's Angels. Exactly."

"How close is *not* exactly?"

"Well, income opportunities may not always be completely above board."

"Oh God."

"No. Don't get me wrong. It's nothing that would hurt people. Sometimes the law meddles in people's lives when it shouldn't."

She stared. "I'm afraid to ask for details."

"Wouldn't do you any good, because I don't know details. I'm not a member."

"No?'

"Nope."

"Why?"

Brant looked at her expectant face for a long time before answering.

"There's a difference between what's legal and what's moral." She nodded her agreement. "Since I can make enough money to cover my needs, it seemed pointless to take a chance on a jail sentence."

"Jail?"

Brant nodded. "Yeah. My old man did two stints at Huntsville while I was growin' up. Every time he left, he was somebody else when he came back. Decided pretty early on it wasn't for me.

"Dad formed the club with six other guys who'd been to Nam. It's grown. They're about seventeen now. Plus a couple more who aren't full-fledged members yet."

Garland still looked as wide-eyed as if she'd just come upon the James Gang, which made Brant chuckle. "You curious?"

She closed her mouth and thought about it. "Well, yeah. I think I am."

"How curious?"

"Where's this going?"

"Well, next Friday night they're havin' a Pig Party."

Garland narrowed her eyes. "You mean where all the

guys bring the ugliest woman they can find and the one with the ugliest gets a prize?"

It was Brant's turn to look wide-eyed. "Uh no. I mean where we roast a pig and eat barbeque sandwiches."

"Oh. Okay. Go on."

"Everybody will be there. My friends and my family. Naturally, I'd love a chance to show you off."

"So it's just sandwiches? No arrests? No pictures for the papers?"

He laughed softly and crossed his heart. "Scouts' honor."

"You were a Scout?"

"Absolutely. Do your best. That's the motto."

"Are you making that up?"

"No!" He laughed. "That's the motto. My mom was a Cub Scout Den Mother. Do they really have parties where guys bring ugly women for prizes?"

"Unfortunately yes. Sometimes money creates a veneer of gentility that scratches off easier than a lottery ticket."

"You've bought lottery tickets," he said drily.

"We used to get them as prizes for stupid stuff at sorority parties."

"What kind of stupid stuff?"

"Okay, well, going with the pig theme… you might get a prize for being the one who could sing "I Want Your Sex" with a pig mask on."

Brant stared at Garland for a full minute before saying, "Babe. You and I come from two different worlds."

"Right now that doesn't matter to me. When it's just the two of us together, the rest is just..."

He leaned in and lowered his voice. "Just what?"

"Not important."

Brant reached over and ran his finger down her cheek. "So you're in for a Pig Party?"

She grinned. "Do I ever say no?"

He threw some money down on the table and said, "I'm hopin' not today. Let's get out of here."

CHAPTER 6

BRANT HAD ENOUGH money saved to live on for a while without needing to earn. Knowing the end of summer was closing in like an executioner made him want to spend every second he could with the heiress either in his bed or on the back of his bike. He and Garland spent the heat of the days in the cool dark cocoon of his bedroom. Mornings and evenings, he showed her all the reasons why he loved Austin and explained why he couldn't see himself ever living anywhere else.

When they foraged for food, Garland insisted that Brant try curry. He insisted that she try crawfish. They learned the only thing that they could agree on wholeheartedly was Mexican food. And Brant's Hamburger Helper.

Garland loved going out on the bike at night. She reveled in the way the warm air seemed to turn soft when they sped through the darkness. Sometimes she wished she could freeze moments and simply remain in stasis, preserving the feeling forever.

On Thursday, the day before the club party, Brant received an unexpected phone call.

"This is David St. Germaine. I'm Garland's father."

"I know who you are. What do you want?" Brant was unapologetically hostile.

"This is more about what you want. It's occurred to me that you might want something more from my daughter than a tawdry summer fling. So I think it's time we talked face to face."

"I can't think of one reason why that would interest me."

"Because you care about Garland."

Brant paused. "Where and when?"

"Tonight at the Headliners Club. It's..."

"I know where it is."

"Well, aren't you full of surprises? Eight o'clock. I'll send a car."

"Send a car if you want, but I'll be drivin' my own."

"If you prefer."

He saw a flash of disappointment on Garland's face when he told her he had something to do that night, but she covered it up quickly.

"Sure. I need some time to figure out what I'm wearing to the, um, party at your club."

"Not my club, babe."

"Okay. At your dad's club then. So. Any hints? What do women wear to these things?"

When he got an image of what women wore to club

parties, he could have kicked his own ass for having ever suggested taking Garland. He was busy thinking of new ways to call himself an idiot, when he realized Garland was talking.

"Hello? What should I wear?"

"We'll be on the bike. So wear those jeans that I like so much."

"The tight ones."

"Yeah. Those."

"And?"

"And what?"

"Is it a topless party or do you want me to wear something in addition to jeans?"

He stared at her dumbly, thinking she didn't know how close she was when she suggested that it might be a topless party. Jesus, he was a dumb son-of-a-bitch.

"How about that pink thing?"

She looked confused. "The rose-colored halter top?"

"Yeah. That's the one. But wear a jacket over it for ridin'."

"I know the drill. You look jumpy, Brant. What's wrong?"

"What? Nothin'. Come on. Let's get you home."

BRANT ARRIVED AT Headliners at five past eight. He hoped he'd be making David St. Germaine wait for him.

"Lookin' for David St. Germaine."

The maitre d' looked him up and down. "Mr. Fornight?"

"Yes."

"I'm afraid you'll need a jacket. I believe we have something you can borrow."

The man disappeared behind a door that was disguised as raised-grain paneling, but returned in under a minute with a black coat that fit Brant like it had been made for him. It was the first time in his life that Brant had experienced having another man hold a coat for him, and he couldn't say he particularly appreciated the experience. Nonetheless, he tried to be gracious and said, "Good eye," in acknowledgment of fitting him perfectly with nothing more than a look.

Magically one of the staff, who was wearing a white coat rather than black appeared at reception. "Mr. Fornight is Mr. St. Germaine's guest. He's already seated at 17."

"Right this way," said white coat.

Brant followed the waiter into the club. It had a regal ambience of money, success, and power. The walls of the outer rooms displayed framed historical events. Remington statues appeared here and there with such casual disregard that their presence assured members they had "arrived".

St. Germaine sat in a corner by a window that overlooked the Capitol, which was entirely lit at night. The view was stunning. He gestured toward the chair opposite him.

The waiter said, "Would you care for menus now or may I get you something from the bar?"

"Please bring my guest a drink. What will you have?"

Brant looked at the waiter and, for some reason, remembered the waiter from the Ragin' Cajun who was missing a tooth that, no doubt, had been tobacco-stained like the others.

"Whiskey. Neat."

The waiter nodded once and left.

"Not a cocktail man, hmmm?"

"Not here for small talk. For the second time today, you're forcin' me to ask what you want."

"So you don't like wasting time."

"I like wastin' time. I just don't like you."

"Fair enough. I'll get to the point. I've asked you to meet me so that I can explain Garland.

"She lives life at a level you can't begin to imagine. You see this club? It's the best your town has to offer. No doubt it's the site of routine political deals that affect millions of lives. Maybe yours. Money changes hands here. Power changes hands here. And yet, to Garland, there's nothing remarkable about having a drink in an exclusive place like this. If she were here, she'd probably be thinking this club is commonplace, nothing special."

Brant looked down at the thick white linen tablecloth and the china with emerald band and gold border.

"That doesn't sound like the Garland I know. She loves new experiences, even those that really are commonplace."

St. Germaine laughed out loud. "That's just it. Don't you get it? *This* is her norm. What you're showing her is *your* norm. It's all new to her, but that newness will wear off fast and she'll be longing for the luxury and security of her real life.

"She lives in a three story penthouse worth forty-two million dollars. She wears four-thousand-dollar dresses once and gives them to charity." He sat back to assess the effect his words were having.

Brant kept his features perfectly non-committal, although the picture Garland's father painted caused his stomach to burn like it was full of acid. When Brant said nothing, he continued.

"The private jet that brought her here, the one she'll be leaving on in three weeks, belongs to me. I paid twenty-five million for it and don't get me started on how much it costs to maintain it or fly it around, not to mention the crews' salaries.

"What I'm trying to tell you is that this is Garland's center point. When she skis, it's on snow in the Alps. Not behind a cheap boat on Lake Travis. How long do you think it would take for her to get tired of long necks and tacos?"

St. Germaine seemed to be studying Brant's reactions. That was why Brant was intent on not giving him any.

"I'm sure the idea of someone like you is exciting to her. You're a novelty, but fascination with novelties wears off very fast. Don't you agree, Mr. Fornight?"

Brant didn't falter or look away. "It's not important whether I agree or not, David. The only thing that matters is whether or not Garland agrees. Her future isn't up to me. And it sure as fuck shouldn't be up to you."

St. Germaine sat back with narrowed eyes. "I'm hoping we can arrive at an understanding like gentlemen. I'd hate to have to pull out any more stops."

"You've already taken my job and Garland's transportation. What's next?"

"Remember when I said that all kinds of deals are made in places like this? Well, it might amaze you at how easy it would be for your father to be pulled over for a simple traffic violation, like say, a broken tail light. If he, a convicted felon, happened to be found in possession of a firearm, I understand that the sentence in Texas could be, what? Two to ten?"

Brant's blood was boiling like the juices in his stomach, but his eyes were ice cold and steady. "I haven't asked Garland to stay here with me. But I will. And I hope like hell she understands that it'd be a shame for a girl as special as she is to have to live in the gutter with you and your kind."

He stood, took off the jacket, dropped it on the chair, and walked out.

THE NEXT NIGHT, Brant picked Garland up at eight o'clock. She'd been listening for the distinctive rumble of the Harley and came running out the door like he was back from a war. Her exuberance was just one of the things he loved about her.

At that time of year the sun wouldn't set for another hour. So Brant got the full visual experience of Garland in her rose-colored halter top with a hem that floated around her hips like magic. The thing left her shoulders bare and shiny from the healthy tan she kept by swimming every day. He loved running kisses over the smooth skin of those shoulders, but was regretting telling her to wear that, as he imagined fighting guys off of her. His eyes touched on the slight hint of cleavage and ran over her hair, which was pulled into a braid that highlighted the white-blonde highlights she'd gotten from the combination of sun and pool. But what made him instantly hard was the extra flush in her cheeks that said she was sincerely glad to see him.

"I look okay?"

Brant snorted. "Fishin' for compliments?"

"How else am I going to get any?"

He turned over his shoulder. "No. You don't look okay. You look like a dream."

"A good one."

He laughed about the fact that she was pushing for clarification. "Listen. About tonight. Sometimes the parties get a little wild."

"No arrests. No photos."

"I think we can manage that. But stay with me. Don't go wandering off."

"Why?"

"Well, ah, sometimes local girls come to the parties because they want to find out what it's like to be with, you know, somebody rough around the edges. If you're not with me, you could be mistaken for one of them. I'm not sayin' you'd be in danger, but assumptions might be made."

"I get the picture. Glued to your side. Will you hold my hand if I need to go to the little girls' room?"

"No. But I will stand outside the door."

"You're serious."

"Yes ma'am."

WHEN THEY PULLED past the gates and parked the bike, Garland took off her jean jacket.

"You can leave that here. It'll be safe," Brant said.

She nodded then pulled the elastic that was holding her braid away and finger combed her hair out. It had been wet when she braided it and the air had dried it on the way over. The result was a fall resplendent with shiny waves that made her look like a goddess.

"You're staring," she said.

"We're leaving. No one can see you looking like this."

"No sir. I'm not leaving until I see what you do when you're not with me."

She started walking toward the music coming from the other side of the building, which made Brant have to jog to catch up.

He grabbed her and brought her to a stop. "Garland. I'm seriously not kiddin' around when I say I need you to stay *with* me."

"I wasn't going far."

He pulled her into his side and they walked around the corner of the building. A group of the guys were standing around an open fire pit, with a pig on a spit that was rigged to constantly turn like a huge rotisserie.

They were talking quietly, holding beers. Every one of them wore a sleeveless leather vest with the same artwork on the back. In the center was a depiction of a Corinthian temple with Hydra's heads emerging from the columns, snarling at the viewer. Above the artwork was an arc of text that said Sons of Sanctuary. Below was an inverted arc that said Texas.

THE EVENING WAS eye-opening for both Brant and Garland. He introduced her with pride, but noticed that some of the guys raised their brows at him as if to say, “What the fuck you doin’ with a woman like that?”

Brant introduced her to his father, his mother, and his older sister, who was married to somebody named Doobie. As the night became dark and the drink flowed freely, the mood of the party changed from a family picnic vibe to something else altogether. At one point Brant watched Garland taking everything in and tried to imagine his life through her eyes. That’s when he knew she wasn’t going to stay.

It didn’t stop him from trying.

WHEN THE CALENDAR ran down to seven days left, he made his play.

“I don’t want you to go. Stay here. With me.”

“I can’t.”

“Why?”

“Because this is your life. Not mine.”

“But it could be ours.”

“No. It couldn’t. It would always be me trying to fit into yours.”

She cried. She told him she loved him and always would. She cried some more. But in the end she left with her father.

CHAPTER 7

BRANT SAT ON his bike on a patch of grass at the southern end of the airport and watched the Germane jet take off. The sleek plane was beautiful and Arctic white, but looked miniscule sandwiched between a 747 and an Airbus on the runway. He watched it climb until it was out of sight.

Some guys would have crawled into a hole with a bottle. But Brant rode to Chuy's, took a seat on the patio, and ordered a frozen Margarita with fish tacos.

His life would be forever divided into before and after that summer. Before Garland, he'd been a simple man with simple needs. After she left, he was a man on a mission called money.

When the table server came to check on him, he put cash in her hand and stepped out the patio gate. Fifteen minutes later he was walking past the bar in the Sons of Sanctuary club house.

"Where's the old man?"

"Office," said Digger, looking up from his beer.

Brant knocked twice. When he heard his father say, "Open," he stepped in.

"Make me a prospect."

F.J. Fornight looked his son over. "What brought this on?"

"I got my reasons."

After staring Brant down for a full minute, he said, "Okay. I'll sponsor you. You know the rules. No favors."

"Got it."

"Church day after tomorrow. Seven o'clock. I'll put it to vote, but everybody has to agree."

"I know. I'll be here."

Brant had his hand on the door, when his father said, "This have anything to do with that beauty you brought by?"

It had always been impossible to get anything past his old man.

"Reasons are my own."

F.J. nodded and went back to what he was doing.

EPILOGUE

GARLAND WAS THREE weeks into the fall semester at the Wharton School when her pregnancy was confirmed. Her initial panic was assuaged when she reasoned that lots of women go to school while pregnant. She'd have to take off spring semester because of her due date. Her father would have to be told. And Brant. She couldn't decide which she dreaded most. The single saving grace was that she could do it by phone and wouldn't have to see either of their faces.

It took four days to work up her courage. She took a hot tea out onto the balcony of her University City apartment that overlooked the Schuykill River. She pulled the hoodie up on her red, boiled wool jacket because it was chilly out. If there was going to be serious unpleasantness, she wanted to deal with it outside.

The phone call with her father was every bit as awful as expected, especially the part where he insisted that there was a quick fix that could resolve the problem for everyone. It left her shaken, and thinking it was a mistake to plan to make both calls on the same day.

The phone rang three times before Brant answered.

Since she was intimately acquainted with how small his house was, she almost hung up.

"Hello."

Her breath caught, hearing the sound of his voice. It was like a blow to her solar plexus and caused her to close her eyes. "It's me."

There was a long pause before he simply said, "Garland."

She heard the lingering pain in his voice and hated herself for causing it. "I have news."

"Okay."

"I'm pregnant."

Another long pause. "I thought you were on the pill?"

"I am. Was. It's not guaranteed."

"So what do you want to do?"

"I'm having a baby in April."

"You're keepin' him."

She heard relief in Brant's voice. "Of course I'm keeping it."

"No. I didn't mean keepin' him like that. I meant you're not thinkin' about adoption or any shit like that. Because I have dibs."

"Dibs?" She smiled. "You're calling dibs on the baby?"

There was a part of her that was thrilled that Brant wanted to be father to their child.

He let out a long breath. "Yeah, if you didn't want to raise him, I would make it work. Somehow. Gonna be hard for me to be part of his life if you stay in Yankeeland."

"I guess. Okay, then. I just wanted you to know."

"Garland." His heart seized with panic knowing she was about to hang up. He didn't know what to say. He just knew that he didn't want to let go of that little piece of Garland, her voice on a phone that was fifteen hundred miles away.

"Yes?"

"How are you?"

She sighed into the receiver. "School is okay. I like business better than I thought I would." Pause. "How about you?"

"I miss you. I wish you'd change your mind. Especially now."

"I think about you a lot. But we made the right decision."

Brant barked out a laugh. "*We* didn't decide this. *You* did."

She sighed again. "Let's don't fight. I called Dad first and it was… hard."

Brant relented and backed off, as he always did. He couldn't stand to think about her hurting. Fucking David St. Germaine had some karma coming and Brant fantasized about being the one to serve it up.

"Okay. Are you… stayin' in school?"

"This semester. At least. Next semester… well, with an April baby…"

"Yeah. Let me know if you need anything?"

"Sure."

"Or just want to talk?"

It was her turn to pause. "Hearing your voice just makes it harder."

"Yeah." Brant wasn't accustomed to the sting of tears threatening. He was a bad-ass second generation biker. Not a slobbering little pussy-face bitch. "I'm here if you change your mind. At least give me regular updates about the baby."

"Okay, bye." She started to hang up and then called out. "Brant?"

He heard her voice and brought the phone back to his ear. "Yeah?"

"Why do you keep calling the baby 'he'?"

He smiled.

ON MAY 1ST, when the sun resided in the constellation of Aries, Garland St. Germaine gave birth to two big beautiful boys. Identical twins. She named them Brandon and Brannach.

When she'd learned that the 'baby' was actually babies, she and Brant Fornight had many long late-night talks before deciding that he would take one home to Texas and she would keep the other. The first time she saw the boys, she regretted that decision with all her soul. But she was also grateful for the gift of that choice because the look on Brant's face when he held Brannach told her that it was the right thing to do. She knew that little boy would help heal the scar that she'd left on her biker's heart.

They decided together that it would be easier on the boys to not know about each other. So, on the birth certificates, Brandon was given the surname St. Germaine and Brannach became a Fornight.

It was 1988 when Brant boarded a plane for Austin with a brand new baby and an ache in his heart that never went away.

TWO PRINCES

The Biker and The Billionaire
Sons of Sanctuary MC, Book 1

"I was minding my own business, buying peanuts at the H.E.B., when I saw this asshole on the cover of "NOW" Magazine. He was wearing a pinstripe suit... and my goddamned face."

—Brash Fornight

Two brothers, one a player, one a playboy, are on a collision course with destiny and a woman who thought she'd scored a coup when she was allowed a look inside the Sons of Sanctuary Motorcycle Club.

Brigid was a graduate student at the University of Texas. It wasn't hard getting her thesis approved, but finding a Hill Country motorcycle club willing to give her access to their lifestyle was starting to look impossible. Then she got a lead. A friend of a friend had a cousin with family ties to The Sons of Sanctuary. Perfect. Or so she thought.

What she wanted was information to prove a scholarly proposition. The last thing she had in mind was falling for one of the members of the club. Especially since she was a feminist academic out to prove that motorcycle clubs are organized according to the same structure as primitive tribal society.

Brash was standing in line at the H.E.B. Market when his world tipped on its axis. While waiting his turn to check out, his gaze had wandered to the magazine display and settled on the new issue of "NOW". The image on the cover, although GQ'd up in an insanely urbane way, was… him.

After reading the article, he threw some stuff in a duffle and left his only home, a room at The Sons of Sanctuary clubhouse, with a vague explanation about needing a couple of days away. He left his truck at the Austin airport and caught a plane for New York, on a mission to find a mysterious guy walking around with his face.

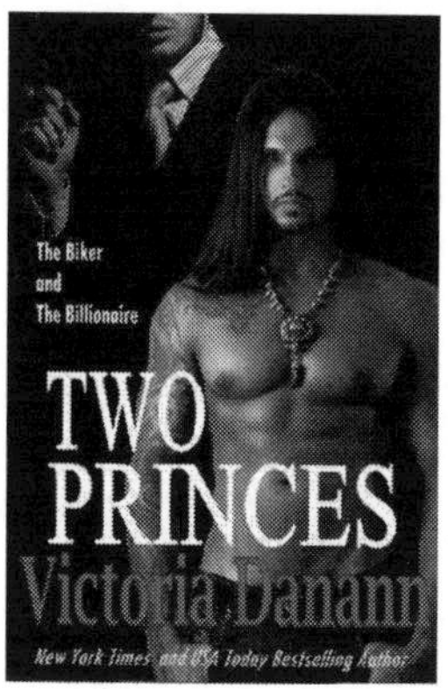

CHAPTER 1

"SIR?" BRASH FORNIGHT gradually became aware that someone behind him in the grocery checkout line was trying to get his attention. "Sir?" He refocused and glanced behind him. The woman leaning on a cart overflowing with chip bags and cookie boxes nodded toward the cashier indicating that it was his turn to move forward. Brash looked her in the eye and had to give her props. Most people wouldn't have the balls to try to herd a guy wearing Sons of Sanctuary MC leather.

THE CLUB EMPLOYED a woman who cooked and did grocery shopping several times a week as part of her job description, but Brash didn't like to explain his semi-constant craving for peanuts and he liked being teased about it even less. He didn't know whether it was the Vitamin B or the fat or just because he liked the taste, but he couldn't imagine going a day, or even half a day, without them.

THAT'S HOW HE came to be standing statue still in the grocery checkout line, being prompted by some woman with more nerve than sense. While he was waiting, his eyes drifted over the magazine display and settled on the cover of "NOW", on the Most Eligible Bachelor edition, no less. The debonair figure staring back was wearing Brash's own face and body. His style was radically different. He had short hair and wearing a designer suit with the shirt fashionably open at the neckline, but the similarity between them was inescapable.

ON IMPULSE HE grabbed the magazine and tossed it onto the conveyor belt with his week's stash of peanuts.

HE STUFFED THE bags into the saddlebags of his bike and roared toward home, nervously tapping his fingers on the handlegrips as he waited at red lights with one foot on the pavement. Eventually the anxiety overrode caution and he resorted to riding on shoulders to keep from slowing down. He was anxious to get to the privacy of his own room and read more about Brandon St. Germaine.

TWO BEERS, ONE jar of peanuts, and one "NOW" article later, Brash was sitting on the edge of his bed looking at the wall, without seeing it. His mind was buzzing with heavy thoughts. It didn't take long for him to make a decision. He hadn't gotten the nickname "Brash" because he lacked spontaneity. He pulled out his phone, Safaried a website, and waited on hold for ten minutes to hear the time of the next flight from Austin to New York.

THERE WAS A flight to Newark in a little over three hours. He looked at his watch and calculated the time it would take to drive from Dripping Springs at that time of day. As he booked the flight, he stood up, walked to the small closet, grabbed a duffel bag, and began shoving stuff into it. Ten minutes later, he closed his door and locked it, threw the duffel over his shoulder, and headed straight for the office downstairs. He dropped the duffel on the hallway floor beside the closed door and knocked.

"YEAH?" BRASH LOOKED inside, glad that his dad was by himself, and stepped in. "What's up?"

"I'm takin' personal time, Pop. Gonna be gone for a couple of days."

"What the hell is 'personal time'?"

The gruffness made Brash smile. "It means I'm not gonna be here if you call and I'm not tellin' you why."

The Sons of Sanctuary President looked up at Brash, over the top of his readers, and narrowed his eyes. "You got a secret?"

"Everybody's got secrets."

Brant Fornight studied his son for a minute. "True enough. Is it the kind of secret that could affect this club?"

Brash shook his head. "Don't see how."

"Well, then. See you… when did you say you'd be back?"

"I didn't."

"Bein' purposefully vague, are you?"

Brash grinned. "That's why they call it personal time. But I expect to be back Friday."

"You gonna have your phone with you?" When Brash nodded, Brant looked back down at his ledger in a deliberately dismissive gesture. "Well, get outta here then."

BRASH PARKED HIS bike in the airplane hangar. The structure had already been on the property when the club had bought it and turned it into a compound twenty years earlier. They used part of it for vehicle maintenance and repair and part for parking.

Some of the guys who were working looked over and shot curious glances his way when Brash threw his duffel into his pickup and started it up, but it wasn't their way to ask questions. The Sons figured that if somebody wanted you to know something, they'd tell you.

BRASH TOOK A cab to a midtown hotel, wondering all the way why human beings would choose to live in such a place. As he slid his credit card across the hotel counter to the agent on duty, he glanced at the name, Brannach Fornight. It seemed unlikely that it was a coincidence that the mysterious look-alike's first name began with the same four letters. He ordered room service and pulled out his laptop.

GETTING BASIC INTEL on the guy was easy. Within an hour Brash knew where Brandon St. Germaine worked, what kind of car he drove, what kind of women he dated, who his tailor was, and where he liked to dine. There was no shortage of photos online, but the one that grabbed his attention wasn't one of the many with starlets or debutantes on his arm. It was the one taken with his arm around his mother as they were arriving together for some red carpet fundraiser. Brash had an almost irresistible compulsion to reach up and touch her face on the screen in front of him.

OF COURSE, WHAT Brash needed wasn't basic intel. What he needed was everything there was to know. Maybe more.

The knock on the door signaled that room service had arrived. He signed the check, but gave the guy a cash tip. Five minutes later he wheeled the service cart out into the hall on his way out. The food cost a fortune, but looked and tasted like shit. It didn't take long to make a decision to close the laptop and go down to the street for a walk to clear his head and find something edible.

Brash had always been a little vain about his "nose" for eateries and it wasn't misplaced. He did seem to have a sixth sense that rarely failed him.

He looked through the window of a deli that didn't look like much. Zero ambience. Couple of tables. But the food in the case looked fresh made and the aromas called to him like a siren. He ordered a corned beef sandwich on wheat bread with mayo. The guy behind the counter just stared at him.

"Somethin' wrong?"

"Well, yeah. We don't sell corned beef on wheat with mayo. We sell corned beef on rye with brown mustard."

Brash couldn't help smiling, partly because of the New York accent and partly because of the guy's attitude. He could appreciate taking pride in work. His father had taught him that.

"Corned beef on rye with brown mustard it is."

"Coming up," said deli man as he began weighing corned beef on a scale covered in saran wrap. "What're you having with it?"

Brash looked over at the beverage case. "Bottle of Beltzings."

Deli man looked at Brash with a little more respect. "Excellent choice. Eating in or taking out?"

"Taking out. Why don't you throw in one of those apples and a piece of that pie there."

"Which one?" Brash pointed at the dessert carousel and deli man nodded.

The sandwich was big enough to make two meals. It

was also unforgettable. Brash ate in front of the computer while going over the same photos again and again.

EARLY THE NEXT morning, he called Jon Matlack, a Black Hat the club used when they needed information. It was nine central time, but Jon sounded sleepy.

"Still in bed, slacker?"

"Who is this?"

"Brash."

"Fuck, Brash. Why're you callin' in the middle of the night?"

"Got a thing that can't wait."

"What?"

"We'll get there in a minute. Right now I need to hear somethin' about loyalty to the one who's payin' your bill. Know what I mean?"

Jon paused for a few seconds. "You mean you don't want the old man to know."

"I mean I don't want *anybody* to know, *especially* not the old man. If you're not good with that, tell me now. 'Cause if you take this job and betray my confidence, your last meal will be your own balls."

"Jesus, Brash. No need to go graphic on me. The answer is yeah. I can keep your secret." Black Hat was sounding more awake, which was good with Brash. "What do you need?"

"Everything you can find on Brandon St. Germaine. And I need it in six hours."

Brash could hear a female voice in the background.

That was followed by a muffled sound, like Jon had put his hand over the phone and said something to her.

"I'm up and on it."

"Hold on. What's the charge?"

"Between five and nine, depends on the risk."

"Okay. Call me back at this number. Be prepared to walk me through it on the phone. Don't want anything sent electronically."

"Yep. You got it. Later."

AT FOUR O'CLOCK, Brash stepped out of the elevator into the top floor offices of Germane Enterprises, wearing sunglasses and a hoodie pulled up to cover his long hair. The receptionist looked at him with more curiosity than disdain.

"Can I help you?"

Leaning on the counter, he glanced at the name plate next to her keyboard. It said Diane Nix. She was cute. Blonde with an athletic body. Just his type.

"Yes, you can, Diane. I'm here to see Brandon St. Germaine."

"Do you have an appointment?"

"I do." He made a show of looking at his sports watch. "I'm a couple of minutes late. The elevator stopped on every floor."

"Your name?"

"Brash Fornight."

She lifted the receiver of the interoffice phone system. "I'll just check with his assistant."

"No need. I know the way."

Of course he didn't know the way, but he picked a hallway and started walking. Diane called after him to wait and he suspected she would be making a call to security next. He hoped he could find the Big Dog House and get inside before uniforms arrived. He passed dozens of offices encased in glass walls, but didn't look right or left. His goal was the big double doors at the end of the hall.

Brandon St. Germaine was sitting at his desk, talking on the phone, when Brash charged in looking like a carjacker. He walked straight to the edge of the executive desk, tore off his sunglasses, and waited for "eligible bachelor" to register the unique character of the event.

Brandon barely stifled a gasp when he looked up into eyes that were so very like his own. So much like his own they were… identical. "I'll have to call you back, Phil-lippe."

When two security guards rushed in, Brandon calmly held up his hand signaling that there was no alarm.

"Trouble, sir?"

"No," said Brandon. "Just a misunderstanding. Thank you for your quick response. Please close the door on your way out."

The guards looked at Brash's back with suspicion, and glanced at each other uncertainly, but complied and backed away, closing the door as requested.

Alone in the large office overlooking the east river, Brash and Brandon stared at each other for a long time without moving. Finally, Brandon said, "Who are you?"

"Brannach Fornight. I saw your picture on a magazine." He glanced around and saw the "Now" cover. Nodding toward it, he said, "That one. Flew here from Austin to try and sort this…" He motioned between the two of them and his gaze drifted to a large bowl of peanuts sitting on the desk. That caused him to smirk and shake his head. "Have a craving for peanuts, myself." He pulled a bag from the pocket of his hoodie as if to demonstrate. Brandon continued to stare in silence. "I can see you're surprised. I know how you feel. I've had a couple of days to digest the possibilities. You haven't."

Brandon cleared his throat. "Yeah."

"You want to have a conversation?"

"Yeah." Brandon blinked a couple of times like he was forcing himself to be fully present in the room. "I have something I have to do now." He looked at his watch. "How about dinner?" Looking Brash up and down, he said, "On me."

"Alright."

"Meet me tonight at eight at Pollegro's." He had taken a pad with his name printed at the top and was scribbling. "It's in Little Italy. Any cab driver will know where it is. When you get there, give them my name and they'll seat you."

Brash took the note Brandon handed him. "You're not going to stand me up. Right?"

Brandon rose and couldn't help but notice that he was exactly the same height as Brannach Fornight. He pulled out his cell phone and handed it to Brash. "I won't stand you up. But put your number in just in case there's traffic."

Brash handed over his own phone to reciprocate. Each programmed their names and numbers into the other's phone. Brash put his sunglasses back on. "Eight o'clock."

Brandon nodded.

THE RESTAURANT WASN'T the typical Little Italy tourist stop. It was a hole in the wall with a barely readable sign a block and a half off Mulberry Street. Brash had located it and taken up a post across the street by seven forty-five. He had strong suspicions about his relationship to the guy who had his face, and voice, and well, his everything, but the dandy was still a stranger. So he wasn't going to be first to arrive. He stood under the awning of a closed cobbler shop to keep out of the drizzle and waited.

Ten minutes later a sleek black, long wheel base Range Rover pulled up in front. Its polish either defied rain or else the rain amplified the shine. Either way, Brash knew that Brandon St. Germaine was going to get out of the car before he did. When the car pulled away, Brandon's gaze swept side to side like he was looking for something. After a couple of seconds he locked on Brash standing across the street. Brandon jerked his head toward the eatery behind him then turned and disappeared inside the door.

Brash waited for a couple of cars to pass and jaywalked toward the nondescript door. Once inside, he did a quick scan. Nothing fancy. Small bar up front. Small rooms with a few tables in each wearing checkered tablecloths. It was quiet. Cozy. Even intimate.

Brandon didn't wait for the hostess. He made his way to a corner booth in the farthest room in the back. Brash followed and slid in opposite his doppelganger.

A young waiter wearing a white apron appeared in seconds. He looked between the two with intelligent black eyes, but didn't comment. Brash had already figured out that it was the sort of place where friendly questions weren't welcome.

"Whiskey neat."

Brandon looked at Brash in invitation to order.

"Same," Brash said in his economy-of-words biker speak.

"And menus," added Brandon.

The waiter nodded and left without a word. Brandon turned his full attention to Brash.

"You first."

"I live in Austin. Texas. I was at the grocery store gettin' peanuts." He offered a slight smirk to punctuate the point. "Waitin' in line when I saw that magazine, like I told you. I took it home. Read it. Then got on a plane to try and find out why some asshole in a pinstriped suit is walkin' around with my face."

Brandon replied with his own smirk. "What made you think I'm an asshole?"

"As far as I'm concerned, unauthorized walking

around wearing my face is an asshole activity."

Brandon nodded. "Yeah. I can relate to that. You walking into my office, my reaction was pretty much the same. So what are your thoughts?"

"We could get a DNA test, but I think we already know what the result would be."

The silent waiter waited a few feet away until Brandon nodded to indicate that he could approach. He set drinks then menus down on the table and took two steps back.

Brandon looked over at him. "Give us a minute."

The man nodded and disappeared behind a two-way swinging door with a head-height porthole window.

"You know what you want?" Brash's brows drew down over his eyes and he gave Brandon a confused look. When Brandon realized he hadn't been clear, he said, "To eat. What do you want to eat?"

Brash looked around, everywhere but at the menu in front of him. "What are you havin'?"

"Special of the day. No matter what it is. The chef's a treasure."

"Sold. Make it two."

Brandon nodded and set the menus aside. "Have you been to New York before?"

Brash shook his head. "Can't say I have. You been to Austin?"

"I haven't," said Brandon. "Even though we own a property there. A place called the Yellow Rose Resort."

Brash nodded. "Yeah? It's close to where I live. Fifteen minutes or so." Brash took a sip of whiskey. "That's good stuff."

"So what are you thinking?"

"Same as you. My pop knew your mother *really* well twenty-nine years ago."

"If our conjecture is true, then technically that would be *our* pop and *our* mom."

"I asked Pop if he'd ever been to New York. He said no. How long has your company owned the Yellow Rose Resort?"

Without saying anything, Brandon pulled his cell out of his breast pocket and selected a phone number from contacts.

He held the phone to his ear. After a couple of seconds, he said, "How long have we owned the Yellow Rose Resort in Austin?" to an unnamed someone who had answered.

"Hold on a second." Brandon's eyes met Brash's as he waited for the answer. "Since May of 1988."

"Thank you."

Brandon ended the call and put the phone down on the table. "May of 1988."

Brash's interest seemed to ignite. "You good at math?"

Brandon smirked. "Reasonably so. Enough to figure out that a summer fling could make March babies."

"If our mother visited the property that summer…"

"I know Pop worked as head mechanic at the Yellow Rose for a little while."

And there it was. They both studied each other with even more intensity than before.

Brash cleared his throat. "Is your mother married?"

"No. She never did. What about..."

"No."

"What did he say when you asked about your mother?"

"That she didn't want us. It was hard as fuck to get that much out of him. The subject was closed tighter than a nun's knees. But I can tell you this, he left no room for doubt that he wasn't happy about the arrangement. What did she tell you?"

"She just said it didn't work out and wouldn't say more. I didn't like bringing it up." Brandon took a drink and looked over at Brash. "Because it made her sad."

"Did you ever consider looking?"

Brandon nodded slowly. "I thought about it. More than that. I always planned to do it. Just never followed through. I guess living got in the way."

"Yeah."

"What you said about her not wanting you... It doesn't sound like Mom."

Brash's eyebrows went up and he looked dubious. "Well, like Pop likes to say, actions speak louder than words."

Brandon's knee jerk reaction was to want to defend his mother's character, but the guy across the table was right. He didn't have an explanation as to why his mother would have kept him and sent his brother to the exile of godforsaken Texas. But what really hurt, the thing he was having trouble coming to terms with, was the fact that his brother had been kept from him. It felt a lot like betrayal and it had been done by the one person who should have his back. His mother.

It explained a lot about the lifelong nagging feeling that he was missing something… big. A chunk of himself. The minute he'd looked up at Brannach he'd known exactly what he'd been missing.

"Yeah. I know how it looks. Fathers can't be counted on. But mothers…"

"Hold on. Don't be throwin' Pop in the bin with deadbeat dads. He ain't like that."

"Okay." Brandon agreed, but Brash thought it sounded insincere.

"Christ." Brash sat back and stared at his brother like he was trying to read his mind.

"I guess we've both got brand spanking new issues with parents."

"Hmmm. Mine are not so new."

"Fine. Speaking for myself then."

Brandon noticed the waiter keeping a discreet distance. He motioned the man over with two fingers and asked for the specials. "Two Soffici Cuscinis and a bottle of Tenuta dell'Ornellaia Masseto."

"We have several years in stock."

"What do you recommend, Mercutio?"

"2001."

"Bono." He turned back to Brash. "I guess you'll never know what it's been like to have Mom as a single parent. But she's done a good job of it if I do say so myself."

"Ditto. For you and Pop."

"You know that's a ridiculous thing to call your father. Right?"

Brash looked offended and his expression clouded over. "I didn't pick it."

"Who did?"

Brash looked thoughtful. "I don't know. It's one of those things that's part of the way the world works. Like the sun coming up in the morning." They sat in silence for a few minutes. "You know what you were sayin' about me never knowin' your mom like you do?"

"Yes. What about it?"

"Well..."

"Stop right there. You know it's a bad idea."

"Why?"

"Because it would be like betraying our own parents."

"Oh and keepin' us from knowing about each other was just fine?"

"I'm not defending that."

"Well, good. 'Cause there's no defense for it."

"We don't know that."

"Let's just get 'em on a video conference call and find out then."

"We're not doing that."

"Well?"

"You're suggesting what I think you're suggesting?"

"Trading places. Yeah."

Brandon considered his brother for a few seconds. "It's tempting, but really brash." Brash barked out a laugh and followed that with a series of chuckles that came in waves with alternating shakes of his long mahogany hair. "What?"

"It's my name. I mean my legal name is Brannach, but everybody calls me Brash. Always have."

Brandon's smile gave Brash a funny feeling. He'd never been much for approval-seeking. So he was surprised to find out that he liked making Brandon smile.

The waiter took the lull in conversation as an opportunity to open the wine. He poured a splash and handed it to Brandon. Brash was glad to see his brother didn't make a show of smelling and swishing. He took a sip and nodded. That was it.

Two glasses of dark red Italian merlot were poured. Like magic, the waiter was back with steaming plates before Brash had taken a sip.

"Is there something else, sir?"

"For starters," Brash answered, "you can tell me what the hell I'm lookin' at."

"Certainly, sir. It's gnocchi, pancetta and red onions tossed with spicy creamy vodka sauce, topped with Parmesan and basil." He said it like he'd memorized the dish from a menu listing word for word.

"Jesus, Mary, and Joseph. What else you got back there? This is an Italian place, right? How about some plain old spaghetti and meatballs?"

"Of course," said the waiter without ever changing expression.

When the man was out of earshot, Brash looked from Brandon down to the plate sitting in front of him and back up again.

"Well, go ahead. Just because I'm waiting on actual food doesn't mean you have to let that crap get cold."

"Thanks," Brandon said drily as he picked up a fork and speared a round of pork belly. "So is that what you want to be called? Brash?"

Hearing his brother call him by name made Brash smile. "Works for me."

"Okay."

They both started to speak at the same time.

"You first," offered Brash.

"We should think about it. Not go charging into something so…"

"brash."

"Yes. As brash, for instance, as trading places. I mean, aside from the fact that we have entirely different styles…" Brandon looked pointedly at Brash's long hair. " …we have entirely different *everything*."

"Like what?"

"Like, what do you do for a living?"

"None of your business."

Brandon had to chuckle at that reaction. "None of my business? Really? In one breath you're proposing that I impersonate you and the next you don't want to tell me your occupation? You see anything wrong with that picture? If we were going to switch places, we would have to know *everything* about each other then practice pretending."

"For somebody who wants to *think* about it, seems like you've already given it a lot of thought."

"Well, that's part of what I do for a living. Thinking."

Brash narrowed his eyes. "What was that supposed to mean?"

"It's supposed to mean that, for all I know, you could be a professor of physics or a hog caller."

"A hog caller." Brash repeated drily, but grasped Brandon's meaning nonetheless. "I see your point."

"Okay. Well, I don't exactly have a job title. My… our… Christ! That's gonna take some getting' used to. *Our* father's organization owns businesses in Austin. I kind of float around and make sure they're all runnin' the way they're supposed to." Brandon looked a little stunned. "What?"

He put down his fork. "It's just that…"

"Just what?"

"It's just that, that's kind of what I do. On a different scale no doubt."

"No doubt." Brash couldn't argue. He'd seen estimates of the St. Germaine net worth.

"What kind of businesses?"

"We don't own resorts." Brandon just looked at him and waited. "A few bars. A club on 6th Street. A few wrecker and auto repair outfits. We have part ownership in various and sundry small businesses." He barked out a laugh. "Really, I think that if Austin knew how many pies we have fingers in, they'd be worried. Pop's baby is an auto restoration place that's kind of famous." His smile gave away the pride he felt about that. "And last, but not least, my personal favorite, the movie production vehicle supply."

"What's that?"

"Lot of movie companies film in and around Austin. That was just taking off in the late eighties. My, our, dad positioned himself to be the go-to for vehicles. Whether it's a caterpillar or a 1968 Stutz Blackhawk, we make it happen and the payout is sweet."

"What you said about our dad's 'organization'. What did you mean by that? His corporation or LLC?"

Brash raised his chin. "No. It's not a corporation. It's a motorcycle club."

Brandon let his mouth fall open then repeated what his brother had said earlier. "Jesus, Mary, and Joseph. I'm related to a biker gang?"

As if to punctuate that, the waiter set a bowl in front of Brash that had a generous helping of spaghetti and marinara and one half pound meatball the size of a softball. He looked up at the waiter, "Thank you."

The waiter bowed slightly, hesitated long enough to get a nod from Brandon, then disappeared again.

"Now we're talkin'," said Brash, happily diving into his giant meatball.

"Not a vegetarian I take it."

Brash smiled around a big bite of sauce-covered

ground beef. "Hardly."

"So. Where were we?"

"I was just about to tell you that the organization is not a gang. It's a club. In this case it also happens to be a business enterprise. Instead of board members, we have club members."

"Uh-huh. Who ride motorcycles."

"Ever tried it?"

"No."

"Almost as good as fucking." Brash looked up. "Don't tell me you haven't tried that either."

"Funny. So how many, uh, *board* members are there?"

"Thirteen. There are a couple of kids who may be inducted someday if they prove themselves to be useful. And loyal. But just thirteen who get to vote." Brash chewed for a minute, looking thoughtful. "If you're gonna be me, you're gonna have to learn about all of them."

"Let's just set that aside for now. Right now we don't look enough alike to pass for each other. You've got all that hair."

Brash jerked his chin toward Brandon. "Yeah? Well, cuttin' off my hair wouldn't hurt me nearly as much as the pain you'd be feelin'."

"What do you mean?"

Brash grinned. He stepped out from the booth, looked around to make sure they were alone, then unzipped his hoodie and pulled his Henley over his head.

He laughed as he watched Brandon go pale. Brash's right arm and shoulder were completely covered with brightly colored tattoos.

Brandon swallowed. "Forget it." He turned toward the garlic bread, while Brash put his clothes back on and acted like he thought the subject was closed. "I'm not doing that. Nobody I know would ever buy that I just decided to become a walking mural one day."

"Walking mural." Seeing Brandon bite into the garlic bread made Brash want to try it. He tore off a piece with his teeth and hummed his approval.

"What was that?"

"What?"

"That humming thing. My... *our* mother does that when she eats sometimes. When she really likes something."

Brash didn't know how he felt about that. He'd spent more than two decades with unpleasant feelings directed toward some faceless woman who birthed him into the world and then left him because she didn't want him.

"Don't read into it."

"Okay." He eyed Brash. "I guess it could be worse. I should be glad you don't have piercings." Brash stopped eating and grinned again. Brandon groaned. "Where?"

Brash just continued to grin and shoved half a meatball into his mouth.

"No. You didn't." Brandon was scandalized.

"What can I say? I like the women. They like me. And they like me even better as the enhanced version. Brash

1.2."

"You are killing me."

"Come on. You wouldn't need to worry about the piercing. We're never going to fuck the same woman. That kind of brotherly love has no appeal for me."

"No. I'd just have to get half my body inked!"

"I can't have a brother who's a pussy. Maybe we need that DNA test after all."

"If you call me that again, you'll be going to the hospital and it won't be for a DNA test."

Brash laughed. "Good to know you won't take shit. You really know how to handle yourself?"

"If I have to."

Brash grew solemn. "Good to know. That's one less thing to worry about."

"How long did it take you to get all that done?"

"The ink? Hmm. A year maybe, but I wasn't on a time sensitive schedule." Brash took a swig of wine. "That shit's good." He looked at his brother. "You're thinkin' about it aren't you? Curious about Pop and our life in Austin."

"It would be hard to not think about it."

"I think we should do it."

Brandon smiled. "I know you do." As he took another sip of wine he was thinking that it amazed him how much he felt like he'd always known this other version of himself sitting across from him in a red leather booth. Brash was so like him, but learning to *be* him would take some doing. On one level, that was part of the appeal of the whole idea. "How much money do you make?"

"Me, personally? Why?"

"I want to know how much of a lifestyle change I'd be making."

"If we're seriously considering, I think one of the things we need to agree on is how long. How long would we pretend to be each other before we come clean with the, uh, folks."

"The folks? I'd have to undergo a serious personality makeover before it would occur to me to call my parents 'the folks'."

Brash scoffed. "You strike me as a smart guy. I think you'll pick up the ins and outs of being me without too much trouble."

Brandon smiled. "You do, huh?"

"I think one of the big questions for you is, you gonna trust me with makin' decisions about your billions?"

"That's not as much of a factor as you might think. When you're talking multigenerational wealth, well, at some point investments kind of take on a life of their own, so that you'd have to be trying to destroy it. I guess an heir with a big enough gambling problem could do it, but it wouldn't be easy. You'd have to spend a long time and try really hard to get rid of everything."

Brash turned his wine goblet thoughtfully. "Almost wish I could say the same. But keeping our businesses in the black takes concentrated effort and constant monitoring. A big part of my job is mentoring entrepreneurs."

Brandon smiled. "So you're saying that I *could* lose

everything you've got. Then I guess you'd be facing the biggest risk."

Brash rolled a shoulder in a display of unconcern. "Nah. If you lost all the club's assets, I'd just write a check as you. I bet we have the same signature. Then I'd sill an SUV full of cash, leave the suits behind, and start over."

Brandon laughed. "Looks like we're both covered. Cash wise. Now business relationships. That's something else."

"What do you mean?"

"There's this guy on the board, mid forties, named Thomas."

"Say no more. A guy who would go by Thomas has to be a douche."

"Exactly. He's the sort who baits and needles and makes trouble."

"I've got a counterpart. Hell, maybe everybody in the world has got a Thomas. Maybe each one of us is paired with a needler at birth."

"That's deep. What's his name?"

"Edge."

"Somebody named their baby Edge?"

"No. Of course not. Just like I'm not *really* named Brash. His name is really Edgar, but one of the club members is dyslexic or some shit like that. He saw it in print and pronounced it Edger. People started calling him that and eventually it got shortened to Edge."

"What's Pop's name?"

"Brant."

Brandon chuffed out a breath. "Our mother must have liked him or she wouldn't have named us Brandon and Brannach."

Brash's head was bobbing in a slight but repetitive nod. "Yeah. They almost got away with it. If it hadn't been for that magazine… What?"

"There's some irony. I didn't want to do that bachelor piece, but Mom wanted it so bad I ended up agreeing just to please her."

"Life is strange."

"Concur. Hundred percent."

PLATES WERE CLEARED away and Brandon was reaching for a credit card.

"Let's split the tab," Brash suggested.

"I got it."

"At least let me get the wine."

Brandon looked up from the bill and gave his brother a broad smile. "The wine was more than dinner."

Brash's eyes widened slightly. "I'll get the dinner. You get the wine."

Brandon chuckled. "Deal."

When the waiter left with the check, Brash said, "So we're decided?"

Brandon stared for a few seconds without answering. "The rational side of me says we need to slow down and think this through."

"What's the other side say?"

"That, no matter how long I take to think about it,

I'm still going to do it."

Brash reached across the table and gave his brother an affectionate slap of affirmation on the shoulder. "So what's next?"

"If we're doing this, we need a serious plan. How long would it take me to…", he fake shuddered, "…get that much tattoo?"

"You're tough. I think you could do it in a month."

"That's a long time to be away. Do *you* have that kind of time available?"

"Not really. You know if we found a good artist, I think he could do a lot less and nobody would notice. We might trim it down to… three weeks, but we won't know until we ask. Better plan on a month."

Brandon grimaced. "It would take some planning, but I think I could manage it. If we went somewhere remote for four weeks, we could do a crash course on learning each other's lives."

Brash nodded. "Serious catching up. It's a plan. When we leave from wherever we decide on, I'll come to New York as you."

"And I'll go to Austin as you."

They both grinned at the same time.

"How long do you need to get ready?"

"A month?"

"Okay. I'll start hunting down a place where we can hide out and get you inked."

"And get you a decent haircut."

"And teach you how to ride a bike."

"Hold on. Who said anything about that?"

"How do you think I get around at home? Motorcycle Club? Remember?"

"What's the name of it?" Brandon's high was short-lived. He was pouting about the prospect of learning to ride.

"The Sons of Sanctuary. Don't worry, brother. You've got the genes of a badass. Guaranteed."

"Right. So you're heading back to Austin."

"Done what I came for. You got my number."

"What?" Brandon asked when Brash hesitated.

"Are you kind of, I don't know, mad at them?"

Brandon sighed and looked away for a minute. "They definitely have some explaining to do."

They stood up and looked at each other for a minute, finally deciding on a semi-awkward man hug.

"I'll leave first." Brash pulled his hood up over his head and walked away.

CHAPTER 2

BRIGID BAILEY DROPPED her backpack next to the corner table in Starbucks where the SSGM met nightly at ten o'clock. Or thereabouts. Members of The Society of Social Sciences Graduate Students Meet Up, affectionately known to themselves as Bitch Out, met when they could to support each other through the nightmare of sleep deprivation and the cross-eyed existence of being expected to devour six books a week.

Lots of places close to campus in Austin stayed open late. It would probably work for students if first classes started at noon.

The tiny support group found that a ten o'clock boost of venti concentrated caffeine and a little support from others in the same boat helped get them through the wee hours. Within a second of hitting the door, she had scanned the corner for who was there. Everybody. Jeff, the psychologist, whose baby face was masked by a dark thick beard. Tara, the researcher, who struggled daily with two annoying roommates, which was all she could do with her tiny housing stipend. June, the social worker, who never complained and wore a beatific serene smile to a fault. Mark, the funny political scientist, who wished he could draw cartoons. And Rausch, the economist, who claimed that his professors knew less about economics than anyone.

It was elite company if you were talking about academic achievement. A tiny percentage of graduate school applicants received acceptance to the hallowed halls of the University of Texas.

Brigid was a social anthropologist. The demand for social anthropologists has never been high and she knew that wasn't likely to change. In fact, the scope of prospective employment was pretty much non-existent, but she'd made her choice. Against the concerned advice of every practical minded person she'd ever met.

Everybody looked up when she slumped into the empty chair. Six chairs were always reserved even if only two people showed.

"S'up, Bright Eyes?" Mark asked. He, like the other two males, had an interest in Brigid that went beyond the boundaries of peer support group functions. It would be impossible not to notice her copper-colored hair or the intelligent flash of her wide amber eyes. But her reserved manner and refusal to respond to flirting had left no doubt that she was all business. So they had settled into the role of friends and kept their fantasies to themselves.

"I can't find a motorcycle club to talk to me. My thesis is approved and I'm running out of time."

"My dentist is in one of those clubs. He even wears a Sturgis tee shirt."

It was only the fact that June was so sweet and trying to be helpful that kept Brigid from giving her a dirty look.

"Thanks, June, but the kind of club I'm trying to get inside of is different."

Jeff laughed. "You're insane, Bridge. After what happened in Waco, I'd think you'd want to be hundreds of miles away from that shit."

Brigid scowled. "Even if I thought you were right, I've spent too much time on this. Changing my thesis topic at this point…"

"Yeah. We get it," Mark said.

"What are you gonna do?" Rausch was rarely interested enough in other people's problems to ask that kind of question.

She sighed. "I don't know." A small smile touched her lips. "But, hey, if you wouldn't mind learning to ride and pledging your life to a club, say, in the next forty-eight hours, I'd owe you one."

"Sure. No problem. You buy the Harley and the clothes. I'll supply the attitude." Everybody laughed a little too hard. "What? You don't think I have a badass persona? You want to see my James Dean?"

"Who?"

BRIGID TOSSED HER cup on the way out and stepped out onto 24th Street. She was lucky enough to have an apartment a couple of blocks from campus, close enough to walk. She pulled on her backpack and went round the corner toward her place when she heard Tara call to her.

"Hey. Wait a second." Brigid turned and waited. Tara was a little out of breath even though she'd only jogged half a block. "One of my roommates… well, her uncle is in a club. You know, the kind that don't cater to dentists." She rolled her eyes. "I could ask her if she'd introduce you."

"Tara. I'm not into girls, but I could really kiss you right now. Yes! Please! And thank you! This is the closest I've gotten."

"No promises. And don't get too excited. You're gonna owe me, because that bitch will make me do her grocery shopping forever. Or worse."

Brigid threw her arms around Tara. "Anything. Make it happen, Fairy Godmother."

"Dinner tomorrow night. On you."

Brigid couldn't stop nodding. "Yes. Anything."

Tara smiled. "I'll text you where and when."

BRIGID FELT A hundred pounds lighter walking the rest of the way home.

The next day, monitoring a freshman class that she T.A.'d, she got a text from Tara.

8:30. Trudy's Texas. She had to smile. She'd expected Tara to pick some place exorbitant. *Dinner WITH Margaritas. You pay.*

She checked around before answering. Reading a text in a class she was supposed to be monitoring was one thing. Returning a text was something else.

Yes. I pay. C u there.

At 8:15 she was standing inside the door at Trudy's shifting her weight from foot to foot with nervous energy. The hostess had already told her she wouldn't seat the party until they were all there. So she decided to wait in the bar.

"What'll it be, pretty lady?" The bartender looked about her age. Good looking enough to earn nice tips, she imagined.

"Margarita?"

"Sure. We've got Cuban Martinis for six dollars on Wednesdays."

"Do you give free samples?"

He grinned. "Not usually. But it's just too hard to say no to somebody who looks like you."

She thought that was cheesy, but cute. He made a Cuban martini, then poured it into six shot glasses. He set one down in front of her and then shouted, "Who wants a sample of Cuban martini?" A rush of takers came out of nowhere. "Sorry. That guy took the last one."

She took a sip and pursed her lips. "Don't hate me, but can I just have a plain old Margarita. Frozen. No salt?"

He laughed. "Coming up."

She passed the time chatting easily with James, who had come from Michigan to study geological engineering. There was no mistaking when Tara arrived. She could be heard arguing with her roommate over the bar crowd.

"That's my cue," she told James, picking up her Margarita.

"Come back soon," he said amicably.

She smiled, nodded, and headed straight for Tara. She didn't want her chances sabotaged before they'd even ordered dinner.

Tara glanced at Brigid, but finished the not-so-nice thought she'd already begun. The roommate was a cute blonde with a button nose and cornflower blue eyes. At first glance, she didn't look capable of being a roomie from hell.

Brigid pushed her way in front of Tara and stuck her hand out.

"Hi. I'm Brigid. I'm so glad you came."

The girl took her hand, but looked a little wary. "Hi. I'm Beth."

Brigid went on as if Tara wasn't glaring at Beth. "I hope you like Mexican food."

"Yeah. She said I could pick the place."

"Wonderful choice. I love it here." Brigid looked at Tara. "Don't you, Tara?"

Tara hadn't finished her glare fest, so Brigid elbowed her. "You love Mexican. Right?"

Tara refocused her attention on Brigid. "Sure. Who doesn't love Mexican?"

Brigid laughed. "Well, there you have it."

She tried to stay in between Tara and Beth on the walk to their table. When the hostess tried to seat them out in the middle of the room, Brigid said, "Don't you have something a little quieter? We need to talk."

The hostess looked put out and huffy, but gathered

up the menus and flounced to the corner, assuming they were following.

Brigid found an opportunity to lean into Tara and say, “Be nice or no favor,” under her breath.

Tara sniffed and jerked her head a little.

After the waiter took drink orders, someone left a basket of corn tortilla chips and two kinds of salsa.

Brigid looked at Beth. There were only two starting points for conversation. If she led with, “So you’re Tara’s roommate,” that wasn’t likely to steer Beth in the direction of a helpful frame of mind. If she went with, “So tell me about your uncle, the biker,” she might appear to be rushing, possibly to the point of rudeness. She decided on a third option, putting off the inevitable with small talk.

“Beth, are you a student?”

“No. I’m part owner of We Sell Resale.”

“Oh.”

Tara sniggered. “Say that five times fast.”

Brigid’s knee nudged Tara under the table.

“That sounds interesting. So you’re a native of Austin.”

She brightened a little at that. “Fourth generation.”

“Well, that’s something. So your whole family lives here?”

The waiter set drinks down for Tara and Beth and asked if they were ready to order.

“Need another minute,” said Brigid. She watched Beth raising the on-special-today Cuban Martini. “If you don’t like that, feel free to get something else.”

Beth took a sip and then licked her lips. "No. It's good. Really good."

Brigid offered her most congenial smile and opened her menu. "So what kind of Mexican do you like? I'm having mixed fajitas." Tara sat sullenly nursing her Mexican martini. "What are you having, Tara?"

"Tacos." She looked at Brigid. "As many as I want."

Brigid laughed at her. "Yeah, Tara. Go for it. Many as you can eat, but you have to eat what you order," she added, as if Tara was a child. And also appropriate considering her current behavior.

When Beth closed the menu, Brigid deftly guided the conversation back to point. "I was asking if you have a lot of family here?"

"Uh-huh," said Beth.

While Brigid waited, hoping for something more than a two syllable answer, the waiter returned. Beth ordered a combination plate. Having apparently abandoned the idea of all-you-can-eat tacos, Tara practically created a new dish by the time she was finished making adjustments to the menu.

When they were again alone, Brigid thought perhaps she might introduce the point of meeting for dinner.

"So Beth, Tara tells me that you have an uncle in a motorcycle club."

Beth more or less sneered at that. "He's not in *a* motorcycle club. He's in the Sons of Sanctuary." She said it with as much pride as if she was declaring that her uncle was the ambassador to Great Britain.

Brigid knew that the SSMC was prestigious from a certain point of view and could imagine that someone might think it was glamorous to have an uncle in that lifestyle.

"I see. I've heard of them."

"Everybody's heard of them," she said. "Gotta tell you that this is a first, takin' me out for food and all. People have been askin' me to get them into one of the parties since I was thirteen. So that's sayin' somethin'." Beth looked pointedly at Brigid's raspberry Henley and her cotton infinity scarf. "But I'm tellin' you right now that, goin' like that? You won't get past the gate."

Brigid cocked her head. "I'm not sure what you mean."

Beth looked at her like she was stupid. "You *do* know how biker babes dress. Right?"

Brigid flushed a little, which was embarrassing for a twenty-four-year-old. "I think there's been a misunderstanding." Beth managed to take a drink of Cuban martini while looking curious. "I don't want to go to a club party as a… um, woman. I want to go for research. I'm hoping for permission to observe their habits for a protracted period of time."

After Beth's eyes first widened and then narrowed, she turned to Tara, who had been quietly consuming the entire basket of tortilla chips. "What is this?"

"She's a graduate student. Like me. A social anthropologist who needs a sample biker society to study for her thesis."

Beth stared at Tara for several beats before she looked at Brigid and burst out laughing. When she quieted, she said, "Do you know *anything* about motorcycle clubs? *At all*?"

"Yes. But not enough to write my thesis. I need *firsthand* knowledge."

"Look. If you knew anything about them, you'd know that's never gonna happen. Bikers are so secretive they don't even tell their old ladies what they're up to. They're the farthest thing from, what do they call it? Transparent."

Brigid was undaunted. "All I need is an introduction. If your uncle can get me in, I'll take it from there."

Beth went back to eating. "Yeah. This is good, by the way."

Brigid glanced at Tara who shrugged in response. "Glad you like it."

After a couple of minutes of uncertainty, Beth said, "So what you really want is to talk to the Prez."

Brigid put down the fork she'd been using to play with the food on her plate. She was too anxious to eat, but wanted to appear to be in control. "Yes."

Beth met her eyes. "Let's just say that I'm able to arrange that. No guarantees about the outcome. What's in it for me?"

Brigid smiled. "You mean besides dinner?"

"Yeah. Besides that."

"What do you want?"

Beth looked at Tara, then back at Brigid. Without further hesitation, she said, "I want her out of the apartment, but I want her part of the rent paid for the rest of the year."

Tara looked at Beth with her mouth wide open. "You want to get me kicked out of the only place I can afford? Why you little…"

"Hold on." Brigid intervened, putting her hand on Tara's arm. "Beth, how much is Tara's part?"

"Five hundred a month."

Tara looked a little panicked. "I can't find another place this close to campus that I can afford. You…"

"Calm down, Tara. Nobody's putting you on the street. I'm considering having you move in with me, rent free."

"Rent free? You mean you're going to pay the troll's blood money and not charge me anything?"

"Right."

Tara squealed and gave Brigid a kiss on the cheek. "I *love* you!"

"You should," she said to Tara," because I *hate* the idea of living with somebody else."

"No matter what, I'll be a better roommate than her." She jerked her head toward Beth, who snorted as she covered a bite of enchilada with pico de gallo and shoved it in her mouth.

"Nobody's going anywhere yet." Brigid looked between the other two. "Beth, I will agree to your terms if I get a meeting with the, uh, Prez and get him to agree to give me access to ask questions of the members and research the way the club is organized."

Beth looked directly at Brigid while she contemplated. Brigid knew she wasn't stupid. Anybody who can make a go of a small business in the twenty-first century isn't dumb.

"Okay. I'll press my uncle to get you a meeting. If the Prez says yes, Tara has two days to get out and every month on the first you pay me five hundred in cash to cover her part."

"Ending December first of this year."

"Yeah. That's the deal."

Brigid stuck her hand out, being careful not to let her sleeve touch the food. "It's a deal. We have a witness. So we don't really need anything in writing. Right?" Once they shook, Brigid handed over her cell phone. "Put your number in and make a note of mine. When do you think I'll hear from you?"

As Beth programmed her name and number into Brigid's contacts, she said, "Probably Friday. Depends on whether or not he's in town. If he's not, I'll let you know. If he is, I should have an answer by Sunday latest."

Brigid looked down at the food that had gone from sizzling hot to room temperature and suddenly felt famished. Thinking that cold fajitas are still fajitas, she wrapped chicken strips, onions, peppers, pico, grated cheese, and sour cream into a flour tortilla and smiled at Tara as she took a bite.

Beth finished her food and gathered her purse. "Thanks for dinner. I'll be in touch," she said to Brigid.

After glancing at Tara, she added, "I really hope this works," right before she left.

"What did you do to her?" Brigid asked.

Tara shook her head. "That girl and her evil BFF have put me through it. They're demon spawn. Both of them."

"Okay."

Tara's eyes twinkled. "You better pull out all the stops to get the 'Prez'," she made air quotes, "to agree to be your monkeys."

"Tara. You don't have to put it like that."

"Why not? Isn't that what you're doing?"

Brigid smiled. "No. When human beings are observed in the wild, they're still humans."

"In the wild?" Tara laughed. "From what I've heard, that fits. Biker equals human in the wild. I don't know what's most appealing. Getting away from Beth, getting free rent, or reading your thesis on humans in the 'wild'."

She put 'wild' in air quotes.

"There are a couple of big hurdles between here and having any one of those things become a reality. And the biggest one is apparently called 'Prez'."

Tara looked thoughtful. "Hey. Have you really thought through what getting down and dirty with bikers might look like? I mean, the whole Waco thing…"

"That was 'Wacko'. This is Austin."

"I know, but… just sayin'."

"Appreciate your concern. Don't worry. My interest and involvement are purely scientific."

Tara nodded, then got a twinkle in her eye. "I've never been to our place before. What's it like?"

Brigid laughed.

SUNDAY AFTERNOON AT five thirty, Brigid got a text from Beth.

You're on for tomorrow morning at eleven. He'll talk to you at the shop. Ask for Mr. Fornight. And make it good.

Brigid was supposed to be teaching a class that hour, but she'd explain to her supervisor and get out of it. If she got into the club, she was going to have to get out of all of her other obligations for the duration, which was to be determined. Like everything else. But since they were only a couple of weeks away from summer, it would be less of a hardship. Some first year grad student would be getting early exposure to freshmen, courtesy of Brigid's thesis.

She texted Beth. *Okay. Where do I go?*

Beth replied with the address and a parting, *Good luck. You'll need it.*

Brigid felt butterflies forming in her stomach and already knew she wouldn't be getting much sleep. Tara's concerns came to mind and she wondered if she really did know what she was doing.

She Googled the "shop" and learned as much as she could about Hollywood Rides and Wrecks. There were lots of pictures of Brant Fornight with big name celebrities and the cars or motorcycles he'd custom made for them or movies they were starring in. She supposed he must be the Mr. Fornight to whom Beth referred.

CHAPTER 3

Monday morning, 11 am

BRIGID PULLED UP to the Hollywood Wrecks and Rides building in her hybrid. She decided to get things on the right foot and leave no misunderstanding. So she dressed as professionally as if she was planning to argue a case before the Supreme Court. She wore a black suit with pencil skirt and a starched white blouse with pearl buttons. She softened the look slightly with a long silk scarf with a cream and black pinstripe pattern, then finished it off with three inch pumps.

Hollywood Wrecks and Rides was an impressive place. The front door opened to a two thousand square foot showroom displaying various hip cars and bikes. It wasn't like anything she'd ever seen. There was a vintage hotrod Lincoln painted with a buxom blonde shooting flames from her mouth, and a Harley painted so that it looked exobionic. She was so caught up in looking at the amazing display of vehicles that she startled when a deep voice growled, "Help you, ma'am?"

She turned expecting to see a biker with long hair, beard, and giant belly. But the owner of the gravelly vocal chords was a wiry guy with dark hair, blue eyes and a Pistol Pete mustache. He wasn't exactly handsome, but he had a look about him that could be interpreted as mischievous or conniving.

"Yes." She cleared her throat. "I'm here to see Mr. Fornight."

Pistol Pete looked her up and down unapologetically. "You the new lawyer?"

Brigid's brows drew into a momentary scowl, but she recovered her neutral look quickly.

"No, but my business is with Mr. Fornight. If you are not he, will you please let him know that Ms. Bailey is here to see him?"

Pete's mustache twitched. "Ms. Bailey to see Mr. Fornight? My. Aren't we formal?"

"Do I need to walk around yelling his name?"

Pete barked out a laugh. "Keep your panties on, Missy. I'll get him for ya. But come see me when you're done. We'll go over to my place and have a cold one."

He winked and walked away while she shifted her weight to one leg and rolled her eyes at his back. She went back to looking at the wonderland of vehicles. Each one was a piece of art and, she supposed, that was what she was looking at – an art gallery. A loud whistle startled her for the second time since she'd walked through the door.

She looked around and saw a man in the far corner standing outside an open door. When she looked that way, he waved her over. As she walked in that direction she recognized him as being the man in the photos, the one behind the success of Hollywood Wrecks and Rides.

Her heels clicked as she walked across the polished floor. When she was within ten feet, she said, "Mr. Fornight?"

He answered simply, "Ms. Bailey."

She entered the office which was nicely furnished, but gave the impression that it was never used. No books or computer. No stacked papers. Not even a trash can that she could see. The only evidence that would suggest someone had used the room was an open newspaper and a generic brand, cardboard cup of coffee.

He motioned toward one of the chairs in front of the desk, but didn't ask her to sit with words. Nor did he offer a tasty beverage. Not even water.

He was wearing faded jeans and a dark gray tee shirt that showed off a flat stomach and arms that were both tan, cut, and would not seem out of place on the body of a much younger man.

She sat and waited patiently for him to speak.

"What do you want?"

She immediately regretted not being the first to speak. Because that was no way to begin a friendly negotiation. Still, it revealed that the man liked direct and she could do direct.

"I want access to the Sons of Sanctuary Motorcycle Club."

He sat back and really looked at her for the first time. "What the hell do you mean by *access*?"

"I'm a graduate student at U.T. and I'm writing my

thesis on the structure of, um, motorcycle clubs. In order to make my findings authentic, I need to be able to observe. Personally."

Brant Fornight stared at her for a full minute. His face broke into a grin that was infectious, if not entirely friendly, and Brigid could see that he must have been a beautiful heartthrob some, say thirty years, in the past.

"Look, Ms. Bailey. I'm doin' a favor for my sergeant-at-arms. He has a niece with a pouty mouth and big blue eyes and apparently he can't say no to her. I've done what I promised. You've enjoyed a full five minutes of my time. Now get out."

"Wait. Not so fast. This means too much to me to get the bum's rush so fast. Let's negotiate."

"Sorry, darlin'. Non-negotiable. Door's right behind you. Close it on the way out."

"There must be something you would exchange for letting me talk to club members and ask a few questions."

The president of the Sons of Sanctuary Motorcycle Club prided himself on patience. The Devil only knew it had taken a lot to bring up his wild ass son. But he was beginning to get annoyed. He was accustomed to having people respond when he dismissed them. Immediately.

He sat back and looked at her through hooded eyes. "I see you're working on the theory that everything's negotiable." He cocked his head. "And maybe that's right. So. Okay. Here it is."

Leaning forward slightly, eyes shining with intensity, he said, "Two hundred and fifty thousand dollars cash.

Plus you sign a lifetime non-disclosure agreeing that you will *never* reveal the name of the club, any of its members, their family members, people you meet in association with the club or any of the businesses owned by the club. Likewise, you will not talk to employees of club-owned businesses or their friends and families. What I'm sayin', in case I'm not perfectly clear, is it's pure anonymity or nothin'. That offer is good for exactly one minute." He looked at his watch. "Startin' now."

Brigid pursed her lips, looking very unhappy indeed. Brant made a show of looking at his watch, wondering if he was going to have to physically remove her from the premises.

He looked up when she said, "Alright. But I have to have free access for three months."

Brant's expression was priceless. He forgot all about watching the time on his watch. The last thing he'd expected to come from that meeting was a nice infusion of cash coupled with somebody nosing through club business, where nobody's nose belonged.

He was wondering first, how he could have stumbled into a trap of his own making, second, how he'd never considered that she might say okay, and, third, how high he could have gone!

Narrowing his eyes at her, he said, "You blowin' smoke, girl?"

"I assure you I am not, Mr. Fornight. I have accepted your terms. Do you accept my condition?"

He ran scenarios in his head. The movie season had

wound down and the economy was depressing demand for toys that were cool and expensive. He'd worked too hard to make the SSMC a hub of legitimate business enterprise to go back there. In short, the two fifty would help keep the coffers overflowing, just the way he liked it. Convincing the other members that it was a good deal. Well, that would take some serious finesse.

"Do you understand that the non-disclosure is a tie that binds. If you break it, we won't sue. Do you take my meaning?"

Brigid swallowed. She didn't have any intention of breaking the waiver. Or suing. Still, having her life threatened, if she 'took his meaning', was a new and somewhat unsettling experience. She met his stare. "I believe I do. Does that mean you accept my condition? Three months?"

Brant wasn't convinced she actually had that kind of money, but decided to play along. "I don't think there's three months' worth of dirt to dig on us, but if you want to become a hang-around, that will probably be okay with the boys. They like girls. Don't know how the women will feel about it. You're not exactly gonna fit in."

She ignored that. "When can I get started?"

Swiveling his chair to look out the window toward the clubhouse, the fingers of Brant's left hand absently tapped on the desk. The next meeting was scheduled for Wednesday. He couldn't give her a definite yes without letting the club vote.

He turned back to her. "Okay. First lesson on… what

did you call it? Club structure? No individual has the authority to make a decision that affects the club. It's a democratic outfit. We vote." She nodded. "I'll bring it to a vote at our meeting on Wednesday. If they say yes, and, mind you, that's a very big if, you can move in on Friday. We're having a barbeque Friday night. Would be a good chance for you to meet everybody."

Her eyes were wide as a child's. "Move in?"

There was a part of Brant that thought having her around could be amusing. Her every thought was betrayed by her expressive face and complete ignorance of how to disguise emotional reaction.

"Yes, little girl. Best way to get to know us is to live with us. You asked for it. I'm gonna make sure you get your money's worth. There's a spare room, with shower bath, in the compound. It's minimal. Military style. But you're not lookin' for a luxury vacation. Right?"

He could see she was past the surprise and settling into the idea.

"Right. Friday," she said with a determined set to her mouth.

Brant pushed a pad and pen in her direction. "Write your number down there. I'll let you know one way or the other."

As she wrote her number on the top sheet, she felt like the dog who caught the car he was chasing, and realized for the first time that there may have been a part of her that wanted him to say no. It would certainly be a good excuse for not following through on what might very well prove to be a hair-brained idea.

Her parents had died on an anniversary trip to South Africa in a bush plane crash when she was seventeen. She'd gone to live with a kind, but elderly great-aunt who was a retired schoolteacher. Though her aunt meant well, she was inactive physically and out of touch with both current events and current social problems of adolescents. That meant that, for practical purposes, Brigid had been on her own.

All things considered, she'd done a pretty good job of raising herself. One of her best qualities was a keen awareness of the behavior of others. She found that, if she kept her eyes open, it was easy to figure out what to do and what not to do. That interest in behavior eventually bloomed to fruition in her chosen field of study, which was all about observing and analyzing the behaviors of cultures, large and small.

She gained control of her inheritance when she turned twenty-one. Most of the money, which included the proceeds of substantial life insurance policies, was being managed by a mutual fund company, but she could get hold of two-fifty quickly. She could have paid more without putting her future in jeopardy. A lot more. But it would have taken longer to free up. So far as she was concerned, she was lucky he took her for a struggling grad student and asked for an amount that was easily manageable.

"Brigid?"

Her eyes darted to his. "Yes?"

"Was there something else?"

"What? Oh. No. Um, thank you, Mr. Fornight."

"Second lesson. People who end up in motorcycle clubs are informal types. You can call me Brant."

She nodded enthusiastically, feeling flustered, like every bit of the aplomb she'd worn on the way in had disintegrated the minute he said yes to her proposal.

"Thank you. Brant. I'll, uh, just go now."

His mouth twitched. "Door's still in the same place as before."

"Right. So. See you."

She stood quickly and closed the door like he'd asked. She was hyper aware of the ridiculous clacking sound her heels were making as she walked quickly toward the front. Pistol Pete was waiting by the front door. He grinned as he opened the door for her. That gesture, made by another man, might have looked gallant, but on Pete it looked predatory.

Refusing to return his smile, she offered a simple, polite, "Thank you," while looking past him at her destination – her car in the parking lot. She could hear the sounds of hydraulic tools coming from behind the showroom. She was tempted to walk around to the back and see where the magic happened, but decided it would be more politic to wait until written permission to snoop was bought and paid for.

TWELVE OF THE thirteen members were present at the Wednesday business meeting, everybody except Brash.

Eleven men sat at the table while Beth's Uncle Rock stood behind and off to the side of where the president sat at the head of the table. It wasn't a requirement, or even a tradition, but sometime after Rock was named sergeant-at-arms, he took up a post leaning against the back wall and never gave it up. For years Brant hadn't known that anyone who disagreed with him was treated to Rock's silent intimidating stare. Since Brash suspected that his dad was unaware, he told him that discussion might not be authentic because the S.A.R. was glaring the club into submission. So he took it upon himself to bring the old man up to speed.

Brant responded by taking Rock out back to the picnic table that sat alone under the cottonwood tree, along with a quarter bottle of Jim Beam to share. While they listened to the peaceful music of cottonwood leaves rustling in the breeze, Brant explained to Rock that every member should feel free to voice his opinion.

"I don't wanta be some asshole dictator. I want to be fair."

Rock had said, "Doin' what you think we should do *is* fair."

It was hard for Brant to argue with that logic. The reason he'd picked Rock for S.A.R. was because he'd recognized that the man was loyal as a dog.

"Appreciate that you feel that way, but the *right* thing is to let everybody have a say. Even you."

"Me!"

"Yeah," Brant chuckled. "You get a say just like everybody who sits at the table. You got somethin' to add or argue, you speak it out. Loud and clear."

Rock looked like he wasn't too sure about that, but nodded his head anyway. "If that's what you want," was all he said.

When everybody was present at meetings, five members sat on each side of the long, worn conference-style table, with the president at the far end. The end opposite Prez was reserved for the oldest active member who, in that case, was also the club's historian.

Brant waited until after reports on the businesses and on the prospects to bring up the proposed deal.

He cleared his throat. "There's one other item to be considered. I was propositioned by a young lady this week." That was followed by hoots and hollers. "Yeah. Yeah. Settle down. I know I'm sexy as fuck, but it wasn't what you think.

"As a favor, I met with this girl who knows Rock's niece. She's a student at U.T. who wants to do research on a motorcycle club." The room went instantly still as they waited for him to go on. "She wants what she called access to see how things operate and ask us questions. Old ladies, too, I guess." The room was so quiet a pin dropping would have sounded like a disturbance. "Naturally I showed her the door. At first.

"Then she asked me what it would take. I told her two hundred and fifty thousand dollars with a signed agreement to never disclose the name of the club, members, family, or businesses. I figured that would be the end of it.

Then she said okay.

"I mean she was all dolled up, but I still didn't take her for havin' two-fifty to buy her way in. Anyhow, I told her there was no deal until after a vote. So that's what we're gonna do now.

"If you want my opinion, I was against it at first, but then I got to thinkin'. It's not like back in the days when we really had stuff to hide. These days we're practically the Austin Chamber of Commerce. But just to be sure we're protected, I also stipulated that she could not talk to any employee of Sanctuary Enterprises or their friends and families. We'll get Grayson to draw up an air-tight agreement. Look, two-fifty is more than we clear in a year from the taco shack and the snowcone hut combined.

"I told her absolute anonymity, guaranteed with her life. The look on her face said she believed that if she reveals identities, she dies. And as we all know, everything is about perception.

"So talk it over and, when you're done, we'll take a vote."

Edge was first to talk, "Christ, Prez. She's what? Like a reporter? We're gonna spill our guts to a loose-lipped coed?"

"I saw her the other day. She brightens a room, if you know what I mean." Rescue grinned at the others.

Brant interjected. "Let me stop you right there, brother. Let's make it clear from the jump go, she's not one of your holes. You know as well as I do that *all* money gets earned one way or the other. The price of *this* money is you ease out of your comfort zone and answer questions that maybe you like and maybe you don't, you give the woman some respect, and you keep your fuckin' hands to yourselves." The room went quiet again. "Sorry to interrupt. Just had to be said."

"You want us to make our old ladies sit down for interviews? What if they don't want to?"

Brant smiled at E.R. shaking his head. "If any one of you can tell me you've ever met a woman who wasn't eager to talk, then we'll consider that a potential problem."

There was some good-natured laughter, followed by a question from Rescue. "How long?"

"What's that?" asked Brant.

"How long would she be around? Getting' access."

"Oh. She talked about three months. I told her that, if you vote yes, she could move in Friday."

There was a rush of noise as several people tried to talk at once.

"An outsider *livin'* here? I don't get it. What are you thinkin'?"

Brant turned to Car Lot calmly and said, "I'm thinkin' it's a lot of money for not doin' much of anythin' and that maybe it wouldn't hurt to see ourselves through a different lens."

Car Lot threw up his hands in exasperation. "Different lens! What the fuck?"

"How far does this go, Brant?" asked Eric. "You lettin' her in here?"

"Got somethin' to say, Prez."

Brant turned to look behind him. "Go ahead, Rock."

"When hell freezes over. That's all I got to say."

Brant turned around. "Well, there you have it. The answer is no. This room's off limits. We can tell her what goes on in here, but that's it."

The discussion went on like that for another half hour. Some said that putting up with an outsider, even an outsider who was a woman, wasn't worth the trouble. Some said nothing was worth that and that they would be a disgrace to all MCs everywhere if they allowed it.

When Brant was satisfied that everyone had a chance to put their opinion forward, he took charge. "Motion for a vote."

"Second," said Rock.

Brant took the vote member by member then brought the gavel down. "Seven to five for. Motion passes. I'll ask you to remember that everybody is bound by majority rule. That means you will be polite and respectful to the young woman. And you will answer her questions within reason. Who knows? You may even like gettin' interviewed, as Eric calls it.

"Motion to adjourn."

"Second," said Rock.

"Adjourned." Brant brought the gavel down again and members began shuffling to their feet.

When the room had cleared, Arnold was still seated. "Hope you know what you're doin', Prez. This is the kind of thing that gets hard feelin's started."

Brant sighed. "I guess we have to be better than that, don't we? If Sanctuary could be pulled apart by one little copper-headed girl, then it's not sayin' much for what we've built here."

Arnold smiled. "Yeah. Guess you're right. I know just the thing to take the worry away."

Brant watched as Arnold stood and made his way to the open door. He was the youngest member. Younger even than Brash, but he had a good head and the club was lucky that he was hiding a genuine geek behind those good looks.

BRANT RETIRED TO his real office, the one behind the bar at the clubhouse, and pulled out his phone. When Brigid answered, he said, "You're in, kiddo." He gave her directions and instructions on what to say at the gate. "I'll have papers for you to sign when you get here. If you don't have the cash with you, it'll be a short stay."

"I understand. What time should I, um, be there?"

"Round noon. That'll give you time to settle in and meet the key players before the party starts."

"Okay. And thank you."

Brant laughed. "It'll be interesting to see if you're still thankin' me when your three months is up, little girl."

He hung up.

She had to agree.

It would be interesting.

She dialed Tara.

"Hello."

"Guess what?"

"No way."

"Yes way."

Tara let out such a high pitch squeal that Brigid had to jerk the phone away from her ear.

"Tara?"

"Yes, roomie?"

"If you ever do that again, I will murder you in your sleep."

"That's not a problem because nothing as exciting as getting out of here is ever going to happen to me again in my life."

"I truly hope you're wrong about that. I've got more news."

"More news?"

"And you're gonna like it."

"What? I need to pee. Don't drag it out."

"I'm moving into the clubhouse for the next three months, which means that…"

Tara squealed again. "I'll have your place all to myself."

"You better sleep with one eye open."

"Oh, sorry, but that was almost as exciting as getting out of roommate hell."

"Okay. Go pee. The clock is ticking. Beth is giving you two days from now to get out. Coincidentally, I happen to be moving out in two days. So…" She heard Tara take in a deep breath. "Don't. You. Dare." She heard Tara let out a deep breath. "Do you want to let Beth know that the mission was a success or should I?"

"I'll tell her when she gets in tonight. She'd get suspicious when she sees me packing up. So I might as well tell her. Oh. What's my new address?"

Brigid laughed. "I'll text you and have a key made."

"You're my hero."

"Your standards need to be reimagined."

"Gotta pee."

"Okay. Bye."

AT NOON ON Friday, Brigid pulled up to the gate of the club compound after going past the turn three times. They were located on the far west side, just outside the Austin city limit, at the end of a long drive lined with large old mesquite trees. Someone came shuffling out, taking his time, while she waited.

"Help you?" he said when she rolled down the window.

"Yes. I'm Brigid Bailey. I, um, live here now?"

The gigantic redhead in front of her said, "Oh. So you're the one."

"Maybe. What am I admitting to?"

"Bein' a pain in our butts for three months, if I heard right."

"Yeah. I guess that would be me." She smiled, hoping that would soften the preconception of her as pain-in-the-butt.

"Name's Eric."

"Eric. That fits."

He snorted. "Well, yeah, dumb ass. That's the point." She wasn't sure what he meant by that, but she filed it away for future reference. "You can park over there until you unload." He pointed toward a large wood door that looked like a replica of a medieval castle entrance.

The building, which sat on a hill, appeared to be made out of concrete blocks. She knew it was too high to ever be in danger of flooding and surmised that it would withstand even a direct hit by tornado. Or a siege. In fact, the word fortress came to mind. She made a mental note to write that down as soon as she was situated.

She grabbed a large rolling suitcase and followed Eric. She was glad she'd given up on the idea of keeping her look professional and had traded the suit and heels for jeans and tire tread sandals. While she struggled to get the bag up the two steps to the door, Eric watched but didn't offer to help. Not only that, but he looked amused by the difficulty she was having.

"No. That's okay," she said. "Really. I can get it."

He snorted again and added a smirk this time. "Agree. Exactly why I'm not offerin' to help."

"Well, then, what can I say to that?"

"Nothin', but you bein' a woman, that probably won't stop you."

She wanted to say nothing just to spite him, but couldn't manage it.

"Let me guess. You voted no."

She didn't wait for a response. With a grunt and a monumental effort, she maneuvered the bag up the last step and extended the handle so that she could roll it.

The first room of the clubhouse looked more like a bar than anything else. The long expanse of wood was backed by a mirrored wall with an impressive display of alcoholic beverages to suit any taste.

"Wait here," said Eric.

The guy at the bar waved. He was cute in a young Arnold Schwarzenegger way.

She waved back. "I'm Brigid. Brigid Bailey."

He smiled and said, "Arnold."

As she looked around the room she muttered, "What are the odds?" under her breath.

There was considerable open space between the bar and what appeared to be a lounge area with several leather sofas, large chairs and ottomans and a television screen the size of a small movie theater. No surprise there. Her understanding had been that motorcycle club houses were an expansion of a bachelor's dream party house.

She jerked when a voice right behind her said, "Come with me." She turned to see that Arnold had some serious stealth skills. "Whoa. Jumpy. Aren't ya'?"

"I just didn't hear you coming up behind me."

"Well, most women moan when I come up behind them." He treated her to what she suspected was an always-get-my-way-with-the-girls smile.

"Um-hmm. I'm sure they do, uh, Arnold."

He motioned with his head to follow and she did. With the building all but deserted, the wheels on the bag seemed to be making a lot of noise. Was that an echo?

They walked down a short hallway to a closed door. Arnold knocked and waited for a reply. He opened the door and motioned Brigid inside.

The office, which she supposed must be Brant Fornight's real office, couldn't be more different than the one at Hollywood Wrecks and Rides. This office was tiny, cluttered, and looked like it had been that way for a hundred years. She could barely get inside with the suitcase and close the door.

"You bring the money?"

"Yes. I did."

Brant waited. When it appeared that she wasn't going to produce it voluntarily, he said, "Well, Brigid. Where is it?"

"Oh." She seemed to suddenly remember where she was. "It's here. In my bag."

After waiting an inordinately appropriate time, he said, "That's good. Would you like to give it to me?"

She looked down at her bag like she'd forgotten what she came to do, then bent over, unzipped a large front pouch, and withdrew twenty-five bundles of hundred dollar bills with a count of one hundred each. She put them on his desk in front of him.

"You have something you want me to sign?"

"Right here." He put a document in front of her. "You can sit down if you want to read it."

It was three pages of legalese, but she read it carefully because, after all, her life depended on it. When she was satisfied, she looked up.

"Questions?" he said.

"No. It's exactly what we agreed to."

He picked up the phone and pressed a button, which she noted, thinking that it was interesting that they had an in-house phone system.

"Notary," was all he said, then he hung up.

"Can I have a pen?"

"Wait for the witness. I want to call your attention to the fact that your exit date is contractual, but of course you can leave at any time before that."

She wasn't sure how to respond to that. "Thank you?"

Brant's mouth twitched in spite of himself.

There was a soft knock on the door. "Come in."

Car Lot stepped in and closed the door. He had a book and a stamp with him. After nodding at Brigid, he said, "I need to see your drivers license."

She pulled her wallet out of her purse and handed him the license. After writing information in the book, he said, "Okay. Go ahead and sign."

Brigid signed on the line under her printer name, Brigid Allison Bailey, and noted that she had not told them her middle name. She assumed that meant they'd run some kind of background check on her. She wondered if they were worried about her working undercover for either press or police.

When Car Lot placed his stamp on the document, Brant said, "Send Arnold back to show our guest to her quarters."

The 'witness' left without a word.

Then Brant looked at Brigid. "First thing you need to understand is that some of the guys are used to being sorta free with women. Everybody's been told to cooperate with you and keep their hands to themselves, but if anybody forgets, you let me know." Brigid simply blinked. "Do you understand?"

"I believe so. How likely is it that your, um, members will forget themselves?"

"Not very, but we do serve drinks here and some people worship drink more than others."

She cocked her head. "Do you disapprove of the bar?"

He laughed. "So you think you're gonna have a go at me first? Get your feet wet. Learn the ropes. When your questions start to pile up, then maybe I'll talk to ya.

"We have a woman who cooks breakfast and dinner. You can eat what she makes, fix your own, or go out. You're on your own for lunch, but she keeps sandwich stuff and soup around. Prospects clean the rooms, but I imagine you'll want to take care of that yourself."

When the door opened, Arnold looked first at Brant, then at Brigid. "Right this way, ma'am."

Arnold shot Brant a shit eating grin, indicating that he'd noticed the new business venture was a knockout. Brant was shaking his head as Arnold closed the door, wondering if he'd just made a very big mistake by agreeing to let an outsider shine a light on the SSMC.

SHE FOLLOWED ARNOLD down a long hallway lined with

doors, hotel or dorm style, trying not to notice that his hind end was exceptionally well-muscled. He came to a stop at the end of the hall in front of a larger wood door.

Arnold pointed to the door. "This is what we call the Presidential Suite. Guess who claims the most square footage?" Brigid rolled her eyes. "That's right. Let the big dog eat first. The Prez has an apartment-sized presence here at home base."

He turned to the door on Brigid's right. "This is what you might call the Guest Suite. It's not big, but it's been cleaned since Brash moved out. The room across the hall is the biggest one next to the Prez Pad. So when Rock moved out and got his own place, Brash moved across the hall."

When the door swung open, she had to agree that it was minimal, as Brant had indicated. She was comforted by Arnold's assurance that it had been cleaned. So it would do.

"Kay. Thanks."

She rolled the suitcase that was two hundred and fifty thousand dollars lighter into the room and flipped the light switch on. There was a window that spanned the length of the room at ceiling height. It was wide but shallow, meaning it let light in but offered no visibility. She couldn't see out, but neither could anyone see in. Unless they were on a ladder.

"You got anything else in your car?"

"Um, yes. A couple more bags, but not as big as this one."

"Did you lock it?"

"No."

Arnold grinned at her. "Trusting. I like that."

He disappeared, leaving the door standing open. She hoped he was actually going to get her other stuff. She had figured she'd get settled and, if she needed anything else, she'd bring it from home. He was right, though, it was dumb to leave her laptop in an unlocked car even if she was visiting a fortress surrounded by chain link and barbed wire.

She sat down on the bed to test for firmness and decided it was okay. Then walked over to the bifold door that she assumed was hiding a modest closet. No hangers. That would be number one on the list of stuff to get from her, make that Tara's, apartment. At least it might as well be Tara's for the next three months.

Hearing a rustling behind her, she turned to see Arnold setting the other two bags down.

"Here you go. Everything look okay?"

"I guess. I'm going to need to make a trip to my place for hangers."

Arnold's eyes went to the closet. "Maybe I can scare up a few. Most of the rooms are empty right now."

"Why's that?"

"And so the interview begins?" He smiled. "Right now only the single guys live here full time, but some of the others keep rooms here…" He trailed off and seemed to become disinterested in finishing that thought.

"How about the president? Is he single?"

Arnold cocked his head. "You interested in Prez?"

She laughed. "No. You'll find my curiosity knows no bounds and is usually not personal."

He nodded and leaned against the door jamb. "Anything else you want to ask me?"

"You can count on that, but I'd like to get unpacked. Rain check?"

"Sure. Prez asked me to introduce you around." He looked at his watch. "Place'll start gettin' crowded soon. The old ladies will show up any time now to start helpin' May with cookin' and gossipin'. Lot of people come to these barbeques. People who are associated with the club, guests, and people we call hang-arounds."

"Looks like I'm diving right into the deep end then." She blew out a breath and looked away.

"You scared?"

She met Arnold's piercing look. "Should I be? Arnold?"

He laughed. "Course not. We're as tame as little lambs. Let me see if I can steal some hangers."

Fifteen minutes later Arnold returned through her still-open door with two big handfuls of wire hangers. Brigid couldn't remember ever hanging her clothes on wire hangers, but it was better than throwing them on the floor.

"Here you go," he said as he placed them on the closet rod. "I'll be back in two hours. If you don't mind me sayin' so, if you wear what you've got on tonight, you're gonna stick out like a sore thumb."

Brigid looked down at her clothes. "Why?"

"You got anything a little more... form fitting? Maybe one of those, what do you call them... halter tops?"

"No. I do not own a halter top. And I'm not sure what you mean by 'form fitting', but I left my swimsuit at my apartment."

He barked out a laugh then shook his head. "You're somethin' else, aren't ya? I'm startin' to think this is gonna be fun. So okay. Go as you. Nothin' wrong with different."

Just before he closed the door, he turned and did a passable impression of Terminator. "I'll be back."

Giggling at that didn't present the professional image she had sworn to maintain, but, she told herself, no normal person could resist laughing at that. Her inner judge followed close behind with criticism about the momentary lapse. She gave herself a stern reminder that she was there to work and only to work, that the people were a sample, and that making friends would compromise her objectivity.

TWO HOURS LATER she'd put her folded clothes in the dresser drawers, hung her shirts on wire hangers, and set her toiletries on the tiny vanity in the closet-sized bath. She'd charged her phone so that she could record conversations, if the opportunity presented itself. The phone and a small spiral notebook went into the easily accessible front pocket of a messenger bag.

Then she sat down on the bed to wait for Arnold to

come back and get her. When Arnold was twenty minutes late, she, a much-less-than-patient person, was beginning to get annoyed. She hadn't made a deal to be a prisoner and no one had said she couldn't leave her room, her new home, the last door on the right at the Sons of Sanctuary Motorcycle Club. Saying that over in her head made her smile a little.

She reasoned that she was there to get information, not to sit on the bed waiting for a cutie named Arnold to call for her like it was a date.

When she opened the door, she could tell immediately that the energy of the place had shifted. Both music and voices could be heard at the other end of the building. She walked down the hall the way she'd come.

A door opened to her left and a guy she hadn't seen before stepped out into the hall. He did a double take and stared openly. She nodded and said, "Hello." He said nothing, but she could feel him continuing to stare at her back as she walked down the hall.

When the hall opened into the wide bar slash gathering area, she immediately saw Arnold holding a glass bottle of beer and laughing with a couple of men wearing cuts. One was the guy from Hollywood Wrecks and Rides. The two men looked her direction which caused Arnold to turn around.

"Oh, there you are!" he said, as if he'd been waiting for her to show up. "Come on over here and meet some of the guys." He took her arm and pulled her over. "This is Car Lot."

Brigid nodded and stuck out her hand. "Brigid." Car Lot shook her hand.

"And this is…."

"We've met."

"You have?" Arnold sounded surprised.

"Yesterday at the showroom. But I didn't get your name."

"There's a story behind how he got that name. Maybe I'll tell it to you," Arnold said. "But first, why don't you guess what we call him. I'll give you a clue. It's not the name his mama put on the birth certificate."

"How many guesses do I get?" Brigid asked.

"One," said Arnold. He was clearly having a good time with the name game.

"Well, if I only get one guess, I'm going to have to go with Pistol Pete."

After two seconds of silence Arnold and Car Lot began laughing so hard they had to lean on each other. Edge, on the other hand, didn't appear to be enjoying the joke. In fact, his cheeks and ears had turned red.

He glared at Brigid. "It's Edge," he said through clenched teeth.

"Well…" Brigid smiled brightly. "That suits you, too."

Edge looked away when he heard Car Lot over at the bar saying, "She called him Pistol Pete!" just before another round of laughter ensued.

Turning back to Brigid with a hard look, he said, "Looks like you scored some points with my brothers."

He raised his chin and added, "At my expense," before turning his back and walking away.

She was trying to imagine what damage control might look like where Edge was concerned. For a smart girl, it was extra stupid to make an enemy of one of the members on the first day of a research project that could make or break her future as a social anthropologist.

After Edge walked away she was left standing alone, but not for long. Arnold drifted back over. "You ready to make the rounds?"

"Yep."

He stuck out his arm for her to take, which stymied her. Being introduced to club members and their families, on Arnold's arm, would set up all kinds of signals that were wrong.

"I'm with you, but I can't look like I'm showing partiality in any way."

He grinned. "So. Not my date for the party then?" Arnold watched the surprise flick across her expressive face. He leaned in close. "No worries. I'm just fuckin' with ya."

Brigid couldn't help thinking that fucking with her was exactly what she was determined to avoid, but her body reacted to the warm breath on the side of her face. For the hundredth time that day she wondered if she had taken on more than she was prepared for.

As hard as she tried, it was going to be impossible to remember all the names and put them with the right faces. She met men in Sons of Sanctuary cuts at the bar or hanging around the lounge area inside. She met more standing around the barbeque pit and grill outside along with a few of the wives who were watching the children play. Every single person gave her a thorough visual going-over, head to toe, that made her feel uncomfortable enough to give her self-confidence a little tremor.

Brigid remarked that she hadn't known to expect a family get-together.

"The kids? Oh yeah," Arnold said. "They'll be taken home when it gets dark. Before they see anything they shouldn't see." That was punctuated with a wink.

The last stop was the enormous kitchen with its impressive sea of commercial stainless steel. There was such a flurry of activity with most of the women congregated in one place. Working, laughing, wiping brows.

When she entered it was like a freeze-frame moment. Everything went quiet as they surveyed the newcomer.

"This is Brigid, y'all. Prez says to make her feel welcome."

"Prez indeed!" A woman in her late sixties was making her way past the other women, wiping her hands on her white apron, and speaking as she walked. "That boy doesn't need to tell us to be polite."

She smiled at Brigid and stuck out her hand. "I'm June. You're welcome to join us. Do you know your way around a kitchen?"

Brigid opened her mouth to speak, but Arnold jumped in. "June's old man founded the club. She's Prez's mama."

Brigid could tell from Arnold's tone that he regarded her affectionately.

"Glad to meet you," Brigid said, shaking the hand that was offered. "I'm no French chef, but I've got the basics. Do you need help?"

"Oh, lands. We can always use another pair of hands." To Arnold, she said, "Go on about your business now. She'll be fine here."

Arnold gave Brigid a parting smile. "If you change your mind about bein' my date, look me up later."

June tisked and shook her head. "Way I hear it, that boy'll give you a hard day's night, but won't remember your name in the mornin'."

Brigid laughed at the information and at the twinkle in June's eyes. "So you're the grand dame?"

June elbowed her in a conspiratorial way. "Unlike the men around here, we don't need titles. We just do what women always do. We take care of life while they play their little games."

Several of the other women snickered at that.

June introduced her to seven women, including the club members to whom they were tied and their relationship to them, wives, old ladies, or girlfriends. Brigid catalogued the information that there had been no corresponding mention of women when she was introduced to the men.

It didn't take long to figure out why Arnold had asked if she'd brought something more "form fitting". All the women were wearing clothes that were tight, revealing, or both. That, combined with heavy makeup and big hair did make Brigid look like she was the sheep who had wandered into the goat pen.

"Now if you can drain those pots of boiled potatoes and dump them in here," June pointed to a tub, "we'll start throwin' in the mixin's for potato salad."

"Sure." Brigid's tee had elbow-length sleeves, which she pushed up higher before grabbing some oven mitts to lift the first pot. As she carried it to the deep sink, she was thinking she was glad she found time to circuit train now and then because the pot was damn heavy. One of the other women slipped past her and put a huge colander in the sink so that Brigid could tip the pot and release the steamy water. She smiled at the woman and wished she could remember her name, but it was too many people too quickly to keep them all straight.

She repeated that process twice more before all the potatoes were dumped into, first the colander, then the tub.

"All done!" she announced. "What's next?"

"Marjorie, show Brigid how we make Sanctuary Salad." To Brigid, June said, "Marjorie's got the touch when it comes to potatoes. After tonight, you're going to dream about potato salad. Mark my words."

Brigid laughed. Marjorie appeared to be in her late thirties or early forties. Brigid pictured her with a soccer mom makeover and decided she'd be an attention-getter in any setting.

Marjorie began carving up potatoes with a meat fork

and butcher knife. As she worked, she glanced at Brigid with a look of amusement. "You a biker virgin, honey?"

Brigid had no idea how to answer that. "I… uh…"

Marjorie laughed again. "I'm not askin' if you've fucked bikers. I'm askin' if you've been around 'em much."

Brigid noticed that everything had gone quiet. Apparently everybody in the kitchen was waiting for her reply. "Well, no. Not really."

"Thought so," said Marjorie. "So you see how I'm doin' this?" Brigid nodded. "Okay. You give it a try. When the whole mess has been chopped up so that no piece is bigger than this," she indicated a shape like a half inch square, "come get me and we'll get down to work."

"Okay."

Brigid took the knife and fork and mimicked Marjorie's motions. When she was done, Marjorie added salt, paprika, a ton of Miracle Whip, a little yellow mustard, and some chopped pimentos, "for color" she'd said. She dipped a spoon into the gigantic mixture and aimed it at Brigid's mouth.

"Okay. Try this."

Brigid opened her mouth and let Marjorie feed her. Again, the kitchen had gone quiet as they waited for her reaction.

"Oh my God!" She started talking before she even swallowed the bite. "I *will* dream about this!"

Everybody laughed. Marjorie winked and said, "Have as much as you want. Cook gets first dibs. It wouldn't hurt for you to fill those curves out a little. Bikers like to use their hands and want somethin' substantial to grab onto."

The women agreed, some with laughter, some with, "Amen," or "Got that right".

"Oh, leave her alone," June piped in. "There's a reason why God made things in different sizes. We're not all supposed to be alike."

Brigid appreciated that sentiment and liked June all the more for voicing it. Again, she silently admonished herself for allowing feelings to creep into her research project.

After an hour or so in the kitchen, the women began to relax their guard around Brigid. The novelty of her presence was wearing off and the hum of chatter and laughter resumed. Brigid thought it was the closest thing to being a fly on the wall. Perfect for her.

Car Lot stepped into the kitchen. "Pig's done," he announced as he grabbed a deviled egg half and slid the whole thing into his mouth. "Hmmm." He grabbed a pregnant woman with sandy-colored hair in a ponytail and pulled her close to him. "You make these, hon? Tastes like you."

She giggled. "Yeah. Guess you know my taste pretty well."

The whole room boomed with bawdy laughter. Car Lot smiled as he kissed his wife, but his ears turned pink with embarrassment. Brigid cataloged that as interesting because she wouldn't have guessed a burly biker could be that easily embarrassed.

Brigid helped move the prepared food outside where the women watching the kids had been preparing a buffet table with paper plates, napkins, condiments, and utensils. When Brant Fornight made his appearance, the first thing he did was to acknowledge his mother and give her a kiss on the cheek. She smiled and patted his shoulder.

Brigid got some food and went to find a place to sit down where she could watch without drawing unnecessary attention to herself. She was there for about two minutes before June set a plate and a beer down across from her.

"How 'bout I join you for supper tonight?"

Brigid smiled. "Sure. Love to have the company." June nodded, sat, and picked up a roasted pork sandwich. Brigid nodded toward the children. "The kids are having such a good time they don't want to stop to eat."

"Yeah, it's always been like that. There are a few people here who grew up in the club. I won't point them out because I'm sure you're already overwhelmed with names and such, but you'll find out when you talk to them. I guess you're goin' to talk to everybody alone eventually."

"That's my hope." Brigid tried for an innocent smile that conveyed the idea she wasn't there to hurt anybody.

June was openly studying her. "They told you my old man got this thing started?" Brigid nodded while she chewed a carrot stick. "I've been a widow for about twenty years. Havin' these people, well, it's meant the world. Course I had my hands full raisin' a young hellion.

My son was a single father. Well, I mean he *is* a single father, but the boy's been a grown man for a while now."

Brigid looked around. "Is he a member of the club?"

"He is, but he's not here tonight."

"Oh."

"He's a good-lookin' boy. And likeable. Lord knows the girls like him."

"Do most people raised around the club stay part of the community when they grow up?"

June shook her head. "I wouldn't say most. But I would say that all of them know there's somebody they can go to for help if they come up against the kind of problem they can't fix."

"Like what?"

"Maybe that's a talk for another time. Tonight's about gettin' to see the club at its best. To me, these picnics are the heart of the thing. Bein' surrounded by people who would get up in the middle of the night if we called for help, well, it reminds us that we belong to somethin' worthwhile. And we're not alone."

Brant set a longneck and a plate down next to June. "Mama," he said. "Looks like you're gettin' along with Pain."

"Pain?" June asked.

Brant chuckled. "That's what Eric calls this one," he nodded toward Brigid. "Now everybody's sayin' it. Looks like it's gonna stick."

"You mean me?" Brigid scowled. "They're calling me 'pain'?"

"In our world, when you get a name, you put a smile on and live with it. Unless you're prepared to beat the livin' crap out of any and everyone who mouths a handle you refuse."

Brigid cocked her head. "Is that what happened with you, um, Brant? They tried to give you a nickname and you, uh, beat the livin' crap out of anybody who said it?"

He locked onto Brigid's inquiring eyes, took a swig of Lone Star, then said, "Damn straight."

"Do *not* let him intimidate you with that scary biker shit," June said.

Brant face softened into an affectionate smile as he turned to his mom. "You think I'm not scary?"

June just laughed and patted his face. "Now your dad, *he* was scary."

Brant looked thoughtful as his chin went up once and then down. "He could be. That's a fact."

Not ready to change the subject, Brigid said, "So you're saying that my two choices are to be okay with being called 'Pain' or be prepared to engage large hairy bikers in mortal combat."

Brant looked amused. "Shaved ones, too."

"What's goin' on over here?" One of the women who had been watching the children slid onto the seat next to Brigid.

"This is my girl," June said. "She and Brant are what they call Irish twins. Know what that is?"

"Um, no, I can't say I do."

"They're only a year apart. Joanna's older."

"That's right." Joanna directed her attention toward Brant. "The Prez is my *little* brother." She pointed toward where the children were playing. "Those two little girls in the pink sundresses are my grandkids."

Brigid looked surprised. "You don't look old enough."

Joanna laughed. "People say that all the time. I started young and so did my kid. You met him, I think. Crowley? They call him Crow." She rolled her eyes at that. "Bikers got no respect for the names their mamas give 'em."

"Yeah? Well, respect's gotta be earned," Brant said smugly.

Joanna threw a deviled egg at his head, which he successfully ducked.

"Christ, Sissy. How would it look for the president of the Sons of Sanctuary Motorcycle Club to get hit in the face with a deviled egg?"

She laughed. "I don't know, but I'm takin' bets most of the club would like to see it."

"Funny." Brant looked at Brigid. "I can hear what you're thinkin'."

Brigid desperately hoped not. "You can?"

He nodded. "You're wonderin' if my sister has a man around here."

Brigid had to admit that it had crossed her mind, but that was not the kind of question to ask a stranger. Sometimes the answer was sensitive, personal, and altogether not good.

"It did cross my mind."

"She's a widow. My brother-in-law was in the reserves. Went to Desert Storm. Didn't come back."

"I'm sorry."

Joanna nodded, but her eyes turned red even though it had been so long ago. "He was one of a kind. Nobody like him."

WHEN THE SUN set, the children disappeared, and the music was cranked up louder. Their taste clearly ran to hard driving Classic Rock. Bob Seger. AC/DC. Fog Hat. The night air was far from cold, but they built a fire for light and, as Brigid would later write, probably an age-old call for tribe to gather around the communal fire for rituals and the comfort of togetherness.

A whole new crowd of people showed up. Guys who came to party, not wearing cuts. Girls who responded to the lure of guys reputed to be anarchists.

Brigid stayed off to the side. It was easy to observe without being noticed after dark. Arnold was making out with one of the attendees and didn't seem to care who watched. By ten o'clock most of the women she'd met in the kitchen, including June and Joanna, had disappeared along with some of the members, including Brant.

She lingered until she concluded that she'd seen what there was to see. There was lightning in the distance. The kind that would put out that fire in a hurry if the storm pushed toward them. In any case, she was too tired to stay and find out. She made her way past the crowd in the main room of the clubhouse to her temporary home, the "guest suite".

After a shower, she put on her thin flannel night shirt, the pale blue one with mother-of-pearl buttons, and sat down on the side of the bed to make notes. It was too late to pull out the laptop and set it up, but there were a few thoughts she wanted to be sure she didn't forget.

Lying awake, her head was swimming with first impressions. Some things were exactly what she'd expected to find. Others weren't. The bass was thumping loud enough to vibrate the mattress under her. Between that and the fact that every once in a while a loud chorus of voices could be heard coming from the other end of the building, sleep was an unattainable goal.

Eventually, sometime after midnight, the party noise quieted and she drifted off.

BRASH WAS ON a late-night plane, made later by being diverted to San Antonio because of weather. After sitting on the runway for an hour waiting for it to blow over, Brash demanded to be let off the plane. There was a verbal skirmish between him and the crew that concluded with the threat of calling air marshals to take him into custody. Then quite suddenly, they backed down and let him off the plane.

He rented a car and drove to Austin. It was just getting light by the time he got home. He was tired enough to be bleary-eyed and almost surprised he made it without going to sleep at the wheel. He punched the code into the gate, parked and walked past a still-smoldering fire pit. So exhausted he could barely stand, he'd reached the promised land, the last room on the right at the end of the hall.

He fumbled to find the right key, but got the door open. He managed to pull off his boots, his shirt, and his belt before deciding that he just wasn't motivated to go further. He reached for the covers and saw that there was a woman in his bed. In his barely-conscious state, he supposed it was a club groupie hoping to get a second chance with him. He was too tired to throw her out, whoever she was. So he crawled in. As he drew in a deep satisfied breath, he inhaled the female scent next to him. He didn't remember having been with somebody who smelled that good. Ever. So he turned toward her and was asleep in less than a minute.

BRIGID'S EYELIDS FLUTTERED open when morning light filtered into the room. She was having the best dream. Sexy. Warm. Good. So good she didn't really want to wake up. She squirmed a little, nestling back into the hard body that was spooning hers, then she realized the large hand caressing her breast was no dream.

She came fully awake in an instant and shrieked loud enough to wake the dead.

Brash jumped up, looking around for the direction of the alarm. When he turned back to see a woman standing above him on the bed, he had only a second to take in wide amber eyes and copper-colored hair, before she hauled off and slapped him hard enough to cut his lip on one of his teeth.

She jumped off the bed, ran for the door, threw it open, and began banging on Brant's door with both fists while shouting, "OPEN THIS DOOR, FORNIGHT!"

Brash swiped at the trickle of blood starting down his chin.

"Goddammit! What's the matter with you?!" he roared, sounding every bit as murderous as he looked.

Brigid *really* looked at him for the first time and wondered if she knew him. He looked awfully familiar. "What's the matter with me?! I don't think it's unreasonable to expect to be able to sleep through the night without being mauled by a hairy biker!"

She turned to resume her assault on the president's door, but it flew open before she made contact. Brant stood there in pajama bottoms displaying a surprisingly fit-looking bare chest, messy hair and hellfire in his eyes. He looked between Brigid and Brash, who had come up behind her.

"Problem?"

"I'm not sharing a room," said Brigid.

"I know that." People were beginning to come out of their rooms and congregate in the hallway. He looked at Brash. "You forget where you live again?"

Brash wiped at the blood on his lip with the back of his hand and shrugged.

As Brant was closing his own door, he said, "Welcome back. Don't touch the girl," in an emotionless tone that fit the stereotype of motorcycle club president like a glove.

Brash looked her up and down, then disappeared into the room across the hall and slammed the door.

Brigid stomped back into her room, grabbed the motorcycle boots that had been left haphazardly by the bed and threw each across the hallway, against the closed door so that they hit with an impressive thud. She went back for his shirt and belt and threw them at the door as well. Breathing heavy, so mad her chest was heaving, her eyes locked onto his overnight bag.

She picked it up and heaved it at the door with a mighty, "Oof," and all her strength, just as he jerked the door open. The force of the leather bag hurtling through the air caught Brash by surprise and knocked him back on his ass.

He shoved the bag off his stomach, jumped up and started toward her with a good old-fashioned throttle on his mind, but she slammed her own door in his face before he reached her. He was angry enough to break it down, but was under direct order from his president to not touch the girl.

He turned his defiance on the people who had come out into the hall to watch the show and gave them the finger.

As they shuffled back to bed, he heard Eric say, "Told you she was a pain."

On the other side of the door, Brigid realized why she thought she'd recognized the intruder. He was a younger version of Brant with really long, really gorgeous hair.

She looked at her right hand that seemed to have a memory of wrapping around that hair sometime during the night.

CHAPTER 4

AT TWO O'CLOCK in the afternoon, Brant heard a knock on his office door that was just a little less respectful than usual.

"Come in, Brash."

Brash opened the door. His hair was pulled back in a leather thong. He closed the door and flopped into the chair in front of his dad's desk.

"So. You want to tell me what I missed?"

"Nice to see you, too."

"Had a long night, Pop. Stow the sarcasm and tell me who that is in the guest suite."

"You had breakfast?"

Brash raised his chin and narrowed his eyes. "When you start answerin' questions with questions, I know I'm not gonna like what's comin' next. I saw her sittin' at the bar talkin' up Eric. Looked serious."

"Well, it is and isn't."

Brant spent half an hour bringing his son up to speed on the new arrival.

"Jesus, Pop. Everything about this sounds like a bad idea."

"Well, it's a shame you weren't here to add your opinion before the vote, but you were takin' 'personal time'. I'm puttin' you in charge of seein' to it that she learns just enough to fulfill our part of the bargain. And no more."

"Why me?"

"'Cause she's cute. Maybe even real cute. If I put one of the married members on her, there'd be hell to pay from the old ladies. Tried givin' Arnold that job, but I could see that was a train wreck leavin' the station."

Brash barked out a laugh. "Arnold? What'd you expect? If she's been here a day, I'd be surprised if he hasn't already done that tap dance."

"Then prepare to be surprised, son. She's not that kind."

"Well, why not you? You're single."

Brant looked at his son sideways and smirked. "Not givin' you the job as your pop. This is your president speaking."

"Okay, but I didn't get off to a good start. She may not take kindly to my presence. And I'm only gonna be around for the first month of her contract. I'm takin' off for a month. Goin' on a, uh, sabbatical."

It was Brant's turn to let out a surprised laugh. He raised an eyebrow. "Sabbatical?"

Brash tried to look like he owned the word, but truthfully, that's what his brother had called it.

"Yeah. A sabbatical. I've earned some time off. I'm gonna spend some time fishing. Get my head cleared.

Haven't had a vacation in, well, ever. I want to take it now. So I was plannin' to spend this month makin' sure everything's in order."

Brant tapped his fingers on the desk lightly, eyes darting around, like he was seeing everything that could go wrong with the businesses in his son's absence.

"Fishing, huh?"

Brash almost held his breath. He'd never gotten away with anything growing up. If his dad couldn't read his mind, he did a damn good imitation of it.

"Yep."

"When did you develop an interest in fishing?"

"Everybody needs a hobby."

"And I thought yours was loose women."

"Well. It is. But I'm gettin' older and it's time to branch out."

"Gettin' older," Brant repeated drily. "What's goin' on with you? Really."

Brash tried to hold his father's gaze. He'd been training for a moment of a good lie most of his life. He'd kept his stare steady when he'd been fourteen and taken the 1939 Lincoln hotrod out of the showroom for a joy ride. He'd made himself appear completely sincere when he'd been caught setting fire to a construction site Port O Potty. When he was fifteen, he'd only blinked once when he was asked about fucking a member's daughter, which of course, was way out of bounds. Still, his father knew he was lying every time.

Going with the idea that, when it came to Brant Fornight, honesty was the best policy, he decided on saying, "I need some time off, Pop. Can we leave it at that?"

Brant couldn't argue with it. His son was a grown ass man who deserved no-questions time off when requested.

"Yes. We can. What's your plan to keep things seamless while you're gone?"

"I was thinkin' that if I divide my responsibilities ten ways, give a little bit to everybody but you and Rock, it wouldn't be too much of a burden and shit would still get done. That's why I'm waitin' to go till next month. Gives me time to train everybody on what they're doin'. If anybody comes across somethin' they don't know how to deal with, they can ask you. Right?"

Brant nodded thoughtfully. "I wanna see the *exact* plan, who's doin' what. Don't assign jobs until you get final approval from me."

Brash grinned. "Wouldn't dream of it, Prez."

He got up to leave but Brant had more to say. "About the girl, you're still on the hook for what she does this month. As to who gets the job next month… I don't know yet."

"Pop. How am I gonna train people to do my job while babysittin' the civilian?"

Brant gave him the fuck-you smile. "There's your challenge. Got faith in you, son."

Brash huffed out a breath as he left. His dad played that card way too often. Not that it didn't still have an effect on him. He supposed he'd better go get a handle on the intruder first.

Eric saw Brash emerge from the hallway at the left end of the bar. “Brash. Come on over here and meet Pain. Where you been, brother?”

Brash locked eyes with the copper-headed beauty and saw the immediate change in her expression. Unmistakable hostility. Still, his hand remembered the feel of palming an ample and inviting, flannel-covered breast when she was still warm from being in bed.

He walked straight over without taking his eyes off Brigid.

“Pain. This is Brash. He’s not the toughest or the handsomest or the most entertainin’ of us, but the president is his dad.” Eric laughed at what he believed was consummate witty banter.

Brash nodded at Brigid. To Eric, he said, “Can I have a few minutes with the lady?”

Brigid raised her chin with just enough defiance to make her interesting. “We’re not finished.”

Brash gave Eric a look that said, “I’m waiting.”

Eric shrugged in response and slid off the stool. “Later, Pain. Plenty of time for blab later.”

As Brash took Eric’s place on the barstool, he motioned to the prospect who was tending. “Orange juice.”

The prospect nodded and threw a dishtowel over his shoulder to rest there while he poured juice.

When Brash turned to face Brigid, it was the first real long look they’d had at each other. She was struck by how much he looked like his father, and by the fact that he was beautiful enough to make a woman’s mouth go dry. She was sure that Eric had either lied when he'd said that Brash was not the handsomest of them or he was vision impaired.

Getting his first protracted look at Brigid in the light of day, Brash thought his fleeting encounter hadn't begun to do her justice. The similarity between her eye color and hair color gave her an exotic look that was captivating, at the very least. He could tell by the set of her mouth and the intensity of her eyes, that she was still mad. Even though he was the one with the swollen lip.

When her eyes drifted down to that lip, she had the gall to smirk at him, which made him want to either kiss her into an apology or give her a reciprocal slap on the butt. While turned over his knee. His cock jerked a little at that thought, which translated into a smirk of his own.

"About last night..." he began.

She turned toward the bar and took a sip of her drink. He couldn't tell if it was lemonade or a cocktail.

He started again. "I was road weary and mistook you for club tail."

She turned toward him slowly. "Club tail."

"Yeah, well. I'm sure you get the idea. That's what we call girls who show up for club barbeques or parties hoping to get fucked by a biker. I used to live in that room. I figured it was somebody hoping for seconds, which I don't usually do, but I was too beat to enforce my own rule."

Brigid couldn't help wondering how often Brash had been to the 'club tail' buffet.

"I see. So that's your idea of an apology?"

"I hadn't really planned on makin' an apology. Per se. Was a mistake. I lived in that room for a long time."

"I heard that," she said drily.

"But I'll make you a deal. I'll apologize for mistaking your reason for bein' asleep in my bed…"

"Your former bed."

He smiled. "My former bed, if you apologize for cuttin' my lip and knockin' me down with my own damn luggage."

She stared for a full minute before deciding. "Deal. You go first."

"Okay." He grinned. "I'm sorry for feelin' you up." Then he leaned over and talked close to her ear. "Although I gotta admit it was enjoyable and I wouldn't turn down another chance. If you were so inclined."

When he leaned back, she said, "I accept your apology. Now if you'll excuse me, I have people to interview."

"Where's my apology?"

"What apology?"

"The one you agreed to."

"Do you have that in writing?"

Brash's playfulness had disappeared. "First lesson, lady. We're not criminals, hard core or otherwise. But it's still a very bad idea to fuck with us."

"Do you mind if I record that?"

He picked up the phone sitting in front of her on the bar, set it to record and turned it on. "This is Brash Fornight recording Brigid Bailey's apology."

He held the phone by her mouth.

She smiled just a little. "I'm sorry for busting the big scary biker's lip. And for knocking you on your, um, ass. Although both were satisfying in their own way."

Brash smiled, stopped the recording and put the phone back where it had been. "There you go."

He downed his orange juice all at once, slid off the stool, and walked straight to Eric, who was at the curved end of the bar. She watched as he leaned into Eric. She guessed he was talking about her because Eric's eyes darted in her direction. When Eric gave a nod of his head, Brash strode out the front door without giving her another look.

When Eric returned to finish their conversation, he was more reserved, which had the effect of appearing less friendly.

Brigid's first question was, "What did Brash say to you?"

"Sorry, Pain. Out of bounds."

"Okay. Tell me what you do for the club. Exactly."

Eric described his principle job as head of security for the SSMC's 6th Street night club. He'd been a member since he was twenty-three and couldn't imagine any other sort of life. The club and its satellite community of wives, girlfriends, children, and various other family members were everything to him.

As they sat at the end of the bar and talked, people came and went, always eyeing them with open curiosity. When Eric left, she didn't actively seek out someone to interview. Instead, she made a sandwich in the kitchen, ate alone at one of the immense stainless steel counter-height tables, and thought about what Eric had told her.

Afterward she went to her room to gather up her laptop. She went back to her place at the far right end of the bar because she'd discovered that it was an excellent place to establish Command Central. She could observe all the comings, goings, and interactions with a tiny swivel of her stool.

"Hey, Bradley." The prospect behind the bar gave her a macho chin jerk that seemed out of place on such a soft baby face. She knew he had to be older than he looked. "Could you plug this behind the bar?" She held up the end of the cord.

After plugging in the cord, he looked up. "You want somethin'?"

"To drink?"

He rolled his eyes as if to say, "What else?"

"Can I have a coke?"

"Sure thing."

"Let me ask you something. If nobody was around, would it be okay for me to come around the bar and get my own drink?"

He gave her a crooked grin that suggested he might actually belong among the bad boys. Someday. "You could. But fair warnin'. If you set foot back here, you may be in for more than you bargained for. You might end up servin' drinks for hours."

That's when lightning struck and it was all she could

do to contain her enthusiasm.

“Really?” she asked innocently. “Maybe you should teach me how, just in case that happens.”

Bradley looked intrigued. And perhaps pleased by the idea of instructing. “Yeah. Why not? Come on around.” Bradley handed her an apron. “You don’t need to get Coyote Ugly.”

“What?”

“You never…? What I mean is you don’t need to put on a show. There’s no point, since there’s no tips. And you don’t need to learn to mix drinks ’cause club members have got simple tastes. Beer. Whiskey. Tequila.

“On party nights we might get a stray woman who wants a rum and coke. If somebody asks you for somethin’ you don’t know how to do, just put ’em in their place. Say… Beer. Whiskey. Tequila. What do you want?”

“That sounds easy.”

He snorted. “I’m just gettin’ started. So somebody says they want beer. You need to know which ones we have cold and ready to hand over. If they say whiskey, you need to know which kind.” He pointed to the shelf behind him. “We keep seven brands in stock. Sometimes folks want it straight. Sometimes they want somethin’ with it.”

As he went through the options, Brigid was thinking it was a good thing she was a quick study and had no problem with audio learning.

“And you need to know how much to give ’em. So this is a shot glass.”

She nodded even though she had already known what a shot glass looked like. He ran through the options of what people were mostly likely to ask for.

"What happens if we're out of something?" she asked.

"We better not be out of somethin' because I'm in charge of makin' sure we're not out of somethin'. If we run out, you'll see my head mounted up there." He pointed to the space above the mirrored wall behind the bar.

And that was how Brigid Bailey became the SSMC new and unofficial tender of the bar.

By the time Brash returned that evening, Brigid was beginning to feel at home on the flip side of drinksville. She'd learned how to pop beer tops quickly, operate the taps, and keep the premises mostly clean. She was looking at an old mixed drink manual someone had left behind the bar instead of watching club member interactions.

Car Lot approached the bar with Edge.

"Pain," Car Lot said in simple acknowledgement, acting like it was the most natural thing in the world for her to be wearing a waist apron, bartending in the Sons of Sanctuary MC clubhouse. "Porter," was all he said indicating that he'd take a Pecan Porter beer.

"Okay." She looked at Edge.

"Peacemaker." He winked. "I like it pale."

Brigid caught the innuendo directed at her complexion, but a guy like Edge would never get a schoolgirl blush to bloom. She didn't react in any way, which she supposed would be Edge's worst nightmare – inattention.

She pushed napkins their way, popped tops, and set a bowl of nuts between them.

"So you two are friends?"

They both smirked, but Car Lot answered. "Yeah. Club members are more than that."

"But maybe you're tighter with some than others."

Car Lot looked at Edge then shrugged. "Maybe."

"What happens if you have a disagreement?"

"The usual."

"What's the usual?"

"You know, depends on what it is. We might settle it in Circle. Sometimes Prez decides how things are gonna be for us."

"I know this is going to sound like a dumb question to you, but what's the circle?"

Edge leered at her openly. "It's like cage fighting, but the cage is made of people instead of bars or chain link."

"You mean like MMA?"

Car Lot laughed.

"No. More like a bar fight. Even if we'd had training in Asian chop chop, we couldn't use it in Circle. Wouldn't be fair."

She thought that over for a second. "So you settle your differences with fights, but there are rules."

"Exactly," said Car Lot. "Hey. How come you're behind the bar?" He said it like he'd just then realized something was out of place.

Brash took a seat at the other end of the bar. She knew he was there, but she was enjoying pretending to ignore him. Finally he got tired of waiting. "Little service!" he demanded.

She took a deep breath and walked slowly to the end of the bar.

"What'll it be?"

"We still have some of that Aged Hellfighter?"

"I think so."

She returned in a minute with a napkin, a beer, and a bowl of beer nuts.

As she was pouring the beer, he said, "Looks like you found a way to make yourself useful."

"I did. How about you?"

"You're askin' if I found a way to make myself useful?" He chuckled. "You know I just can't stand it. I gotta know where you got two fifty to spend on askin' bikers questions."

Brigid studied him for a few seconds. "You want to trade answers?"

"I'm takin' that to mean it's a good story."

"I'll tell you what you want to know in exchange for a twenty minute interview right now, nothing off limits."

By the look on his face, she could see he was entertained, by the prospect or the negotiation, she couldn't tell which.

"Seven minutes. I'll tell you anything I'm allowed to share."

"Who picks a number like seven?"

"Me. You're evading."

"Fifteen minutes. No hemming. No hawing."

"Hawing?"

"Straight talk. Right now."

"Ten minutes."

"Done."

"Hawsome."

She laughed and then tried to cover it with a scowl, which made Brash smile even broader. Getting a laugh out of the buttoned-up scientist felt like a little victory. He had no idea why he'd care about that, since his lip had been throbbing all day. Worse, everywhere he went, people had stared at it like he hadn't been able to duck a punch to the face. Which, technically, he hadn't.

"So?"

"What do you mean 'so'?" she asked.

"Answer my question. Where'd you get the cash?"

"My parents were killed in a plane crash when I was a teenager. They both had life insurance policies." He watched her features carefully. Her tone was matter-of-fact, almost emotionless. When he didn't respond, she added, "It was a long time ago."

"Okay. You got ten minutes. Starting now." When he looked at his watch, it reminded her of her first meeting with Brant Fornight.

"You know you look a lot like your daddy."

He grinned. "So they say. They also say he's a handsome devil." When she didn't respond, he said, "Interview over?"

"Pain!" She heard someone call the new 'name' from somewhere behind her. She looked over her shoulder at

Eric, who smiled and said, "How 'bout a brew?"

She turned back to Brash. "Put that stopwatch on pause and meet me outside at the picnic table."

"Yes, ma'am."

On her way around the bar, she took off her apron. "Sorry, Eric. I'm taking a break. Get your own."

By the time she got to the picnic table under the big mesquite tree, Brash was waiting quietly with his beer. He looked at his watch and said, "Go."

"How long has your father been president of the club?"

"Twenty-four years."

"Do you ever remember a time when he wasn't president?"

"Not really."

"Was he a good father?"

"The best."

"Did anybody else help raise you?"

"My Gram. Her name is June. You probably met her."

"I did. Did you live here growing up?"

"No." He looked at her like she was crazy. "Children don't live at the club."

"Okay. So did you live with your grandmother and your dad lived here?"

"No. They bought a big piece of land a little bit south of here and built three houses on it. One for Gram, one for my Aunt Joanna, and one for the two of us. It was a big job, raisin' a kid and keepin' the club in line. I guess he was lucky that my grandmother and aunt were in a position to help. And were willin'.

"He was four years younger than I am right now when I was born. Christ. I can't even imagine."

"You can't imagine having a child or being a single father?"

He gave her a strange look. "Of course I can imagine havin' kids. But raisin' one up from infancy? Alone?"

"So you have a lot of admiration for him."

"More than I can say."

She nodded. "He told me you were a handful."

Brash grinned. "Did he?"

"How'd you get your biker name?"

"It's usually called a road name, but I've had it since my tricycle days."

"What's your real name? I mean, your birth certificate name."

"Brannach."

"Hmmm. Brant and Brannach. I sense a trend." Brash didn't respond, but he thought about Brandon. "So you were nicknamed Brash because…"

"Guess."

She laughed. "So you and your dad still officially live somewhere else?"

"No. When I became a patched in member, I started spendin' more time here and I think Dad liked the convenience of bein' thirty paces from his office. So, when my cousin, Crow, started a family, it seemed like the right thing to let them move into our house. It worked for my grandmother and Joanna, bein' close to those girls. And it worked for Crow's wife, too, 'cause she got lots of help."

"Have you ever been married?"

Brash lowered his eyelids and smiled. "This the personal part? No. I've never been married. Thought I might once, but it didn't work out. Now I'm glad."

"Why?"

She saw the moment he decided to laugh it off instead of giving a serious answer.

"'Cause then I wouldn't be free to flirt with you, darlin'."

Ignoring that altogether, she forged ahead. "What's the best thing about living at the clubhouse?"

"Good food. Somebody to clean and do my laundry. No strings attached other than earnin' my cut of the paycheck."

"What's the worst thing?"

"Lack of privacy."

She nodded. "Anything else?"

"Too much of a good thing, the togetherness I mean."

"It's kind of like living at a bar?"

He laughed. "Yeah. From your point of view, I guess it looks that way. Hell. Maybe it is that way."

"What do you do for the club?"

"I supervise the businesses we own and operate."

"Can you be more specific?"

"I don't know. What are you lookin' for?"

"Well, you left here this morning. You came back at

suppertime. What did you do in between?"

He cocked his head. "You lookin' for an invitation to ride around with me?"

He caught the flash of surprise coupled with excitement. "I wasn't. Could I?"

"I'll think about it. You sure you can get away from your new job?"

"My new job?"

"Behind the bar?"

"I'm a volunteer. So. Yes."

He nodded. "I'd definitely say okay in exchange for sexual favors."

"Two hundred and fifty thousand dollars isn't enough? You want sexual favors, too?"

"Well, see, it's like this. My mind understands money. But my dick don't understand money. He just understands there's a beautiful honey-colored woman in front of me with a lush body I'd like to get lost in."

Though she made a valiant try to keep from getting an image of that, the pictures in her mind caused her to flush. She remembered how slapping Brash had hurt her hand, but she also remembered the feel of his hands on her body before she'd gone Irish-woman mad.

"Is that a blush?" He chuckled. "Christ, Brigid. You really *are* buttoned up, aren't you?" He hoped his teasing didn't give her the wrong idea. Because he liked the fact that she wasn't easy. A lot. "How about you? You ever come close to gettin' married?"

She shook her head. "No. I've been concentrating on

getting grades ever since I was in the ninth grade. That's what it takes to get into grad school at an institution like U.T. All work. No play."

"You have regrets about that?"

"Hey. Who's asking the questions here?"

He held up his hands in surrender, but went on. "Not even a serious boyfriend?"

"You can buy an answer to that with another ten minutes of your time."

He chuckled. "Much as I'd like to take you up on that, I got someplace to be. I'll take a raincheck. Can I walk you back in?"

"No thanks. I know the way."

She watched him walk off, knowing that he knew she was watching. He swung his leg over one of the monster machines lined up facing the club, and started the engine with a roar. One of the prospects was on gate duty and opened up without needing to be asked. Brash gave him a two-fingered wave as he went through.

Bradley had been lucky enough to escape a 'road name' so far. The gate prospect hadn't been so lucky. He'd been dubbed Gulp and she hadn't needed to ask why. He had a nervous habit of swallowing made worse by a thin frame and an extremely pronounced Adam's Apple.

Brigid leaned her elbows back on the picnic table and breathed in the soft evening air as she listened to the sound of the motorcycle fade away. As she lingered, she watched the ones who lived at the club come back for the day, alone or in pairs. From the picnic table she could watch unobserved. She could hear voices, but couldn't make out what they were saying. Still, it was plain that the members enjoyed an easy camaraderie.

As Brash was making the rounds the next day, his thoughts drifted back to Brigid. That first night, even with a smashed mouth, he couldn't help noticing the way she looked in that thin blue nightshirt. It wasn't the kind of thing a woman would wear to seduce a man, but the way she filled it out caught his attention and, apparently, kept his attention.

It hadn't taken long for him to figure out that she was an early riser. Every morning she was already at the far end of the bar, typing away on her laptop. He usually ate in the kitchen with whoever was there, but that day he decided to get a plate and see if he could annoy the redhead into showing him the spark he'd seen in her eyes the night she busted his lip.

Brigid was making notes when she saw a plate of scrambled eggs and bacon being set down next to her where the bar curved. She'd gotten into the habit of writing in the mornings unless someone volunteered to be chatty. After she made herself a salad for lunch, she'd put her laptop away and bartend.

She stopped typing and looked up at Brash.

"You had breakfast?" He took the seat and reached for his fork.

"Hours ago."

"Hours ago? How early do you get up?"

"Well, that depends on how much sleep the house lets me get, but I like to be up by six at latest."

He nodded thoughtfully. "So what were you writin' just now."

When she didn't answer, he swiveled the laptop screen toward him and read out loud.

"At the same time, tribal societies exhibit a remarkable economy of design and have a compactness and self-sufficiency lacking in modern society. This is achieved by the close, and sometimes unilateral, connections that exist between tribal institutions or principles of social organization, and by the concentration of a multiplicity of social roles in the same social persons or offices. There is a corresponding unity and coherence in tribal values that are intimately related to social institutions and are endowed with an intensity characteristic of all 'closed' systems of thought. Tribal societies are supremely ethnocentric."

Brash looked at her like he was trying to read her mind.

"Your eggs are getting cold," she said, glancing at his plate for emphasis.

He turned the laptop back to its position facing her and said, "You got lots goin' on in that gorgeous head, Pain."

"Look. I know this is a losing battle, but I really wish you'd call me Brigid."

He studied her carefully. "Has anybody ever pointed

out that Brigid rhymes with frigid?"

She narrowed her eyes and set her mouth. "Yes. The same people who pointed out that Brash rhymes with gash."

He almost choked on the piece of bacon he'd just put in his mouth. "Real mature."

"You started it."

When he grinned the light shining in his eyes was so captivating she caught herself leaning forward a little.

"Guilty," he said softly. "I see you're pickin' up the lingo, but I warn you. Pop doesn't approve of disrespectin' women. *This* club has kind of strict rules about the way women are regarded. Even the ones who don't care."

"Should I take that to mean that your club is different from most? In that regard?"

"Take it any way you want, but it's a fact. This club is different from most. In that regard."

"Okay."

"So why are you curious about us?"

"I'm gathering evidence to prove a theory."

"What theory?"

She smiled and looked away for just a second. She hadn't expected to ever be asked.

"My theory is that we, as a species, are hardwired to seek a community organized according to the most ancient social structures, tribes. In the modern world, we have civilized constructs that exist outside of instinct. Layer after layer of rules and guidelines, intellectual experiments in culture, that operate in direct opposition to human instinct."

"What's that have to do with us?"

"Don't you see? I think motorcycle clubs have attempted to reconstruct what was lost, at least in part. Tribal society."

He cocked his head and shoved the plate away. "You romanticizin' us, Pain?"

"Maybe I am, Brannach."

He smiled. He hadn't known how she was going to answer his question, but he hadn't expected that answer. At all. He'd gotten it all wrong. He'd thought she looked down on them and wanted to prove that they were primitive throwbacks. He supposed that was part of what she was saying, but the way she said it made it sound like a good thing. "You talked to Nam yet?"

"Nam? No. I don't think so."

"You'd know if you had. He's the… in your terms I guess he'd be the tribe elder. He's the oldest active member of the SSMC and he's also the historian. Everything about the club's formation, what's happened since when, where, how, who… he knows it all. Got it in his head.

"Next time he wanders in here lookin' for a sip of whiskey and some company, you pull his chain, he'll talk for hours. The MC is his favorite subject on earth."

Brigid's eyes were sparkling like he'd just offered her a lottery win. "That sounds… perfect. What's he look like?"

"Old. Gray. Wiry build. Has long hair. He's clean

shaved when he thinks about it. Other days he's got a bristle on his face that's part black part white."

SHE LEARNED THAT general meetings of the membership were held on Wednesday afternoons and that women weren't allowed inside. Brash had given her a tip that members usually stuck around to talk and drink after. So she took her place behind the bar, and waited patiently with Bradley.

"You know, Pain," Bradley said, "it'll be nice to have your help today. They run me ragged after church."

"Church?"

"The Wednesday meeting."

"Oh. Well, I'm glad to help. I'm not doing anything else."

He laughed. "Yeah. Sure."

She didn't have time to ask him what he meant. They heard a chorus of voices talking when the door down the hall opened and the members headed straight for them.

"Bar's open," Bradley said. "Look alive."

All thirteen members were present. Most asked for longnecks and drifted over to the lounge area or pool table, but a few slid onto bar stools. She had compromised her dress code when Brash had told her that men will give up more information if they have a hint of cleavage in front of them.

Cleavage was not a problem for her. She'd been blessed in that department. Showing the blessing was the problem. She was the furthest thing from an exhibitionist, but decided that, if she could get the members to talk more about cogent details with a little skin, she'd make the sacrifice.

She bought a couple of knit tops that dipped enough to erase all doubt that she was a woman. One black. One blood red. That day she wore stretchy skinny jeans with the red one and lipstick to match. That was another concession. The red lip gloss looked good with her hair and eyes, and she knew it would also draw attention, but not too much attention.

A black apron tied around her waist completed the ensemble.

When the guys first sat down at the bar, they gawked and ogled. But she smiled in return, as if she was there to earn some extra money, and after a few minutes they became involved in their own conversations and forgot she was there. She bustled around the bar, sometimes pretending to do things that didn't need doing so she could eavesdrop without appearing to eavesdrop.

They talked about wives, kids, nephews, and yard work. Not the sort of thing one would expect from anarchists and desperados.

When the flurry of activity died down, she walked over to stand in front of the stool where Nam was sitting. She set a fresh bowl of nuts in front of him and replaced his beer with a fresh cold one.

"Hi. I'm Brigid."

"Not what I hear."

"What'd you hear?"

"That your name's Pain. 'Cause you are one."

She shrugged. "People are entitled to their opinion, I guess."

He grinned. It was clear that he hadn't been worried about teeth whitening as the years progressed, but he still had all his teeth.

"Is Nam your real name?"

"What do you think?"

"I suspect it's short for Vietnam?"

"That's right. D'you learn about that in school, little girl?"

"As a matter of fact I did. I bet they left some things out of the textbooks though."

"Got that right. I could tell you stories..."

Edge took the stool in front of her. "She's not interested in your stories, old man. Give me a shot of Jack." He said it with a mean grin to show that he knew exactly what he was doing.

"I'll get your Jack, Pete. But I would like to hear what Nam has to say."

Nam looked at Edge. "She called you Pete." He looked at Brigid. "This here's Edge."

"Well," she smiled at Nam. "I call him Pete," she said as she poured a shot from a whiskey bottle with a black and white label.

Nam thought that whole thing was funny. So much so that Edge took his drink and left. As soon as he was gone, Brigid said, "Thank you," to Nam.

The old man nodded. "Now. Where were we? Oh.

You were saying that you know you haven't heard the whole story."

An hour and a half later, Nam was explaining that Vietnam vets were responsible for curb cuts, that in prior wars people who lost their legs usually died, but in Vietnam, helicopters scooped them up and got them to med in time to save their lives, if not their limbs.

"All of a sudden, we had a whole bunch of guys in wheelchairs with no way to get inside a courthouse or even roll down a sidewalk because they couldn't take the chairs over curbs. And handicapped parkin' places. That was us, too.

"People who were our own age, civilians, they hated us because we fought in a war we shouldn't have been in, but like the song said. There was a draft and I weren't no senator's son. So what were we supposed to do? Well, sure, some went to Canada, but…"

Brigid had given up tending bar and had come around to sit next to Nam. Brash came around on his other side, put a hand on his shoulder and said, "You monopolizin' the beautiful girls again?"

Nam chuckled. "Can't help bein' a chick magnet."

Brash smiled, but he was looking at Brigid the whole time. "Can I borrow her for a minute?"

"I suppose, but bring her back, 'cause I wasn't near finished."

"Yep."

BRIGID LOOKED AT Brash with open curiosity. He steered

her over to an uninhabited corner.

"Were you serious about wantin' to ride around with me on errands?"

"Yeah. Of course!"

"Well, see if you can get outta your bartendin' job tomorrow and I'll take you along. Right after breakfast."

"At six?"

He could see the tease in her eyes and gave her a sideways look. "At *ten*." She laughed. "By the way," he fingered the hem of her shirt near her shoulder, "it's nice to know you hear me when I talk."

She pulled a handful of ones out of her apron pocket. "Uh-huh. So far it's been worth…" she looked at the bills, "at least twenty."

"Guess they forgot you're rich."

"I'm not rich."

"Okay. Next thing you know they'll be forgettin' why you're here."

"I'm not here to hurt you," she said softly. "Or the club."

His eyes drifted down to her mouth. "See you at ten or thereabouts."

"Any time after nine is hit or miss as to whether there'll be any bacon left."

He laughed and gave her a pointed look. "There's more than one place to get bacon."

It was clear by the look on her face that he'd killed the good humor. That was when it crossed his mind, for the first time, that the beautiful social scientist might actually be into him, the rowdy long-haired tattooed biker who wouldn't have a high school diploma if it wasn't for GED. After waking up to find her enraged over a little early morning snuggle, he'd been sure he didn't stand a chance.

He walked up to Arnold, who was waiting his turn at the pool table. "You think women are strange?"

Arnold looked at him like he was crazy. "I think it's strange that you'd ask that question. 'Cause everybody knows women are strange."

Having overheard that, Car Lot added, "It don't get stranger."

The others, within earshot, all nodded and mumbled their agreement.

AT NINE THIRTY Brash set his breakfast plate down on the bar next to Brigid, as he had every day that week.

She kept typing, but said, "It's not ten yet."

He put a piece of bacon in his mouth. "I didn't want to miss out on bacon."

She smiled in spite of herself and looked over at him. He was wearing a short sleeved black tee that showed off both his tan muscled arms and the colorful tattoo on the right side. When she'd awakened to him in her bed the Saturday before, she'd seen the entire design in all its glory, but was too livid to appreciate the detail.

"Did that hurt?"

He glanced down to where she was looking at his arm and smiled. "Like the dickens. You have any?"

"Tats?"

Her eyes went wide, which made him laugh on the inside. "No," she said. "Even if I wanted one, I'm a firm avoider of pain."

"That right, Pain?"

"That's right, Brannach."

If she thought calling him that was going to needle him, she was so wrong. He loved hearing her say his given name.

"Well, if you're finished typing nonsense, we'll be off."

"Bait me all you want. I'm not reacting."

"Okay," he chuckled. "You want to leave that on the bar or in my old room?" He nodded toward the laptop.

"I'll be right back."

She returned wearing a tan baby doll top, jeans and Converse with a messenger bag worn cross-body. He held the door open for her and started toward his bike.

"Wait. Where are you going?"

"I thought we'd use transportation today 'cause walkin' just takes too long."

"Well, yeah. But not *that.*" She waved in the direction of his Harley.

"You never been on a bike before?"

She didn't need to say it. He could tell by the way she looked at him, part fear, part anticipation.

"So today's the day. Look. I brought somethin' for you." He handed her a dark pink helmet with daisies painted on it. "Belongs to my Aunt Joanna. She said you can use it."

"Well." Brigid took it and turned it over, waiting for her life to flash before her eyes. "That was, um, nice of her."

She put it on and fumbled with the strap.

"Here," he said. He stood in front of her, fixed the strap, and looked down into her eyes. Suddenly he grinned, knocked once on the top of her helmet, and stepped back. "Okay. Here's what you do. Put your feet right there like that." He took one foot and then the other and physically showed her what he wanted. "And keep them there. Then you put your arms around me and hold on tight. When I lean, you lean the same way. That's all there is to it."

He started the engine and pulled her arms tighter around him. "There. How does that feel?"

"Scary."

He laughed and started forward. When they were on the other side of the gate, she got a chance to hear what the roar was like up close and personal. It was equal parts frightening and thrilling. It only took minutes for the anxiety to level out so that she could appreciate feeling like she was part of scenery as it rushed past with the wind. There was no mistaking the sense of freedom or the appeal.

She supposed that she couldn't write about a motorcycle club with any authenticity without having firsthand knowledge of riding. She laid her cheek against the plane of muscle between Brash's shoulder blades and gave herself up to the experience of being a fender fox. And he smiled. She couldn't possibly know that she was the first woman to ever be invited to ride with him.

He normally rode a Sportster, but he'd borrowed an Electra Glide Ultra just for his special passenger.

First stop was an old-time movie theater on 3rd Street. Brigid got off the bike and fumbled with the helmet, until Brash came to her rescue.

Brigid looked up at the marquee. It read, FRIDAY FILM NOIR. "Double Indemnity" and "Touch of Evil".

He used one of a fistful of keys to open a door to the right of the ticket window. After Brigid entered, he relocked the door.

The lighting was dim inside, but Brigid could tell the antique fixtures had been lovingly cared for or restored, while carpet and displays were pristine and new.

A man in his fifties came out of nowhere and seemed really glad to see Brash. "Mr. Fornight!" he said.

Brash clasped his hand. "Dave. This is Brigid Bailey. She's my shadow today."

Dave shook her hand. "Nice to meet you. Come on back."

They followed him into the office where he immediately began discussing details of the business with Brash. There had been a spike in beef prices, which meant they needed to print new menus. The chef had been snatched away by another restaurant, but the new woman was promising.

Brigid gathered that the interior of the old movie

house had been turned into a dinner theater. They sometimes rented it out for weddings and private parties, but its main purpose was to serve nouvelle cuisine to a crowd of people who wanted to share an interest in good food and old films with others.

After listening for a while, her curiosity led her out of the office, across the lobby and through the doors to the main room. Since the lights weren't on, she had to hold the door open to see, but it was a lovely space. The floor was terraced into sections sloping downward so that all the diners had a good view of the screen. Half round tables were covered in white linen with crescent seating for either two or four diners.

She had lived in Austin for over a year and had passed by the old theatre without taking note. Of course she hadn't really been interested in anything but her studies.

"See something you like?"

Brash had come up behind her so quietly that she jumped a little and laughed. "Yes. I was just thinking that I must have passed by this place. It's kind of, I don't know, enchanting."

"Huh," was all he said. "Well, I'm ready if you are."

When she turned, Dave said, "Let me know when you're coming and I'll reserve a special table for you."

"Thank you," she smiled. "I'd really like that."

Before lunch they visited a used textbook store that she had personally patronized and a real estate management company. Apparently, the club owned some housing rentals.

When they left there, he said, "What do you want for lunch?"

"Surprise me."

He grinned and fastened her helmet.

After stopping at a taco truck parked next to the river, Brash ordered soft tacos and lemonades and motioned to the picnic table under the Live Oak. Maybe it was because it was a Thursday and maybe it was because it was the middle of the afternoon, but they were the only ones there.

"Hmmm. This is the best soft taco I've ever had."

"Well, that's the thing about small businesses like this one. They can't rely on ambience. Although the location can't be beat."

She laughed. "That's true." She turned her face into the breeze and closed her eyes for a minute as if in confirmation. "So. What is it you've been showing me this morning?"

"You don't know?"

"I want to hear it from you."

"The club owns a network of enterprises. The current president has done all this since I was born. Nam can tell you the whole story, but my granddad's dealings weren't always, ah, legitimate, I guess you'd say. Pop came into the club bent on two things; making money, and doin' it clean.

"He figured out that most small businesses fail not because they're bad ideas or because the owners are lazy, but because of either bein' undercapitalized or missin' something crucial. Capitalization is an easy problem to fix if you have the venture capital. The other thing is usually a matter of bein' too close. Small business people have dreams and put their whole selves into it. Sometimes they have to compromise a little to be profitable, but I'm usually able to convince them that that's better than goin' under. You know?"

She nodded. "So you're the business genius?"

"You makin' fun of me?"

"No." She shook her head to punctuate her innocence.

He could see by the big eyes and her surprised reaction that she hadn't been mocking him, and it gave him a warm feeling in his chest to suspect that she might be truly impressed.

"Everybody's got a talent. Sometimes I can see what needs to be tweaked to make a business work. I mean I read some, too. And I didn't figure this out just yesterday. I did what you might call an apprenticeship for a long ass time."

Before the end of the day, they visited a boot and saddle maker and a florist.

When they pulled back into the SSMC and dismounted the Electra Glide, Brigid said, "So that was a typical day in the life?"

"Pretty much."

BRIGID DIDN'T SEE Brash at dinner and, for the first time

all week, he didn't eat breakfast at the bar with her. She knew there was going to be another party that night and figured she'd see him then.

She did. He showed up around ten o'clock with an outrageously buxom blonde hanging on him.

Brash waited until she was watching to lay a kiss on the blonde, with no mistaking there was tongue involved. He maneuvered the woman so that he could watch Brigid's reaction and, Christ. He'd wanted to find out if she was into him, not hurt her. She looked as devastated as if she'd been his old lady.

She'd taken off like there was an ex on her tail.

Brash handed the woman off to Eric and went inside. When he got to his old room, he knocked. Then knocked louder. When he didn't get any response, he tried the door. It was locked, but that didn't stop him. He opened the door and walked in.

She was lying on the bed crying.

He closed the door behind him and locked it.

"Brigid. What the fuck are you doin'?"

She sat up, looking both indignant and outraged. "GET OUT OF HERE!" She threw a pillow at him.

He caught the pillow in one big hand and walked toward the bed. When he was close she stood up and said, "I said GET OUT!" She drew her hand back like she was going to have another crack at him, but he'd already seen her best move. He caught her wrist. When she raised the other hand, he caught that one, too.

Her face was pink from crying and he was ashamed

enough to want to kick his own butt. He hadn't wanted to hurt her. He just wanted to find out if she was interested. In him.

"Baby." He said it softly. She sniffled in response, but went still. "Kiss me."

"No."

"Yeah, Brigid. Kiss me."

"Why?" She sniffled.

He smiled and said gently, "Because you want to. I want to. We want to."

"I'm not kissing lips that have just been on that skank."

He turned and walked into the bathroom. She heard water running briefly and then he was in front of her again. "There. Every trace of skank is all gone."

When she looked up, he took the choice away from her, pressed his lips against hers and let his tongue leisurely tangle with hers. She melted into his kiss, her body recalling how good he'd felt wrapped around her while she slept the night he'd come back from Colorado.

He eased her back onto the bed and trapped her under his body while he continued to pet slowly. As the spark between them started to catch fire, he drew back, drinking in the look of her lowered eyelids and the lust shining back in her eyes.

Brash opened his mouth to say something. "Jesus," was all that came out.

Brigid raised both of them off the bed in her eagerness to arch into him. He sat up on one knee, pulled the tee shirt over his head, and threw it off to the side of the bed. She raked her gaze over his chest and his tattoos and reached out to run her hands down his torso like she couldn't stand to not be touching him.

"Sit up," he said as he pulled her hands toward him. He lifted her black top away. She'd worn it for the party, hoping he'd like what he saw. And he did. He stared at her long enough to make her self-conscious. Just as she was about to cover herself with her hands, he distracted her with a mind-numbing kiss while he unfastened her bra and tossed it onto the growing pile of clothing beside the bed.

He sat back to see what he'd uncovered and, again, the only thing he could think of to say was, "Jesus." He palmed a full breast in his right hand and reveled in the sound of the deep moan she made. He broke the kiss and pushed down to take her nipple into his mouth.

As he swirled his tongue around her areola, teasing the nipple, she took his hair out of the leather thong that held it and let it fall free around her. Brash stopped abruptly and stood up by the bed. Before her mind was fully in touch with the moment, he had stripped away the rest of her clothing, then his.

She thought the flush on his face was the most fascinating thing she'd ever seen, next to the extra-human shine in his dark eyes that picked up even the tiniest light and reflected it back.

She heard each of his heavy motorcycle boots hit the floor one at a time, and waited with breathless anticipation for him to get out of his jeans. The sun hadn't set and there was enough light left in the room for her to see that he was beautiful, and large, all over.

"Brash. Your penis is a masterpiece."

He stared at her for a moment with an open mouth before glancing down. Looking slightly embarrassed, he practically leaped back onto the bed and pinned her giggling figure to the mattress.

"Shut up," he said playfully.

Her hand was itching to learn the feel of him. He let out a satisfied growl when she reached down and palmed his engorged cock.

"Why are you embarrassed about having such a…?" The tip of her thumb found the piercing. "What's this?" She sounded fascinated. "Oh my."

Brash planted his face in the pillow next to Brigid's head to smother his laughter. He'd been in a lot of beds, and situations, with a lot of females, but he couldn't remember ever laughing during foreplay.

"Hey," she said, "I'm over here getting lonely."

He raised his head from the pillow, smiled. "You want to take that thing in your hand for a test drive?"

She nodded. "Yes. Please."

Just before he set about kissing Brigid senseless, he had a fleeting thought it might be a bad idea to fuck the lucrative business venture. It was the sort of internal warning that he used to ignore as a teenager just before he did something very, very stupid.

When his hand found its way to Brigid's swollen nub,

she arched off the bed again, in a sexy and rather athletic display that he was sure he'd never forget. He stretched to reach his pants on the floor and fumbled through the pockets to retrieve his wallet for a condom. Nothing.

"Stay right here and don't move."

"What? Where are you going?" Brigid half sat up.

"Condom. My room."

To her amazement, he didn't bother with clothes. He left her door open while he dashed through to his room and returned without a stitch on his body.

He relocked her door and started toward her, biting off the condom wrapper as he walked back to the bed, dick swinging in a manner that could have been hypnotizing to Brigid over a protracted period of time. Stopping next to where she was waiting, he put the condom on standing up while Brigid looked on, thinking she had to be the luckiest girl alive.

Brash practically jumped her, but when he positioned himself at the entrance, she said, "Wait. Wait. Go slow."

"Why?" he growled in her ear.

"Because it's been a… while. For me."

He raised up on his elbows and looked at her. "How long?" She hesitated. "Answer."

"I'm thinking!"

"Jesus."

"It's been, maybe four years."

"Four years." He said it like it was an impossibility.

"I don't have time to do much but study and school-related stuff. And before you I wasn't all that interested in…" She seemed to get lost in looking at his mouth.

"Baby," he said softly, smoothing one copper-colored curl away from her face. He wasn't sure what it was about him that caused the tousled beauty to decide he was going to be the one to end her abstinence, but he figured he must have done something really good in his life. "Slow it is."

He handled her like glass, entering her just a little at a time until her breathing picked up and she signaled her readiness, verbally with sexy sounds of pleasure, and physically with squirming and grinding against him.

He could have gone off as soon as his tip was inside her, but he used every trick he knew to restrain himself so that she would be glad she'd given him the end of celibacy. He waited until she was at the brink of orgasm, then lightly stroked her into insanity while he let himself go. All it took for him was one last thrust being fully present in the moment, appreciating that the woman occupying his old bed was a treasure worth waiting for.

By the time their breathing regulated, the sun had set completely.

"It's dark," she said.

"Yeah."

"That was…"

"What? It was what?"

"Wonderful."

"What were you goin' to say?"

"That's what I was going to say."

"You were goin' to say somethin' else. I can tell."

She laughed. "I wasn't going to say anything else. I was just thinking about what you said about sleeping in the wrong room, that you thought I was a former lover hoping for seconds. I thought you were a buffoon for saying so. I mean, who says, 'I'm so good in bed that women beg me for more'? But I guess you have a right to your vanity."

"Jesus."

"You say that a lot, don't you?"

"I never did before."

"Before what?"

He smiled. "Before Brigid."

THE NEXT THREE weeks passed by quickly. Brash made good on his promise to cover his duties while he'd be away. He also bought a second phone for the express purpose of giving his business owners a way to reach him and made sure they all had the number.

He spent as much time in Brigid's bed as was possible. If Brigid had been any other woman, he would have just brought her around, introduced her, and that would have been that. But Brigid wasn't a woman to the club. She was one of their more lucrative businesses, and that made their involvement an indiscretion.

As the end of the month drew near, he was torn between looking forward to spending time with Brandon and, ultimately, with his mother, but he was definitely not looking forward to so much time away from Brigid. It hadn't taken long for him to get used to the smell of her shampoo on his pillow or the feel of waking up with her spooned against his back. For the first time in his life he didn't dread mornings, because morning meant breakfast with Brigid.

Sometimes his pop looked at him funny, like he knew something was up. But if he'd guessed, or even seen the two of them together when they thought no one was looking, Brant never said anything about it.

In moments of clarity and self-awareness, as Brash rode on the curving two lane road to town, he knew he had it bad. And didn't even mind admitting it. He wished he could tell Brigid where he was going and why it was so important, but he and his brother had pledged secrecy and Brash knew that was for the best.

When the day came, he had to tell Brigid that he was going to be gone for a month, maybe longer. He knew she might not stay for the full time her contract allowed, and that once she left, she might not have the time of day to give him, but it was a chance he had to take.

"Pop's decided you don't really need a babysitter while I'm gone."

She blinked twice. "Babysitter?"

"Uh, well, when you first came, he thought one of us should keep an eye on you. He thought the old ladies would pitch a fit if it was one of the married guys. And he thought you were too much of a temptation for the single guys." He grinned and tucked a curl behind her ear. "Turns out he was right about that. But he thought I was the best candidate."

Her brow furrowed. “So you’re telling me that all the time you spent with me…”

He shook his head. “Don’t go there. What’s passed between you and me’s got nothin’ to do with business. You’re a woman. I’m a man who wants you. A lot. That’s all there is to it.” She nodded, but didn’t look convinced. “Anyway, it relieves my mind to know that nobody else will be payin’ you so much attention. At least I hope they won’t be. Maybe I should leave a pistol…”

She laughed. “No. That’s okay.”

“You do have a mean right hand. I can almost still feel where you split my lip.” He pointed to the spot. “Kiss it better.”

She kissed all around the spot tenderly, before engaging his mouth in an all-consuming kiss that she hoped he wouldn’t forget. The last thing in the world she wanted was to do drama about him leaving, but a single tear escaped.

He ran his thumb over it to stop its path down her cheek. “Jesus, baby. You kill me when you do that.” She smiled. “I’m goin’ to be out of touch.”

“Okay.”

“But it don’t mean I won’t be thinkin’ about you.” Her lips parted and he realized she looked surprised. Of course she was. He’d never said one single sentimental thing to her. They’d never named what they had going or talked about anything further into the future than lunch. “I will be thinkin’ about you, Brigid.”

“Okay,” she repeated, with more enthusiasm. He

kissed her again and pressed his forehead to hers. He didn't know what he wanted to say about his feelings, but he wanted to let her know… something.

As he pulled out, she waved goodbye bravely, thinking the very last thing she'd ever expected was to fall for a member of the Sons of Sanctuary Motorcycle Club.

CHAPTER 5

BRASH LEFT IN a black pickup truck, pulling his bike in a covered trailer behind him. He deliberately brought the truck with manual transmission because of mountain and off-road driving. He and Brandon had agreed on a place thirteen miles from Telluride, Colorado called the Buffalo Lakes Observatory. At five miles off the nearest paved road, it was the very definition of remote, but beautiful and unique. Brash looked online to see how much it rented for and was glad the billionaire brother was footing the bill.

They'd kicked around a lot of ideas, but had settled on that place for several reasons. Since it was after ski season and spring break, and before schools were out for summer, nobody would be around but locals. The chances of seeing somebody either of them knew were slim to none.

Last, but not least, a legendary artist owned and worked at Telluride Tattoo and Piercing.

It was a little less than twelve hundred miles. If all went well he could jump on I40 and get as far as Albuquerque, which was seven hundred miles or thereabouts.

That would divide the trip nicely, because driving through the mountains always slowed things down, especially pulling a trailer. At least he'd only be doing it one way. He'd be leaving Telluride in a private jet, while his brother would be driving back to Austin alone.

It occurred to him for the first time to wonder whether or not his brother knew how to drive a stick shift. Thinking the answer was probably no, gave Brash a chuckle. He might be teaching his brother how to ride a motorcycle *and* how to drive a stick shift.

The weather was good and the traffic wasn't bad. He stopped in Lubbock for gas, a piss break, and food. Soft tacos, which made him think about Brigid. Not that he'd thought about much else on the drive. He'd turned on the radio, but all the songs were about loving or fucking or both. And every one of them had brought her to mind.

On the north side of Albuquerque he found a motel that looked safe enough. He asked for the room at the end of the building so that he could pull the rig up to the window and know if anybody tried to tamper with it. God help 'em if they did. He had a hot shower and walked across the parking lot to a diner.

Since it was seat yourself, he took a booth that had a nice view of his truck and trailer. He ordered a BLT with French fries and took an apple pie to go. Back in the room, he turned on the TV and checked the new "business" phone for messages from owners. All clear. He wished he could call Brigid, but he knew the best way to handle that was to simply leave it alone until the family thing was resolved.

He ran through the basic cable offerings on TV and settled on the second half of a western that wasn't as bad as he expected. Sometime before the end, he drifted off. He woke up to an audience full of people looking way too excited about a vacuum cleaner. Infomercial. Holding the remote up just high enough, he switched it off and went back to sleep.

The next day's drive was uneventful. There was a little rain around Farmington and, as expected, his mph slowed down considerably once he got to Durango. Even interstate drives are a slowdown when a trailer needs to be pulled uphill.

Brash stopped at Telluride to fill up with gas and stock up on his favorite things. Peanuts were top of the list, of course. He bought twice his normal anticipated supply. He also got beer and enough groceries for a couple of meals while he was at it.

IT WAS ALMOST dark when Brash stopped the truck next to a new white Range Rover. He got out and shook the stiffness out, then grabbed bags of groceries on the way in.

A familiar face came out to greet him. He'd forgotten just how eerie it was to see a face *that* familiar on somebody else.

"Need help?" Brandon asked.

"You take these." He handed the grocery bags off to Brandon and went back to the truck for the beer and his stuff.

"I hope you got peanuts."

Brash didn't turn around, but Brandon heard him laugh.

BRASH'S POP HAD taught him that not much beats Hamburger Helper in a pinch. He made the chili tomato concoction for Brandon, who had never had Hamburger Helper. Ever. That had made Brash shake his head.

Brandon built a fire while Brash cooked. When the sun went down, it got chilly fast.

"Where'd you learn to build a fire?"

"Boy Scouts."

"No. Really."

Brandon laughed. "Seriously. I made it all the way to Eagle before my interest in girls overrode the acquisition of badges."

Brash shook his head, as they sat down at the table to eat. He popped two longneck Colorado beers and put one in front of Brandon.

"This beer is good," he said.

"You a beer buff?"

Brandon shook his head. "Not really. I know a lot about wine though."

"Shit. Really?" Brash was trying to picture himself being prissy about swirling and tasting wine, then using adjectives like woodsy, rosey, happy, dopey, and the like.

"Yeah. That's something that could give us away. I guess you'll need a crash course in how to be a connoisseur."

"Can't wait."

"Try to control your enthusiasm. Just look at it this way. I'm the one who's looking at torture by tattoo gun, possible traction at the mercy of a motorcycle, and learning badass biker vernacular."

"Okay. First lesson. No badass biker would ever use the word 'vernacular'."

"No? Okay. Noted. This stuff is okay," Brandon said as he took another forkful of skillet casserole.

"Food of the gods. This is a nice place you found us. I'll bet there's good fishin' in that lake."

"Um, fishing?"

"You've never been fishin'?"

"Well, I've been deep sea fishing. Many times. I guess it's the same."

Brash just looked at him. "No. It's not. So tomorrow, we'll go into town and look up this tat artist?"

"I guess. Unless there's a way around it. Maybe temporary tats?"

Brash laughed. "I don't think so. But we'll let him know you're a pussy and maybe he can give you a doobie or somethin'."

Brandon reached over and shoved Brash out of his chair and onto the floor, then laughed. In two seconds the two of them were rolling on the floor wrestling like they were eight and not twenty-eight. After a few minutes they both lay on their backs next to the fire, laughing like boys.

Neither of them was going to try to put the moment

into words, but both of them felt like a chasm in their hearts, that had never been recognized or named, was being filled up. They were being made whole.

"It's weird to see what I would look like with hair band hair."

"This is not hair band hair, numbskull. It's weirder for me to see what I'm goin' to look like in a Wall Street cut."

Brandon laughed. "Fat chance of getting a haircut like this one in Three Sticks, Colorado."

"Well, then. We'd better both get haircuts from the same guy." Brash smiled an evil smile when that caused Brandon to look worried. "Right after the tat consultation."

"Look. If you go to New York looking like you've been in a cat fight people are going to suspect you're not me. You don't get on the cover of magazines by being careless with your grooming."

"Okay. I get it. What do you suggest?"

"You found the tat guy. I'll find a stylist that can fake a decent haircut."

"I'll give you a hand with that."

"Whatever."

THE NEXT MORNING, Brash and Brandon stumbled into the kitchen looking for coffee within five minutes of each other. Since Brandon was first, he had dibs on the Keurig single pod coffee maker.

Brash had to listen to the gurgling while waiting his

turn. “Bastard,” he mumbled.

“What was that?” Brandon managed a smile as he took his time retrieving his coffee.

“Just for that, it’s your turn to cook. I like my eggs over easy and my bacon on the crispy side.” Brandon just stared at him. “Don’t tell me you don’t know how to cook.”

“It, ah, never came up.”

“Well, it has now. Come on over here and watch carefully. And you’re on KP.”

“I don’t know what that means.”

“Christ. It’s like talkin’ to an alien. Stands for Kitchen Patrol. Means you have to clean up.” Brandon looked blank. “No. Don’t tell me. You don’t know how to do that either.”

“I, ah…”

“Let me guess. It never came up.”

BRANDON WAS A fairly quick study. After three attempts he mastered cracking eggs without breaking the yoke and caught on to cooking bacon to perfection.

When they dug in, he said, “This food is good.”

“What do you usually eat?” Brash asked.

“Sometimes there are scrambled eggs and bacon. We have fresh muffins, bagels, fruit, that kind of thing. Cook makes really good quiche. She does this ham and cheese croissant covered with mushroom sauce that’s heaven. Sometimes I have a couple of three minute eggs.”

“Three minute eggs,” Brash said drily. “Okay. I’ll bite.

So if I'm you and I ask for a three minute egg, what am I goin' to get?"

"The white is like hard boiled, but the yolk is still liquid."

"Good to know. What would you have with that? Usually?"

"Cranberry scone with marmalade. Coffee. Of course. Sometimes juice. I don't like grapefruit."

"Neither do I. What's a scone?"

Brandon sat back. "It's a triangular pastry that's folded over. It's not light like a popover. It's heavy like, I don't know, sourdough bread."

"It tastes like sourdough bread?"

"No. It's just heavier than other kinds of pastries. They have them in Starbucks. When we go to town, we'll find the Starbucks and I'll get one for you to try. They're not as good as cook's though. She's English. I know people make fun of English cooking, but my favorite food in the world is pub food." He looked at Brash. "I'll bet you like pub food, too.

"What's your favorite? Food, that is."

"Mexican."

"My… *our* mom *loves* Mexican. We go out for it once a week. And she always says that…" He trailed off.

"She always says what?"

"That it's not nearly as good as the Mexican food they have in Texas."

THE DRIVE TO Telluride took forty-five minutes. When

Brash had asked Brandon if he knew how to drive a stick, Brandon had smirked at him.

"I'm a master of off-road."

"Great," Brash had said, tossing him the keys to the truck. "Show me."

Truthfully, Brash was tired of driving. So he hoped his brother wasn't blowing smoke. He unhooked the trailer and climbed into the passenger side.

True to his word, Brandon knew his way around a manual transmission. On the way to town they talked about various aspects and details of their lives, things they'd thought about that might make the other stumble. Oddly enough, both had a list and coded it so that only they could decipher its meaning.

"Why'd you grow your hair long like that?"

Brash grinned. "Seriously? You don't know?"

Brandon shook his head, looking genuinely mystified.

"Because women *love* it."

"They do not."

"Swear to Jesus. You watch today. See which one of us gets the most lingering looks of lust."

Brandon laughed. "Lingering looks of lust, huh? I submit that the most eligible bachelor has shorn locks."

"Just goes to show we're so good-lookin' the sex appeal can't be completely destroyed even with butchered hair."

They found the tat shop and parked on Main Street. It wasn't open yet so they decided to walk around for twenty minutes. A young woman was setting a pot of flowers outside her boutique as she was opening up. She looked up to smile and say good morning, but did a double take when she saw the twins.

Brandon stopped and gave her his best killer smile. "Hey. I was wondering if you could tell me the best place to get hair cut in town."

"You mean a barber shop?" She looked between the two men and seemed to be having a hard time deciding who she wanted to focus on.

"No. I mean, who do people go to when money isn't an object and they want to look spectacular?"

"There's a woman from L.A. at Bliss and Bang Bang. I've heard people like her."

"Where would we find, ah, Bliss and…"

"Bang Bang." She looked as happy about her answer as if she'd just won Jeopardy. "Two blocks down on Colorado Avenue."

Brandon thanked her, thrilled her with a wink, and walked on.

Brash gave her the ghost of a smile and a dip of his chin as they walked on by. After they were a couple of doors down he said, "She definitely preferred me. No doubt about it."

"You're delusional. She couldn't take her eyes off me. I think she forgot you were there."

Brash snorted. "Like it would be possible for a woman to forget I'm there."

As he said that, Brigid came to mind. He hoped like hell it wasn't possible for her to forget him. He made a mental note to tell his brother about Brigid. Just as soon as he figured out how to reconcile Brigid's expectations with telling Brandon he'd die if he went near her.

When they got back to the tattoo shop, the neon OPEN sign was lit up in electric blue. Sitting behind an old reception unit was a girl who had clearly been hired, at least in part, as human advertising. She had coal black hair with streaks of red above a body that had been turned into a colorful mural. Designs covered her arms, chest, neck, and black tipped tendrils licked up her jawline stopping just below her ears, which were accented by silver ring piercings around the outer edges. Lots of them.

It was Brash's turn to talk since Brandon couldn't seem to do anything but stare. He was actually busy trying to count the number of silver rings in her ears.

"We're here to see Axle," Brash said.

"He's busy. Would you like to make an appointment?"

Brandon had gotten bored with piercings and had started looking around the "lobby". The walls displayed an impressive series of photos of work done by the owner/artist along with some framed newspaper and magazine articles mentioning or featuring him.

"Yeah. I want to make an appointment, but I also want a quick consultation." He pulled out two hundred dollar bills and set them on the desk. "Now."

She stared up at Brandon for a few beats before appearing to come to a decision. "I'll ask." When she rose, she took the two bills with her and disappeared down the hallway behind her station.

"See anything you like?" Brash asked his brother.

"Seems like my choices are either get disfigured like you or forget the whole thing."

"I can see you need an attitude adjustment."

A deep voice said, "What's this about?"

Axel Gunn had only slightly less ink than the receptionist. He appeared to be around forty, with intense gray eyes and a hard set to his jaw. He was holding up the two bills.

Brash walked toward him and stopped two feet away. "That's a way to convey the urgency of our business. We've come a long way to see you. We don't mean disrespect and don't want to keep you, but we need a couple of minutes. In private."

Axel raised his chin as he looked from Brash to Brandon, nodded and motioned them to follow. He led them into a room that was white, meaning *everything* in the room was white. If Axel Gunn was going for a clinical, sterile feel, he'd succeeded.

Once inside, he closed the door. "You bought yourself two minutes."

Brash didn't waste any time. He pulled his shirt over his head.

Axel whistled. "Nice work."

Brash just nodded. "We need to know how long it would take to do the *exact* same on him." When Axel looked at Brandon, Brash said, "He's a blank canvas. We need to give him enough that, if somebody saw him shirtless, they would think it's me. So maybe it doesn't have to be *exactly* the same." Brash glanced at Brandon. "I'm kind of tempted to tell you to do it on his other side. Just to fuck with people."

"Brilliant. What if somebody has a photo?" Brandon quipped.

"Yeah." Brash agreed and turned back to the artist. "So how long?"

Axel nodded thoughtfully, lifted Brash's arm, and said. "Depends partly on his pain threshold."

"If that's not a factor…"

"If that's not a factor, one month." Brash looked at Brandon. "If he's tough, we could do the outline in one five hour session. Wait ten days, do some of the color. Wait ten days, do some more. That'll get us to about seventy five percent, which would fool anybody but a wife."

"A month? That really the best?"

"That's got to be my limit. All good conscience."

"Okay, then." Brash glanced at Brandon. "Can you start today?"

Axel shook his head. "No. I'm booked. I might be able to reschedule something tomorrow. For a premium." At that he smiled for the first time.

"How much?"

"Five hundred more."

Brandon could see that Brash was about to negotiate the biker way. He stepped in front of his brother and said,

"That's fine. When should I be here tomorrow?"

"One o'clock."

"I'll be here."

On the sidewalk outside the door, Brash said, "That bastard just stung us. You know that, right?"

"You're the one who let him know there was urgency *and* money involved. I could see that coming as soon as you flashed grease at the walking billboard." Brash couldn't argue with that. "So forget it. Let's move on to the 'salon'."

Brash didn't like the way Brandon wiggled his eyebrows. "If you're talkin' 'bout the haircut, there's no reason to get off into that until it's time to go our separate ways. From what that shyster said, I've got a month."

THE FOLLOWING NIGHT, on the way back to their hideaway, Brandon described his tattoo session as the worst experience of his life, like a billion bee stings.

"How long did it take *you* to get all this… ink?"

"'Bout a year, I guess."

"A YEAR!" Brandon practically yelled. "And I have to do it in a month?"

"Relax and stop bein' such a pussy. You're not gettin' the mirror image. Just enough to get by." Brandon pouted and looked sullen. "Look. I'm gonna treat you like the little princess you are tonight. I'm makin' lasagna Hamburger Helper. I even got some fresh parmesan and red wine."

Brandon managed a little smile. "You bought wine?

This ought to be good."

BRANDON WAS HAPPY to sit on the couch in front of the fire and sip the wine Brash had bought at the San Miguel County Wine and Liquor.

"This isn't bad. I'm surprised."

Brash set a bowl of peanuts down next to Brandon and said, "Full disclosure. I asked the owner what goes good with lasagna Hamburger Helper. Told him my brother's a wine snoot. He tried to sell me a bottle for twenty-four dollars. I'm telling you. People in this town are thieves."

"How much did you end up paying?"

"Eighteen dollars. It was still highway robbery." Brandon laughed. "What's funny?"

"You remember when we had dinner in New York? If I told you how much I've paid for a bottle of wine, you'd probably make me sleep in the truck."

"Well, now you have to tell me."

"No. I don't."

"If the whole right side of your body wasn't on fire, I'd throw you down right now and sit on you until you talked."

"If you think that's possible, claim a rain check."

"Rain check."

"Done."

"Looking forward to it."

"Not as much as me."

"As much as I."

"What?"

"Never mind."

After a few seconds they grinned at each other. For no reason. At all.

THE DAYS WERE cool. The nights were cold enough to justify building roaring fires every night and found that they were experiencing a companionship that transcended all relationships between people who didn't originate in the same egg. At times each thought he could almost hear what the other was thinking.

During the day they fished for rainbow trout in the blue mountain lake just outside their front door. When they caught enough for dinner, they had fresh fish, pan sautéed, with baked potatoes and salad. Brash objected to the greens at first, calling it girly food, but Brandon lectured him on the merits of fresh organic vegetables until he became a convert. Or as Brash claimed, until he'd been thoroughly brainwashed by a yuppie.

While they fished they traded stories, slowly weaving pictures of their lives, recreating their biographies. They talked about school, extended family, travels, and a litany of 'firsts'. They shared music and movies that they liked and were stunned to find out that their tastes in both were similar if not dead on.

Many of the stories sparked questions about their parents.

Brash had an insatiable curiosity about their mother that Brandon tried to fill with his own childhood memories. Like the fact that she loved to tell tales from Greek and Roman myths. He'd said that every year on their birthday, March 31st, Garland had told him about the astrological symbol of Aries, Chrysomallus, the flying ram whose wool became the Golden Fleece and how many adventures it had inspired through the millennia, including quests by knights of the Round Table.

Likewise, Brandon wanted to know everything there was to know about their dad. Brash told him about everything from whippings with the belt to canoe trips on the Colorado River.

At night, during and after dinner, they talked about business. Or beer. Or wine. Brash had learned which white wines go best with rainbow trout. Brandon learned which Austin breweries made the best local labels. Brash's description of barbequed pork with Pecan Porter made Brandon's mouth water.

Brandon took a sip of one of the wines they'd stocked in and said, "Has it struck you as strangely coincidental that we both ended up managing business interests? I went to an Ivy League school for a degree in business administration. You got a GED and I get the feeling that you probably know everything I know. Really, I'm not sure that your hands-on experience didn't give you an advantage."

"I spent ten years shadowing our pop. You might say it was on-the-job training. He didn't care about the GED because he knew that ninety percent of school is bullshit. But he did think education has its place and he does care about laziness. I'm not sayin' I was home schooled, but he gave me things to read, mostly about business, then he'd quiz me while we were drivin' around." Brash got up and stirred the fire. "It wasn't Harvard, but he could be tough. Nobody'd ever accuse him of low expectations."

Brandon nodded. "Sounds like he loves you."

"Never a minute that it was a question in my mind."

"Mom is the same. You'll see."

Brash felt a little flutter in his belly, anxiety about seeing his mother and having her believe he was the child she'd raised.

AS THE DAYS progressed Brash and Brandon came to know each other so well, it was as if they had never been separated.

Each knew that they had to get very clear about the people who occupied the other's immediate environment. In Brandon's case, that would be those who worked closely with him at Germane Enterprises. In Brash's case, that would be the Sons of Sanctuary MC.

During the planning stages, they had agreed to bring photos of people and places along with floor plans and diagrams. Brandon had to learn, not only the names of the club members and their families, but the names of the business owners, where their offices were located and Brash's professional history with each one.

THE TWO OF them sat at the dining table while Brash gave a detailed rundown of club members.

"Sargeant at Arms. Name's Rock and that's not a road name. His mama named him Rocky. She liked that old movie about the leg breaker turned champ. Rock proves that people really do become what they're named. He's hard as hard gets.

"This is Nam. He's the club historian and the oldest active member. He was one of the originals with my... *our* granddad. They came back from Vietnam and started the club. That's where it got its name, Sons of Sanctuary. They didn't feel at home anymore after the war. So they sort of banded together.

"E.R. It's an abbreviation for Easy Rider. He rides a fifties Harley police bike choppered up to look like the one in the movie. He's treasurer, got a head for books like a real genius.

"Car Lot and Eric work together to make sure we have security at the businesses that need it, that would be the bars and the club on 6th Street."

"Why is this guy named Car Lot?" Brandon pointed at the photo on the table.

Brash smiled. "His real name is Dodge Ford. His mother claims to be related to both auto families and is real proud of that, I guess.

"This is Crowley. He's our cousin. Also known as Crow. Tell me what you know about him."

"His mother is our Aunt Joanna, Pop's sister. He's married to Bethany Lynn and has two daughters. Gidget and Gellis." Brandon reached for another pile of photos and pulled out a recent one of the girls together in pink sundresses. "Ages five and six?"

"Close enough. Now this here is Arnold."

Brandon laughed. "This guy looks just like the Terminator. Like a young Arnold Schwarzenneger, but without the bulk." Brash nodded. "He could be one of those celebrity impersonators who work parties."

"Yeah. He's handsome. Women buzz around him like flies. But he's even smarter than he is pretty. He's super good with high tech stuff. And enterprising folks can always find a good use for somebody like that." He gave Brandon a look that said, "You know what I mean?"

Brash fingered a photo. "Here's the guy I was tellin' you about. Watch your back because he's gonna think you're me. The fucker has an issue with that."

"Why?"

"Not sure. Maybe because he'd like to *be* me."

"Well, that's not happening because you're one of a kind." Brandon chuckled.

"Funny. He's only been patched in for two years. Here's one that's worth remembering. Rescue.

"Aunt Joanna was torn up after she lost her husband in Desert Storm and Pop couldn't stand seein' her that way. They were close. Irish twins is what Gram calls 'em.

"Pop was down on 6th Street one night and saw cops pickin' this guy up for vagrancy. He intervened, brought him back to the club, and fed him. When he found out that Rescue was a Desert Storm vet, Pop took on that problem like it was his own. Now we call it PTSD, but they didn't name it back then.

"So, at the time, Gram had a German Shepherd named Bullet after some TV show from the fifties. Bullet was the only creature Rescue would talk to at first. He wanted to eat with the dog, sleep with the dog, and Gram let him.

"She's got a big heart. You'll like her. Everybody does.

"Anyway, it didn't escape Pop's notice, as time went by, that Rescue was gettin' better. Like the dog was bringin' his humanity back or somethin'. Remindin' him of who he'd been before.

"Now Rescue runs K9 Keep. People come from everywhere to buy our German Shepherds and it's fairly lucrative. The tagline is, *Deadly to predators, but safe for toddlers.* He started out by rescuin' them from all over Texas and repurposin' them as family guard dogs. We still take rescues, but we're also a breeder now. Treaty Oak Shepherds. That's part of the reason why the club is out past the city limits."

"What's the other part?"

Brash grinned. "Parties get loud sometimes."

AT THE END of the second week, Brash gave his pop a call.

"Everythin' okay there?"

"Yep."

"Okay."

"By *everything*, do you mean the brainy woman?"

Brash was surprised that his dad read between the lines, but knew he shouldn't have been. Brash still couldn't manage to get anything past him.

"Yeah. That's what I mean."

"She goes about her business. Asks a lot of questions. Does a good job of keepin' the bar stocked and clean. People like her and they're gonna miss her when she leaves to go tell the world about the primitive society of motorcycle clubs."

When Brash ended the call, he was thinking the same thing, that he was going to miss Brigid when she left to go back to her real life. He reminded himself again to come up with a plan on how to handle the issue of Brigid and Brandon.

BRASH HAD TO admit that Brandon had the biggest adjustments to make, between the tattoos and learning to ride a motorcycle like he'd been raised on one. He backed the Harley out of the trailer, familiarized Brandon with the throttle, clutch, and brakes. Since Brandon was a beginner, he taught him the one down, five up shift pattern. The real problem came with Brash's explanation of turning.

"It's easier than it sounds."

"It doesn't make sense."

"Well, I know, but just do it and you'll see. Like I told ya, if you want to turn right, lean just a little and push the right handgrip that direction." Brash tried demonstrating, but reached the conclusion that, in the end, people have to ride to learn.

"If you're gonna fall, be sure to fall on your left side. You don't wanna mess up your ink and get it infected."

Brandon looked incredulous. "Thanks for the encouragement." Brandon stopped. "Which one of us do you think is older? I think it's me."

"Then you'll be in for a letdown because I can tell that you're my *little* brother."

Brash was playing it cool, but was actually a little apprehensive about the first bike ride, and not just because he was worried about the bike. While he tried to make light, beginner accidents weren't that unusual, even on straightaways where shifting wasn't such a big issue. But Brandon figured it out.

In fact he figured it out so well that, twenty minutes later, Brash was ready to get in his pickup and go looking. He'd climbed into the passenger seat when he heard the distant roar of an American-made motorcycle and smiled to himself. At that point he would have taken bets that his brother would never again be happy spending his entire life in enclosed vehicles.

EVERYDAY BRASH WORKED on adding g's to verbs ending in -ing. Brandon worked on drawing out his vowel sounds and dropping his g's from verbs ending in -ing. Spending so much time together helped. Hearing each other speak, their dialects morphed into a sort of amalgamation, which would make it easier to imitate the other.

They quizzed each other relentlessly.

Finally it was hair time.

"It's not going to hurt nearly as bad as needle torture," Brandon said as they stood on the sidewalk outside Bliss and Bang Bang. "Come on."

Every head turned and stared when they stepped inside. And not just because they weren't local. "You have a new stylist from L.A.?"

The hostess smiled brightly. "Yes, we do. Her name is Esmerelda. Do you want an appointment?"

"Uh, does she take walk-ins? We're staying quite a way from town."

They looked around at people receiving services. One had tinfoil in her hair, one was being blown dry, and one was getting a cut.

"Just a minute." She walked back to the stylist who'd been wielding the blow dryer like a weapon, spoke to her, and pointed toward the front where Brash and Brandon waited.

The stylist was a young woman in black; black hair and black clothes, with pale skin and eyes so dark they were almost black. If her lipstick hadn't been light pink, she could have passed for latent Goth. She looked toward Brash and Brandon then nodded to the receptionist and said something they couldn't hear.

On return they were told that, "As you can see she's with someone, but her eleven o'clock cancelled. So she can take you if it's something simple."

"Need a haircut for my brother. Would that be something simple?"

She looked at Brash. "Yes, but what a shame to cut off that beautiful hair."

"That's what I keep sayin'," grumbled Brash.

"But she's going to need to do both of us because we need to leave here looking the same."

The receptionist smiled. "Don't worry. We'll handle it."

FIFTEEN MINUTES LATER, Esmerelda had the two brothers in chairs side by side. "Give me a trim and then make him look *exactly* like me."

She looked between them and said, "Just when I think I've seen it all."

She grabbed hold of Brash's hair, then smiled at him in the mirror. "This really is beautiful. You know that?" Brash was feeling too traumatized to do anything but nod. She laughed. "Don't worry, lover. It's not like he's ugly." She moved her head in Brandon's direction. "Here we go."

Two hours later they were back at their mountain lodge. They stood together in front of the bathroom mirror verifying that they could pass for each other.

"I think your ears are bigger," Brash said.

"You're being ridiculous."

"I feel ridiculous."

"I don't want to hear it. On Sunday you're going to walk out of here wearing a forty-seven thousand dollar Brioni Vanquish suit with tats showing beneath your cufflinks."

Brash just blinked. "There's not really any such thing as a forty-seven thousand dollar suit."

"Yes. There is. And I have a whole closet full of them. You need to expand your thinking."

"Yeah? And you'd better rein it in because the most expensive article of clothing I own is the SSMC cut. 'Bout two hundred dollars. Retail."

THE NEXT MORNING they dressed in each other's clothes, traded phones and ID's, and gave each other a man hug. Both were anxiety walking, but neither would admit that to the other.

"You gonna have trouble explainin' the haircut?" Brash asked.

"No. I'm *gonna* tell *'em* that I decided to be a man. What are you gonna say about the tattoos?"

"I got drunk and, once the damage was done, I had to go a lot further to make it look like it's what I intended." Brandon frowned. "No? You don't like that one? How about this? I've been thinking about it for a long time. Finally decided to go for it."

Brandon shrugged. "Okay. Watch your g's."

"You do the same. Don't get comfortable. That's when mistakes happen."

CHAPTER 6

It wasn't as easy to appear nonchalant about private jets and gourmet service as it sounded like it would be, but Brash concentrated on looking as casual about it as if it was an everyday experience.

Brandon's driver was waiting when the plane landed. Brash recognized the car from his brother's description and the driver from the photo.

"Welcome home, sir."

"Thanks, Charles. It's good to be back."

As they drove into the city, Brash tried to take it all in without looking too curious. When they stopped at his building, he recognized the doorman from the photo Brandon had brought to the mountains. He waited for Charles to open his door.

"Will you need the car in the morning, sir?"

"No. I think I'll walk." Brandon had told Brash that he walked the four blocks to work whenever the weather allowed, but not to be fooled by the number 'four' because east/west blocks were *much* longer than a typical city block. He'd given very specific directions, beginning with, "Turn right when you exit the building." Brash had memorized the map because reading directions would give rise for suspicion if someone who knew Brandon saw him on the street.

They had talked about what to do in case of a random encounter with someone who knew them, but was outside the catalog of usual suspects. They'd decided they'd just wing it, just as people do when encountering a stranger at a party who has memory of a prior meeting.

Brash smiled at the doorman in greeting.

"Nice evening, Mr. St. Germaine."

"It is, Jimmy. Shame I'll be spending the rest in-doors."

Jimmy had rosy cheeks and a jovial nature. "Good night to you then."

Brash nodded. "Good night."

The lobby's grand post WWII architecture was solid and impressive. The result was a euphoric feeling of permanence and well-being.

He made his way to the elevator and put in the key that would access the top floor. The elevator opened into a large foyer, large, that is, for New York, where real estate is sold by the square inch.

Brash flipped on some lights and whistled when he stepped into the living room. Beyond the Steinway studio grand was a view of the east side from across Central Park. He wandered around the penthouse and decided that it was about the size of the entire club house. Maybe bigger.

He smiled when he opened the refrigerator. Brandon

had told him that the housekeeper kept it stocked with food ready to eat for when he didn't want to cook or go out or order in. True to his word, there was a variety of fresh, microwaveable meals. He smiled even bigger when he opened a cabinet to find an entire shelf of every sort of gourmet peanut imaginable.

His self-guided tour ended with the master bedroom, which was decorated in peaceful but masculine shades of brown and olive green. When he opened the door of Brandon's closet, he barked out a laugh even though no one was around to hear. It was bigger than the entire room that was his home at the SSMC.

The walls were lined with closed glass-front California cubbies sporting stainless steel rods and polished wood hangers. The island in the middle was easily ten feet long with drawers on all sides. The wall at the far end was mirrored above the bench seating, which was covered with brown tufted suede.

After exploring, he found a pair of soft jeans and a gray tee shirt, then padded back to the kitchen barefoot. He turned on the kitchen TV and watched the news while he sat at the bar and ate by himself. Afterward he looked around and decided that, since there was nothing to do, he'd go to bed early. After all, he needed to be on his game the next day. It's not every day a guy meets his mom.

He climbed into bed and mentally rehearsed what he was going to do the next morning. He knew the way to walk to work. He knew how to get to his office. He knew to ask his assistant for his schedule. After that, he was pretty much on his own. He wasn't worried about people knowing he wasn't Brandon. He was worried about his behavior appearing to be unusual.

As he lay awake in bed, he couldn't help thinking the quiet was disturbing, as was the knowledge that he was alone. When he was growing up, there were always people around. His grandmother. His aunt. His cousins. Members of the club. After he and his pop had moved to the club, there were even more people around.

Living completely alone was just… strange.

AT AROUND TEN Garland poked her head into Brandon's office. "You taking me to church on Sunday?"

Brash froze at the emotional impact of being in the same room with his mother for the first time. He took her in. Her face, her voice, her manner. She squinted like she didn't understand why he was hesitating to answer.

He cleared his throat. "Don't I always?"

She scoffed. "No. You certainly do not! And you know it."

"Well, this Sunday I'm all yours." He felt his chest tighten as he said that. "In fact, I've been thinking we haven't been spending enough time together. How about lunch?"

"When? Today?" She looked shocked.

"Just you and me." She opened her mouth to respond, but he went on with enthusiasm. "And dinner. Dinner, too."

Garland narrowed her eyes. "What's the matter with you, Brandon? Since when have you been interested in *more* one-on-one time with your old mom?"

"Since I realized that I only have the *one* mom."

She studied him at length. "Are you feeling well? Has something happened?"

He chuckled softly as he got up and walked around his desk. When he got close to her, he picked up the scent of lavender and thought it was marvelous.

"Come on. What could be more important than time together?"

"Well, that's true, but…"

"We'll do Mexican."

She smiled. "Then how can I say no?" She looked at her watch. "Can you do one o'clock?"

"I can do anything I want."

"That's certainly not what Alice would say." Garland turned and walked to Alice's work station in the expanded outer office. "Alice, is my son free for lunch?"

"No, ma'am. He's supposed to meet with the Divetech Marine people."

"Shit," said Brash.

Garland and Alice both turned and looked at him like he'd farted.

"Uh, Alice. Can you get me out of that?"

Alice blinked twice. "They've come from Houston to get this meeting with you." She looked at her watch. "In ten minutes."

Brash opened his mouth, but thought better of what

he'd been about to say.

"Mom. I'm sorry. Can we do dinner instead?"

"Of course, darling. Call me when you're on the way and I'll be ready to go." She started to turn, but her eyes drifted down to his sleeve and flew open wide. "What is that?"

He glanced down. "Oh, the ink?"

She looked up at him. "The ink? That's all you have to say? The ink? Good heavens, Brandon. What have you done?"

"It's just a tattoo, Mom. Not exactly unusual these days."

"Well, it's unusual for you!"

"Not anymore."

"Honestly. The world is going crazy."

"That's what I hear."

"Okay. I'll see you tonight."

"Good. See you then."

She turned back. "Did it hurt?"

He smiled. "Not at all."

"Alright. Later."

He watched her walk away gracefully, like she was an athlete, or had been.

"Alice, can you come in?"

She followed Brash into Brandon's huge ass office overlooking the Hudson.

"What's the nicest Mexican food restaurant in town?"

"I don't know."

"Can you find out?"

"Yes, sir."

"Okay. And make us a reservation for six thirty."

"Six thirty?" She seemed surprised.

"Is there something wrong with six thirty?"

"Well, no. It's just that it's awfully early for dinner."

"I was hoping to have extra time with my mother tonight. Find us a nice Mexican restaurant near a place where we can go for drinks first."

Alice smiled. "Alright."

"Oh. And ask my driver to pick me up at… I guess you need to tell me that after you find the best Mexican."

"Yes, sir."

"Where did you say I'm supposed to be for lunch?"

Her body turned slightly as her eyes wandered toward the hall. "In the conference room, sir. Lunch is being catered."

"Oh. That's right. What else absolutely has to be done today?"

"It's, uh, all on your computer. Like always." Brash just looked at her. "Would you like me to pull it up for you?"

"Yes, please. I, uh, cut my finger cutting a green pepper."

She glanced down at his hand. He put his hand in his pocket.

In less than two seconds Alice had Brandon's schedule on the computer screen in front of Brash.

"There you go. Sorry about your finger."

"It will be fine. Let me know about the plans for tonight."

"I will."

After Alice closed the door, Brash sat down and looked at his schedule then at his watch. He had an afternoon meeting with Uncle Adlay. He had no idea about what. Adlay was actually his great-uncle, his grandfather's brother, but Brandon had always called him uncle.

The phone buzzed. "Do you want to accept a call from Pan Asia?"

"Don't I have a meeting in a few minutes?"

"If you're still on the phone, I will get them coffee and let them know."

"Yes, then. I'll take the call."

"Line two."

Before he picked up the phone, he reminded himself of what Brandon had said over and over. That he couldn't lose all the St. Germaine money even if he tried.

"St. Germaine speaking."

The call posed no problem. Pan Asia wanted to know if Germane Enterprises was open to acquisition. The answer to a question like that is always yes. So he had Alice set up a meeting that Brandon would take, whether he wanted to or not.

Luckily, Uncle Adlay came to him so that he didn't have to wander around the building pretending to know where he was going.

"Brandon. Welcome back. Did you enjoy your time away?"

"I did."

"What did you do?"

"Trout fishing in Colorado."

"For a month? I never knew you liked that sort of thing. Well, you must feel like a new man."

Brash smiled. "You have no idea."

"I wanted to run something by you. The lobby is reporting that the senator from Louisiana might be on board with drilling expansion, but he seems to be dragging his feet. I was thinking about offering his wife a position on the Grane Corp board."

"Grane Corp? What does their board get?"

"Usual perks. A hundred thousand annually, quarterly meetings."

Brash stared at his uncle for a moment while he let that sink in. A hundred thousand dollars for attending four meetings a year. "Not unless he promises to deliver first."

"Very well. Also, the lead engineer on the South China Sea project is pressing for an answer. Do you want to give him a green light?"

"No. Too risky. The region is volatile right now."

Brash figured he could get away with saying that, because it made him sound like he had some kind of insider information. If Brandon wanted something done in the South China Sea, he could send the engineer back later.

"Very wise," Adlay said as he got up to leave. "I'm glad you're back. I've gotten used to having you make the tough calls."

"Anything else I need to know about?"

"I was trying to be kind and let you settle back in. But I have a list and Alice has put me on the schedule for tomorrow."

"Okay. I'll wear a helmet."

Adlay laughed. "Door open or closed."

"Closed," he said as he reached for a handful of Brandon's peanuts.

ALICE ARRANGED TO have Brandon's car pick him up at six to stop by Garland's first, then drop them at Harry's for drinks. When the car stopped in front of Garland's building, Brash got out on his own.

He nodded at Garland's doorman, who said, "Good evening, Mr. St. Germaine. Your mother is in."

Brash walked through the door and stopped at the security/conceierge desk. "Can you call Ms. St. Germaine for me?"

"Sure. You don't want to go on up?" asked the uniformed guard.

Brash felt a moment of panic. If Brandon had told him their mother's apartment number, he'd forgotten it.

"Thanks, but I want to call her down. That way she'll think twice about keeping me waiting." He smiled at the guard as if to say it's a male-togetherness conspiracy to keep women in line.

"Of course, sir." The guard chuckled and picked up his station phone. After a few seconds he said, "Ms. St. Germaine, your son is waiting in the lobby." Pause. "He says he prefers to wait for you here." Pause. "No, ma'am." Pause. "Yes, ma'am." He hung up and smiled at Brash. "She says five minutes."

"Well, then I'm ahead. If I'd gone upstairs it would have been thirty and we'd be late for our reservation."

The guard laughed. "Your team is looking good this season."

Brash was starting to think that standing around chatting was a bad idea. "Yeah. They are." He had no idea which team was his team or even what sport they were discussing. "You know I just remembered I've gotta make a phone call. Will you let her know I'm waiting in the car?"

"Certainly."

When the doorman opened the door, Brash said, "I'm waiting in the car for my mother."

"Yes, sir."

The doorman went around to Brash's driver, asked him to pull up a few feet and pointed to the spot where they should wait.

"Charles, I need some privacy for a phone call. Would you mind waiting outside the car for five minutes?"

After Charles exited the car, Brash called his own phone to get Brandon.

"Yeah?"

"Good impression of me, asshole. Can you talk?"

"Just a minute." After a thirty second pause, Brandon said, "Okay. Go ahead."

"I'm sitting outside our mother's building because I don't know her apartment. Did you tell me?"

"I don't remember but it's the top floor. One of the keys in your possession goes in the elevator."

"Which one?"

"Really? You expect me to describe *which* key fits Mom's elevator?"

Brash growled. "Never mind. What team is your team?"

Brandon laughed. "The Mets. I don't own them. I just like them."

"Okay. I ended a project in the South China Sea. No idea what was goin' on there."

"No problem. I wrecked your bike."

"YOU DID WHAT?"

"Not really." Brandon was chuckling. "But there is…"

"Gotta go. Mom's here."

Brash ended the call just as Charles was opening the door for her.

"Brandon, why didn't you come up? I wanted to show you those photos."

"It's rush hour. We just have enough time to go for drinks and get to our dinner reservation. I knew we'd be late if I came up."

She relaxed. "It's impossible to be miffed at the same time I'm so proud that you're incredibly smart."

Brash smiled, leaned over and gave her a kiss on the cheek, noting that her skin was soft, smooth like a much younger woman, and she smelled like lavender, which was incredibly soothing. He was finding it hard to hold a grudge against a person who smelled like lavender.

"So Adlay said you were gone trout fishing?"

"That's right. Telluride, Colorado. It's beautiful there."

"Well, you do look good. Healthy."

"Thanks." He smiled.

"Except for that." She pointed to the ink coming out of the sleeve of his cashmere Henley. "How big is it?"

He smiled. "You don't want to know."

"I do, but I'm already sorry for asking. You go to the gates of hell to bring a boy into the world and then spend every waking moment making certain that no evil in the world harms that precious skin. And for what? So that he can draw permanent pictures on it later?"

She huffed out a breath of exasperation.

"Let's not fight. I appreciate you bringing me into the world. I appreciate you taking care of me. But now the body is all mine."

She took in a deep sigh, looked out the window, then said, "Yes. You're right. I missed you. A month seemed like a long time."

"Missed you, too. What photos did you want to show me again?"

"Oh. I found those photos of you at the beach when you were three. So precious it hurts my heart. You were *such* a beautiful baby. Not that you're bad looking now."

"Thanks."

THE ATMOSPHERE INSIDE Harry's was like another world compared to the controlled chaos of the street outside.

Brash stepped up to the hostess. "We're here for drinks."

"We're pretty busy. I can get you a table in, perhaps, half an hour."

A man stepped in beside her and said, "I'll take this, Patty. Right this way." He led them to a comfortable booth in a back corner with upholstery covered in French striped silk shantung. "Enjoy yourselves. Always good to see you at Harry's."

"Thank you," Garland said as she put her purse down beside her on the upholstered seat.

"What will you have?" Brash asked Garland.

"Wine."

Brash ordered an Aubert Ritchie Pinot Noir to share. Brash was grateful that Brandon had spent some time drilling him on how to accept, or reject, a bottle of wine.

When he was gone and they were alone again, Brash said, "So, tell me, something." Garland looked at him over the glass as she took a sip. She was beautiful at nearly fifty and he didn't have any trouble imagining what a knockout she must have been when she'd met his pop, but it was obvious that he and Brandon had gotten their coloring and features from their dad. He wondered what it would be like to look every day into a face so very similar to the man you rejected. "Why have you never gotten married?"

"Well, that was blunt. Where did that come from?"

"Just interested in you. That's all. But it's not completely random. It's a fair question."

"But personal."

"Right. But we have a personal relationship. Don't we?"

"Don't be silly. You know we do." She sat back and sighed. "I loved your father, Brandon. Nobody else ever came close enough to be so much as a distant second."

"Are you saying you still love him?" She sighed again, but didn't answer. "Did you ever try to find him? Let him know how you feel?"

"No." She looked around like she was anxious about people overhearing their conversation. The bar was crowded. And noisy. But in an odd way that can be an insulator and create a sort-of inside-out intimacy.

"I guess you're old enough to know the truth." She bobbed her head. "You've been old enough to know the truth for a while. Your grandfather was a man who liked to have his way. No. Correct that. He *had* to have his way, and wasn't above being ruthless to get it. He was against the relationship. He told me he had something on your father that would send both him and your other grandfather to prison, among others."

Garland looked at Brash as if she was willing him to read her mind and her heart, pleading with him to understand. "Your father was not the kind of man who would be okay with being locked up." Brandon looked on, silently agreeing with her. "I let him go. Because I loved him. And, yes. I always will."

Brash sat there, stunned and speechless. Of all the excuses he'd imagined she might make, that wasn't a scenario that he'd considered. "Why didn't you look him up and tell him? Your father's been dead a long time."

"Brandon, so many years had passed by the time your grandfather died. You were thirteen. I'm sure your father found somebody else and made a life. Dredging up the past might hurt him. And it would *definitely* hurt me."

"What makes you so sure of that?"

He saw a flicker of doubt in her eyes.

CHAPTER 7

Brant seemed irritable. "What's the matter with you?"

"What do you mean?" Brandon sank down in one of the chairs in front of Brant's desk. It was a tiny room, full of clutter, but there were three armless chairs available for conversations that required privacy.

"Okay. I'll lay it out. First, you go all mysterious about gettin' away when you've never taken a vacation." Brandon opened his mouth to answer, but Brant held up a hand to stop him. "Or *personal time*. You come back after a month with your hair gone, claimin' you've been fishin'. And if all that's not suspicious enough, now you're bein' clingy as a little bitch."

"I thought you don't like disrespectful words bein' used about women."

"I'm not talkin' about a woman. I'm talkin' about *you*. And I'm askin' you right out. Are you sick? I mean in the physical sense."

"No. I'm not sick. I've just been thinkin' we should spend more time together."

"More time together," he repeated drily. "Since you

turned thirteen all you've wanted out of life is for me to stay the hell out of your way."

Brandon's head moved slowly from side to side. "I... didn't mean to neglect you."

Brant looked incredulous. "*Neglect* me? Boy, you better tell me what's up right now. If you're sick, just lay it out."

"No. I'm not sick. But I've been wondering about my mother."

"Jesus Christ. Not again!"

"Did you ever think about looking her up? See how she's doing?"

Brant sighed deeply, sat back, turned his head toward the window and got a faraway look in his eyes. "Not more than a hundred times a day."

Brandon took a hard look at Brant's face. Perhaps he'd mistaken sadness for orneriness.

"Well, how would you feel about me tryin' to find her?"

Brant ran a hand over his face and suddenly looked years older. "You're a grown man."

"That's not an answer."

Brant's lips pressed together momentarily. "Your mother, she came from money. Lots of it. At first I thought that, if I could make this thing," he waved his hand to indicate the clubhouse, "legitimate and profitable, maybe if I made enough money..."

Brandon was quickly putting the pieces together. Neither of his parents had married. Both wore sorrow like a cloak. Brandon had always known that his mother's smile didn't reach her eyes and her laugh didn't go all the way down. She'd tried to cover her unhappiness with love and adoration. For him.

"You did great, Pop. But things change. Maybe it's time to check in with her and see what's going on?" Brant said nothing. "Aren't you curious?"

"Of course, I'm curious. Also scared."

"Of what?"

"Of having the heart that's hangin' off the end of my sleeve shredded. Again."

Seeing Brant's eyes turn red around the rims, Brandon swallowed hard and said quietly, "But what if she feels the same way about you?"

Brant lost his patience. "Was there somethin' else you needed?"

"Lunch?"

Brant narrowed his eyes. "You forgot where to get lunch? Just turn around, walk down the hall to the second door on the left and make yourself a sandwich."

"I mean maybe we could have lunch together. I'll make two sandwiches. Or we could go out?"

"Go out," Brant said drily.

"Yeah. How often do you go out for lunch?"

"Whenever I'm at Hollywood. Don't you have things to do?"

"Yeah, but nothin' more important than spendin' time with my old man."

Brant looked at Brandon for a long time, then said,

“Chuy’s.”

Brandon grinned. “I’m in. Come on. I’ll follow you.”

Brant looked suspicious. “This ain’t a surprise birthday or some such shit. Right?”

“Is it your birthday?”

“No.”

“It’s just you and me and Chuy’s. For lunch.”

They got on their bikes. As Brandon followed his dad’s motorcycle along the curving two lane road to Austin, he decided it might be the best day of his life. He liked the feel of rushing through the air behind his dad, who gave every indication of being a genuine bona fide badass. Unless he was talking about Garland St. Germaine.

They ordered beers and tacos on the patio. Brandon noticed that people gave them extra-long looks. He supposed it had something to do with the SSMC cuts. They probably thought they were having lunch next to hardened criminals. Something about that was amusing. The looks they were getting from women weren’t about fear though. He knew how to recognize signs of feminine interest and he was learning that an MC cut beat out a fifty thousand dollar suit any day.

“So we were talkin’ about my mother.”

“We were not,” Brant growled as he swiped a tortilla chip through the hatch pepper salsa.

“Look, Pop. You know how you feel about Gram? What if you didn’t even have a face to put with the word ‘mom’?”

Brant leaned back and looked at his son as he took a swig of Lone Star. "I hear ya, but nothin's perfect, Brash. You've always had people around who'd do *anything* for you. I always hoped that would make up for..." He didn't finish that sentence.

"It hasn't escaped my notice that you never got married. You've had a few women friends, but nothin' lasting. Or serious." He watched Brant carefully. "You still love her. That's what you meant by that thing about your heart on your sleeve."

"What difference does it make? Like I said, none of us get perfect outta life."

The food was set down in front of them. Brandon picked up a taco and bit down. Before he chewed the whole bite he was saying, "Oh my God! This is unbelievable."

Brant raised an eyebrow. "Brash. What the hell is the matter with you? You've been to Chuy's at least once a week every day of your goddamn life. Now, all of a sudden the food is un-fuckin'-believable?"

Brandon grinned. "I'm workin' on appreciatin' things more. You. And Chuy's. It *is* un-fuckin'-believable."

Brant just sighed and shook his head.

CHAPTER 8

THAT NIGHT BRASH was watching TV in bed when Brandon's phone rang.

"How's it goin' there?"

"You first."

"Well, as a matter of fact, there is a thing."

"What thing?"

"This woman."

Brash shot straight up and his heart rate did the same. How had it been possible, in a month together with Brandon, that regardless of his mental reminders, he'd never gotten around to addressing the issue of Brigid?

"What happened?"

"Well, she seemed expectant."

"What did you do?" Brash growled into the phone.

"See, that's the problem. I didn't do anything. And she seemed kind of hurt by that."

"Fuck!"

"Forget to tell me something important, brother?"

"Christ!"

"I take that as a yes."

After a lengthy pause, Brash said, "Just stay the hell

away from her. Leave her alone and I'll make it up to her when I get back."

"So she's..."

"I don't know have a name for it yet. It was kinda new and we were figurin' things out. But until I'm done figurin', she's off limits."

"Okay. I mean I'd offer to stand in for you because she's just... well, you know. But I'm afraid she might have questions about my pierceless dick." Brash growled again and Brandon smiled picturing him pulling out the little bit of hair he had left. "Okay. Don't worry. Hands off. Pierceless dick stays in the pants."

"It better."

"There are lots of girls in Austin. I can stand having one of them declared off limits."

"How much did it, uh, hurt her feelings when you..."

"Let's just say you'd better learn to carry roses while you're dancing like Fred Astaire."

"Jesus."

"And one more thing. I think our pop is still in love with our mom."

"Glad you brought that up. 'Cause I think our mom feels the same way about him. What are we gonna do about that?"

"Let me sleep on it."

"Okay. You know, when I get back I'm gettin' a big ass TV like this one in my room."

Brandon laughed softly and hung up, thinking that the next day he'd have one just like that installed in

Brash's room. He'd lived in a room that size when he was in college, but had forgotten what it was like to experience economy of space. The first time he'd opened the bifold door of Brash's three-foot-wide closet, he'd laughed out loud. His brother didn't even own a suit. Aside from his cut and a leather jacket, his brother owned five pairs of jeans. Sixteen tee shirts, ten with short sleeves, six with long sleeves. Three Henleys. And four pairs of boots.

"What else does a guy need?" he'd said out loud to the closet.

BRASH NODDED AT Diane as he stepped off the elevator and headed back to his office, but didn't slow down. He was almost to the double doors when the door just before his destination opened and Uncle Adlay stepped out.

"Brandon. Hold on a minute. Someone I want you to meet."

Adlay introduced him to the head of Houma Rig and Dig. They had a two minute conversation about the future of oil exploration in the Gulf, then Brash excused himself.

By the second day on the job, he had figured out how to pull up his own calendar. Navigating the morning's tasks was a minute by minute challenge, but he found it to be kind of exciting. He didn't know if he was making a mess for Brandon to clean up or blossoming into a global finance genius. Just as long as he didn't blow his cover, he didn't care about the rest.

By lunchtime he was feeling pretty confident. Right up until his office door opened and closed behind a leggy brunette with dark blue eyes and awfully white teeth.

"Bran. I'm here for lunch," she announced.

"I don't see you on my calendar."

She laughed, came around his side of the desk, picked up his phone and said, "Alice. Ginger Michelson is having lunch with the boss."

Brash heard Alice say, "Yes, ma'am."

He didn't have a good enough reason to say no and, even though Brandon hadn't mentioned any girl in particular, he thought he'd better not burn his brother's bridges.

On the way out of the building she threaded her arm through his, giving the distinct impression that she was quite comfortable in his company. She said, "Some of us are going to the Love place in the Hamptons this week-end. Want to come?"

He said, "Got me a Chrysler, it's as big as a whale and it's about to set sail."

"What?" She blinked.

Clearly she wasn't familiar with B52's. "I'm not sure, Ginger. I could be busy."

She gave the sort of open mouthed laugh you'd expect to hear coming from a big busted, bawdy bartender. It was the kind of laugh that was interesting in its uniqueness, but could get old fast. He wondered if his brother was really interested in Ginger.

It turned out that what interested Ginger was society

gossip. The good part was that it became obvious quickly that Brash would not be expected to talk. All he had to do was nod and give an occasional one-syllable reply. So he concentrated on the food and on finishing quickly.

THAT NIGHT, BRASH called Brandon to find out how carefully he needed to handle Ginger.

"Do. Not. Encourage. That. She's clingy as velcro. If you lead her on, I will *never* be able to peel her off."

"She doesn't seem *that* bad." It was all Brash could do to say that without laughing. "Maybe she'd like to experience the difference a piercing can make." Of course he had no intention of following through on that threat, but it was fun to make Brandon squirm.

"You wouldn't." Brandon's teeth clenched of their own volition.

"Oh, yeah, I would." Brash chuckled.

"Just because we missed growing up together doesn't mean I won't still pound you proper."

That only made Brash laugh harder.

Until Brandon said, "You know there's plenty of mischief I could cause around here that could make your life more… interesting."

Brash got very serious, very fast. "Yeah? Like what?"

"Well, I know this brainy hangaround with a super nice ass."

The thought of Brandon talking about Brigid's ass made Brash's temper shoot to imminent explosion levels within a nanosecond, but he didn't want his brother to know just how much he was sensitive about that subject. So he dialed it back quickly.

"Okay. Settle back. I was just havin' a little fun at your expense. Truth is, I'd rather be strangled than have another meal with Ginger. So you been thinkin' about our parents and their predicament?"

"Yeah."

"Did you know that your grandfather blackmailed her into leaving Pop?"

"What? No! She told you that?"

"She said he had somethin' on Pop, Granddad, and some other members of the club that would send 'em all up. Unless she walked the path he'd laid out for her." Brandon was silent. "Guess you didn't know."

"I didn't. But I never really pressed her hard."

"I wasn't brutal about it, but I trapped her at dinner in a public place. By the way, the Mexican food here is shit."

"Preachin' to the choir. I've been to Chuy's."

"Anyhow, she seemed ready to talk about it. She said that after the selfish old monster died, she figured Pop had moved on. Probably married. Maybe other kids and stuff. Readin' between the lines."

"She called him a selfish old monster?"

"That was all me, my interpretation of events."

"Call it Fate, but I got a similar story here. Pop says he never contacted her again because he thought it was too late, but here's the thing. He said he took the club legit and concentrated on profit because he was hoping to make some serious money. The subtext is he was hoping to neutralize that as a reason to be apart. He still loves her. Can you imagine? After all this time."

"She feels the same. We gotta fix this. Hey, look, Adlay is blowin' up this phone. Let me find out what he wants."

"Okay."

Brash hit call back for Adlay.

"Hey, Uncle, what are…?"

"Brandon. I've been trying to reach you. Your mother has had a stroke. She's been taken to Presbyterian Weill Cornell."

"But she's just…" He was going to say that she was just fifty-years-old, then realized that was a dumb reaction. "Didn't my grandfather die from a stroke?"

"You can't think about that right now, Brandon. Get yourself to the hospital."

Brandon felt like he was in a daze. Fate wouldn't be cruel enough to give him his mother and take her away a day later. He pulled on jeans and a tee shirt and threw on his brother's leather jacket.

Stuffing his phone and his keys into his pockets as he ran, he hailed a cab on the street, then tried to remember the name of the hospital.

"It was Presbyterian something."

"Weill Cornell?" the cabbie asked. His accent was hard to understand, but Brash thought it sounded right.

"Yeah. That's it."

When he found the right floor, they showed him to a

private waiting room.

"What…?" Brash started to ask.

"She's not responding yet, but she's alive," Adlay said.

"Can I see her?"

"I think so. Let's go ask."

The room was dark except for the light of the machines. Brash pulled a chair up to the side of the bed that didn't have the IV drip. Every hour or so, someone came in and took readings, made adjustments, and asked if they could get him anything. The first few times he said no, but eventually he asked for coffee.

Even with the coffee, sometime during the night he fell asleep sitting in the chair with his head on the bed next to Garland's hip. He woke to the feel of her hand on his head.

He sat up. "Mom. You're awake."

"Brandon. Do you know how much I love you?"

She sounded weak and looked pale as death.

His voice caught in his throat twice when he tried to say what needed to be said. He finally got it out. "I'm not Brandon, Mom. I'm Brannach."

He could see that she was trying to focus on him and make sense of what he was saying. He could see that her heartrate was speeding up by looking at the graph display on the other side of the bed. She reached for him and he took her hand.

"Brannach. My sweet baby."

Brash's throat closed off completely as tears formed behind his eyes. She *had* wanted him.

"Mom. Why did you...?" He couldn't finish the sentence.

"It was all I could do to give you up, but your father needed you to heal his broken heart. I loved you, but I loved him, too, and I knew you'd be his angel in the form of a beautiful baby."

"He still loves you."

"It was the magazine, wasn't it? I think I was hoping that you would see it." She sounded exhausted and went to sleep before he could say anything else.

LATER THAT MORNING the doctor told him she would recover. She had some slight paralysis on the left side of her body, but it might go away in time, with physical therapy.

Brash called Brandon from the private waiting room before going down to the hospital cafeteria for breakfast.

"She's okay. There's no damage to her memory or speech. She may have to have some physical therapy to get her brain to connect with her left side again. But it's gonna be alright. And I've been thinkin' we might use this to our advantage."

"What do you mean?"

"We're gonna tell Pop what you'd call a partial truth."

"Spill it."

"We're gonna say she's had a stroke and wants to see him. Once they're in the same room with each other..."

Brandon didn't respond right away. "It's as good as anything. Let's do it."

"You'll have to let Pop know you're not me."

"Thank fuck. It ain't easy bein' you."

Brash laughed. "And that's the truth. Now about that girl…"

BRANDON FOUND BRIGID behind the bar, deep in conversation with Nam, who was telling stories from the early days of the Sons of Sanctuary.

"Brigid." She looked up. "Could I have two minutes?"

She looked surprised, suspicious, and above all put out. "I'm busy."

"Please."

She asked Nam to excuse her and untied her apron as she walked around the bar. "What's this about?"

"I have somethin' to show you. Somethin' important."

"What?"

"Guaran-damn-tee you will want to see it."

She followed, but with both prejudice and resentment. Inside Brash's room, he closed the door and said, "You can't be mad at Brash."

"Why not? And when did you start talking about yourself in the third person?"

"I'm not talking about myself in the third person. Because I'm not him. He wasn't the one that made you mad. It was me, the…" he had to smile, "…evil twin."

She turned on her heel and started toward the door, but he caught her wrist and pulled her back. "Hold on. I can prove it."

He pulled out his phone and dialed Brash. When he answered, Brandon said, "Need you on Facetime. There's a girl here who doesn't believe there are two of us." He switched the phone to Facetime and handed it to Brigid.

"Hey, beautiful," said Brash.

She narrowed her eyes at Brandon. "How are you doing this?"

Brash pulled her gaze back to the phone by answering. "He's not doin' it. I'm here in New York. Takin' his fuckin' place."

She looked at Brandon, then at Brash on the small screen in her hand and could see that he was wearing a tie. "That's a… good look for you."

"Yeah? Well, don't get used to it. Look. I'm sorry you got caught in this."

"What is *this*?"

Brash sighed. "It's a long story. We didn't know about each other until a couple of months ago. When we figured it out, we were both curious about the other parent. Brand was raised by our mother." She looked at Brandon, who smiled and waved. "I was raised by Pop."

Her eyes widened as she processed that. "Oh my God. You traded places and your parents don't know!"

"We both wanted a chance to find out what we missed."

"That is one incredible story."

"I know. I'm sorry if you got hurt in the middle of this."

"What made this confession day?"

"Our mother has had a stroke. Brand is gonna tell Pop and bring him up here. We're gettin' our parents back together."

"That's got to be the most romantic thing I've ever heard. What do you need me to do?"

"Nothin'. Just know that I miss you and as soon as this is over I'm comin' back. For you."

"I take it back. *That's* the most romantic thing I've ever heard."

"Does that mean you're gonna forgive me?"

"No. It means you're already forgiven. And I can't wait to see you."

CHAPTER 9

BRANDON KNOCKED ON Brant's office door and heard his father say, "Come in, Brash."

He flopped in a chair in front of the desk. "What made you think it was me?"

"You have a distinctive knock."

"I do?"

"Yeah. What do you need?"

"To tell you that you're wrong. It's not Brash." Brant looked at him over his glasses like he was waiting for the punchline. "I'm Brandon."

Brandon sat quietly and patiently waiting for his father to internalize his words.

Brant put down the paper and took off his glasses. After staring for a full minute, he simply said, "Brandon."

"Yeah."

"That explains a lot."

"I expect so."

"And Brash is?"

"With our mother."

Brant scrubbed a hand over his face. "Does she know?"

"She does now. We'd both planned to have at least a week with the other parent before we came clean, but Mom's had a stroke." Brant looked absolutely panicked. "She's okay. Well, she's out of danger. Her speech and memory functions are okay, but she's going to need some physical therapy."

"So she knows that you…?"

"Yes. And she wants to see you." He tried to keep his voice steady even though that was, by far, the biggest lie he'd ever told.

"She does?"

"Yeah. How soon can you be ready?"

"We need to book a flight."

"All taken care of. Got a jet waiting for us."

Brant smiled. "Of course you do. I'm gonna take a shower." He ran a hand over his face. "Can't take the years away, but I can at least shave."

"You look great, Pop. And I think you know it."

Brandon stood when Brant rose and came around the desk. His father shocked him by pulling him into a bear hug, but he returned the hug and swallowed hard, trying to keep his emotion in check.

When Brant leaned away, he looked at his son, who was two inches taller, and said, "That's why the haircut."

Brandon nodded. "It took a month to get the tattoos."

Brant laughed. "You did all that ink in one month?"

"Yeah. And I'm betting Mom is gonna be pissed about it."

"Well, let's go find out."

"Brash made it better with Hamburger Helper though."

"Hamburger Helper will cure a world of ills."

SEVEN AND A half hours later Brash heard the swish of the hospital room door. Garland was awake. She'd eaten, had a shower with assistance, was wearing a nightgown of her own, and was looking a little more like herself.

Brash smiled at his pop and his brother when the door opened. Brant stood just inside the door staring at the mother of his two boys. He hadn't seen her for almost three decades.

"Garland", was all he said.

His voice was more gravelly, and laden with emotion, but she didn't have to turn her head to know who it was. He had some silver in his hair, but he was every bit as beautiful as her memories. And her fantasies.

When she looked at his eyes, she felt decades slip away.

He crossed to the side of her bed.

"Brant. You're still hotter than hell."

He smiled. "And you're just as beautiful as the day you wandered into the maintenance shed."

She tried to laugh, but coughed instead. "Liar."

"Not about that. Brandon said you wanted to see me."

"He did?" She sounded weak. "Well, he wasn't wrong."

"You mean you didn't ask for me?"

She started to cry softly. "Dad said he would send you

to prison."

"Why didn't you tell me?"

"Because you would have fought him and he would have won. Nobody could win against him. I had to make you agree to not contact me. He would have broken you and that would have broken me. More.

"I told Brannach, when I thought he was Brandon, that I didn't contact you after Dad died because I was sure you'd gone on with your life. I figured that, except for Brannach, you must have forgotten all about me. Our summer romance. We only had a few weeks together. It seemed logical that you would have found somebody else and made a life. Without me."

He sat down next to the bed and took her hand. "That was no summer romance. That was the real deal. And I never stopped lovin' you. Not for a minute."

"God, Brant. I can't believe you're here."

"Brandon told me you never married."

"How could I be interested in anybody after you, biker boy?"

He smiled a little. "I spent years turnin' the Sons into a legitimate business, thinkin' maybe if I made enough money…"

"It never was about money."

Brant's shoulders slumped at that. All that time he'd spent thinking she didn't want him because he didn't have enough to offer, when all along she'd simply been protecting him.

"I know that now. It must have been really hard to let

Brannach go."

In response, she let out a sob just as the door opened and a nurse came in to take vitals and check the IV.

"Are you a family member?" she asked Brant.

"I'm her lover," he said. Garland tried to laugh, but ended up coughing.

"Only family members allowed," said the woman.

"Okay then. I'm her long lost brother from Texas."

The nurse gave him the stink eye, but left without another word.

Everything was quiet for a few minutes after. Brant reached over, took her hand, and immediately began drawing little circles with his thumb, just to remind himself that he had a connection, no matter how tenuous.

"How're we gonna fix this, darlin'?"

"You mean my brokenness?"

"No. I mean *our* brokenness." He paused and changed the subject. "You did a good job with Brandon. He's so much like Brash he fooled me. Mostly."

"Who's Brash?"

"We started callin' Brannach that as soon as he was old enough to show us his personality."

"And he's brash?"

"Can be. Yeah." He looked at Garland adoringly. "He's also good as they come. Smart as a whip. Devoted to friends and family. Got a work ethic that had me questioning him about wantin' a vacation."

"Brandon's not brash. He thinks things through. But he's smart, too. Got top honors in school. He runs

Germane Enterprises. And he's only twenty-eight. Well, I guess you knew that last part." They both laughed softly. "People like him."

"Yeah. People like Brash, too."

"They both look just like you."

"But I see you in Brash all the time. The way he moves or laughs. Even his bad singin'."

She smiled at that. "Looks like we did something good."

"True enough. But we also did somethin' bad. It wasn't right keepin' them away from each other. And it wasn't right not bein' together either."

Brash opened the door a crack and could see that the two of them were talking in low voices, holding hands.

"Looks like they've got some catchin' up to do. Want some coffee?"

"Okay. Now's as good a time as any for you to tell me what you've done to my company while I've been riding your bike and enjoying great Mexican food."

"Chuy's?"

Brandon grinned. "Have you ever had the chicken and guac tacos?"

"No. Sounds girly to me. Speakin' of business. Since I didn't get any calls from you or my owners, I'm guessin' things are steady."

"The worst thing that happened was my stop at the river taco truck. They seemed surprised that I don't speak Spanish."

Brash laughed. "I wish I had a video of that."

"That reminds me. Give me my wallet and phone."

They fished in pockets and switched. "What about the taco truck reminded you of that?"

"That's not what reminded me. It was the word 'video'. You said you wanted a TV like mine in your room at the club, so I went to get you one. But you don't have enough credit on your MasterCard. It was my first experience of being denied credit. Ever. And I didn't like it. I'll take a black American Express any day."

"Uh-huh. How much was the TV you were tryin' to buy?"

"Twelve thousand."

Brash just looked at him like he was crazy.

"TWENTY YEARS AGO I bought a lot up on the bluff above the river. It has a view northeast overlookin' downtown, the capitol, the university. It's beautiful day and night. When I saw it, I knew you'd love it."

Garland smiled wistfully. "I know I would."

"I used to hope that someday I'd get the chance to build a house there. For us. Somethin' you'd like, you know? I don't have billions, but I've got enough to make you comfortable. And happy."

"Brant…"

"You don't have to answer right now. You can think about it, but when they let you out of here, I want to take you home with me."

"Brant. I can't. Maybe last week. Even three days ago. But this isn't a head cold. I can't even walk by myself. I'm not sure that I will I ever…" Her voice broke.

"I don't care about that, Garland. Maybe you'll walk. Maybe not. Either way. You're the only thing I ever wanted, except our sons. And the reason I love them the way I do is 'cause they're part you."

"You say that now, but taking care of a person who's helpless… It's not as easy as it sounds."

"I don't have to do it by myself. We can get help until you don't need it anymore. In the meantime, you'll be busy tellin' the contractors what kind of house you want." The tears started rolling again. "Garland. Why is this makin' you cry?"

"Because I want it so much," she whispered.

"Then stop bein' a pussy and say yes."

TWO WEEKS LATER, Garland was released from the hospital and taken directly to the airport. Brash and Brandon had flown back to Austin together and made the people who lived in the house next door to Brant's lot an offer they couldn't refuse. They figured their mother would like to be close to the house she was building.

They then had the ground floor outfitted for a wheelchair and had their mother's things moved into the first story. While they were at it, they had the upstairs outfitted for two bachelor brothers to visit. They'd also hired a physical therapist and people to take care of the house and help Garland with what she couldn't do by herself.

When the Germane jet landed in Austin, Brash and Brandon were there waiting anxiously.

"She looks happier than I've ever seen her," Brandon said.

Brash nodded. "He looks so much younger."

As they reached the SUV where the boys were waiting, Garland told Brant. "They're so beautiful."

"If you say so," was the most she could get out of Brant, but he did wink at their sons as he reached down to put on the wheelchair brakes. "We have news."

"What?" Brash and Brandon said it at the same time.

"We're gettin' married." Their pop looked like he'd struck oil.

Brash said, "Shut up!" which made Garland giggle.

A YEAR LATER, Garland walked into their new house on her own. It was everything she'd ever dreamed of because it was where she and Brant lived together. She'd made sure there was plenty of space for grandchildren to come and stay. Just in case.

Brandon had moved Germane Enterprises headquarters to Austin. He was working less and enjoying life more since becoming an honorary member of the Sons of Sanctuary MC. Brigid finished her master's degree, but by that time, she was more interested in owning and running a bar than in pursuing a career in social anthropology.

She told Brash, "There's no better place to conduct cultural research."

It took the lion's share of her remaining inheritance to open a bar on 6th and Guadalupe, but she did it with

Brash's assurance that he'd show her how he'd made three other bars profitable.

The two of them sat at the picnic table next to the river taco truck and talked about her future. "And I'll make sure the club shows up regularly to patronize your fine establishment."

"Yeah. That's one of the things that's got me worried," she said.

"You won't have to advertise for Ladies Night. I'll get Arnold and Brand to show up. All the women will come runnin'."

She laughed. "In that case maybe I should invest in a male escort service instead."

"There's only one male escort you're in the market for, and you're lookin' at him."

"Yeah?" she teased.

"Yeah. And I suggest we christen your new drinking establishment by havin' a private party before we open to the general public."

"What kind of party?"

He wiped his hands on his napkin, reached into his pocket, and said, "This kind." When his hand came out of his pocket, it was holding up a diamond ring. "You're the one, Pain. Say yes."

She looked from the ring into the dark eyes that never failed to captivate. "I'm yours, biker boy."

Brash chuckled. It was an inside joke because that's what people close to Brant and Garland heard her say to him so often.

AT THE RECEPTION in Brigid's new, but yet unopened bar, Brandon gave the bride and groom the deed to the house next door to Brant and Garland, saying, "Somebody needs to keep an eye on those two."

Watch for

The Biker's Brother, Sons of Sanctuary, Book 2.

End of Book Shit.

Working on dark.

I even managed to pull off a hopeless ending to *A Season in Gemini.* I was all set to kill off Garland and have her die young of stroke, like her good-for-nothing father. It was all planned. She was going to die while Brash was in New York sobbing by her bedside. The boys were going to have to tell their dad together. Brant was going to be so devastated by the fact that she died before he'd accumulated the cash he thought he needed to woo her back that he was going to retreat into a bottle of Jack and never come up. Ever.

That was the plan.

Then the twins started a *relentless* campaign. They were always in my ear saying, "Please. Please. Don't kill our mom! She's never done *anything* to you."

And I caved!

What can I say? When it comes to HEA's, I'm a sucker for pleas from my characters, especially when lots of shirtless begging is involved.

So, really, I'm not weak-willed when it comes to standing up to the twins. They're just super persuasive. I mean, who could resist two out-of-this-world gorgeous guys pleading with those big dark eyes, wanting to save their mother? Not me.

I don't know how much of a chance I stand against these two. They'll probably just continue to force me submit to their will.

So I'm moving on, setting my trap for CARNAL. And nothing will keep me from the darkness this time.

94192263R00171

Made in the USA
Lexington, KY
25 July 2018